BLOOD BEFORE DAWN

BOOK 2 IN
THE DUNG BEETLES OF LIBERIA SERIES

DANIEL V. MEIER, JR.

BQB

North Carolina

Published in the United States by BQB Publishing
(an imprint of Boutique of Quality Books Publishing, Inc.)
www.bqbpublishing.com

Printed in the United States of America

978-1-952782-35-0 (p)
978-1-952782-36-7 (e)

Library of Congress Control Number: 2021948707

Book design by Robin Krauss, www.bookformatters.com
Cover design by Rebecca Lown, www.rebeccalowndesign.com
Map illustrator: Rosana Keleber

First editor: Caleb Guard
Second editor: Andrea Vande Vorde

PRAISE FOR BLOOD BEFORE DAWN AND AUTHOR DANIEL V. MEIER, JR.

"Meier continues his *The Dung Beetles of Liberia* series with this enthralling installment as Ken Verrier returns to Liberia to buy diamonds. It's April of 1979. When Ken, accompanied by his strong-willed wife, Sam, planned to return to Liberia to buy diamonds, he had no idea the country was entering a devastatingly tumultuous period of political unrest. Will he get out alive? Meier's insights into the ways corruption, injustice, and atrocities hollow out a nation's soul are cleareyed. His prose is intelligent, the narrative engrossing, and his unflinching forays into the African nation's social, cultural, and political atmosphere are realistic. Along the way, he weaves in a high-profile assassination, suspense, and daring escapades, keeping readers invested. From its adrenaline-fueled opening to its surprising conclusion, this poignant novel brilliantly captures the population's unrest and the white-hot fury as they struggle to obtain the basic necessities of life. This is a powerful story of civil unrest, corruption, and the arbitrary division between the masses.

— *The Prairies Book Review*

"... In both books, *The Dung Beetles of Liberia* and this sequel, *Blood Before Dawn*, author Daniel V. Meier, Jr. captures the essence of Africa. It's a continent that is both majestic and undeniably cruel. It's the battlefield where the clash between foreign influence with western ideals of life and a fair standard of living, tribalism, lack of compassion, minimal sanctity of life, and belief in witchcraft meet and struggle. Meier throws the Americans into this mix, who are worried that either China or Russia is gaining inroads into an area they wish to influence, and this lights the touch paper to the revolution. No one is safe; men's basest behaviors are unleashed, destroying lives and livelihoods. . . . The story itself takes the reader on a page-turning, fast-moving exciting ride, and I found myself holding my breath as I flew through the chapters . . . this is another read that will stay with me for years to come."

— Lucinda E. Clarke for *Readers' Favorite* reviews

". . . Daniel V. Meier, Jr. has written another compelling historical fiction narrative in *Blood Before Dawn*. Readers hit the ground running in the beginning scenes (along with the main characters, much to their horror) while the suspenseful and harrowing story of the corrupt political environment and unrest in Liberia unfolds and doesn't subside until the shockingly messy conclusion.

It is evident that the author is a master of writing in the historical fiction genre, whether he is spinning a tale partly from his personal experience as seen in this series, or with his other equally engaging historical fiction works. Readers are not just told a wild, fictional story that might have some basis in history, but they're presented with an entertaining story expertly woven throughout real events in the tumultuous history of Liberia. . . . *Blood Before Dawn*. . . will not only linger in your thoughts, but it also has the potential to awaken your thirst for knowledge."

— Lynette Latzko, *Feathered Quill Book Reviews*

TABLE OF CONTENTS

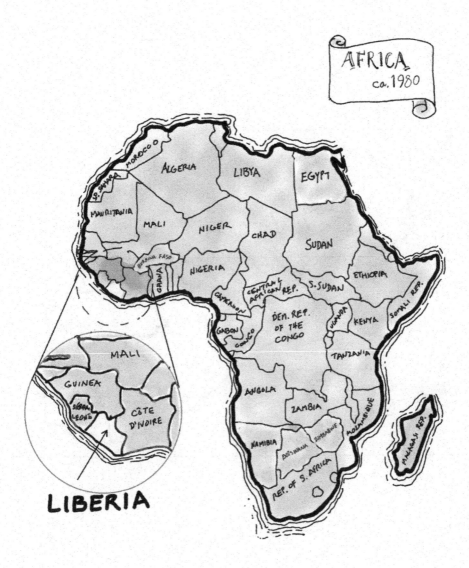

Map Illustrator: Rosana Keleher

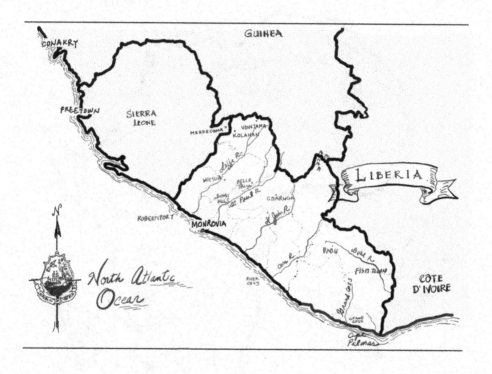

Map Illustrator: Rosana Keleher

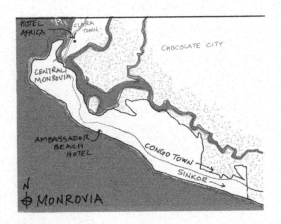

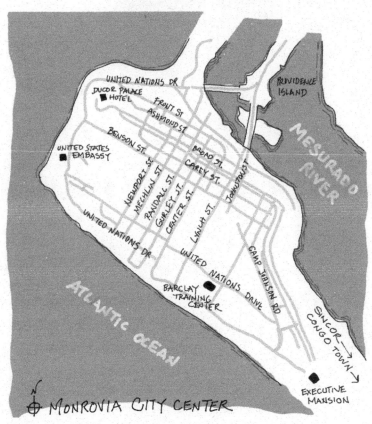

Map Illustrator: Rosana Keleher

ACKNOWLEDGMENT

To Caleb Guard, my editor, for his patience, understanding and professionalism and to Andrea Vande Vorde for her eye for detail.

I would also like to thank Jane Knuth of the The Knuth Agency for being a particularly thoughtful early reader and editor and to Teeja Meier, my wife, for her faith in me and for her love.

CHAPTER 1

APRIL 1979

I'd always known that one could get into trouble just standing on a street corner, but never like this. We had just finished a late breakfast at a new Lebanese restaurant on Gurley Street in center city Monrovia, and were actually standing on the corner of Gurley and Benson when a crowd—more of a roaring mob—swept down the street like a tidal bore. Judging from the signs and posters coming toward us, the throng seemed to be heading in the direction of the Executive Mansion. We watched for a moment, fascinated, just as one might stare at a growing flood, then realized, too late, that we were caught up in this human deluge. We tried to run, but we were already submerged in the tumbling waters of human flesh and the roar of human voices.

Sam and I glanced at each other. "What the hell?" All we could do was lock arms and flow with the mob.

I had returned to Liberia because I needed to raise a lot of cash quickly, and the best way I could do that was to drop in on some of my old friends in the diamond business. It was the beginning of the wet season in West Africa—not the best time to arrive or, in fact, to do anything there. My wife, Sam, had insisted on coming with me. I told her I didn't think it was a good idea—Sam is one of the toughest people I know. You just don't say no to her, not even a maybe. Then, too, I knew she was better at this sort of thing than I was.

It had been twelve years since Sam and I were in Africa, but Sam appeared not to have aged a single day. She still had the same thick red hair that she had cut short for the trip. It would be easier to manage in the heat and humidity of Liberia. Her eyes were still clear and green with the same laugh wrinkles at the corners, and the attractive bridge of freckles across her nose and upper cheeks had not faded. I knew that with her intelligence and insight we had a much better chance of succeeding.

The flights to Liberia had been long and arduous despite Pan Am's latest jet transport airplanes. Sam and I learned a new term on this trip: "jet lag." We experienced it by first falling asleep during the taxi ride to the Ambassador Hotel. Then, after a surreal check-in at the hotel, we went up to our room in a dreamlike state and, without removing our clothes or taking a shower or any of the normal things people do before retiring for the night, collapsed onto the bed and immediately fell deeply asleep until early the next morning when our unexpected adventure began.

The noisy mob, brandishing posters reading, "OUT WITH TOLBERT!", "STOP OPPRESSION NOW!", "WE WANT RICE!" swept us up into their superheated mist and carried us along like two pieces of entwined flotsam. We tried but could not move against the flow. Sam and I began to move laterally through the crowd like two small animals trying to swim across a rushing river.

The noise was deafening until I heard the gunshots in the distance, and the crowd grew silent for a very brief moment. Then screaming started, drowning out all other sounds except the staccato rhythm of automatic gunfire. Sam and I fell facedown onto the pavement, making ourselves as flat as possible. A man, an older man with gray hair, fell on his back in front of us, blood spurting from the front of his head like a small red fountain. As his blood pressure dropped, the gushing slowed to a trickle and the man lay dead. Blood covered his face, slowly filling his right ear. A woman tripped over us and fell, shrieking, still holding on to her protest sign.

Finally, the firing stopped. Soldiers ran toward us, rifles in hand. I couldn't make out what they were saying. They stopped along the edge of the street and shouted at us. They wanted us to leave, and made aggressive waving motions with their free hands. Several people stood up, hesitated as though waiting for something to happen, then started to run. There was no more firing. I looked over at Sam. Her red hair was disheveled and her face was contorted into a snarl, and through gritted teeth she shouted, "I wish I had my goddamn Uzi!"

"I think they want us to go!" I hissed back to her. "I'm making a run for it. Are you ready?"

She nodded. We stood up slowly. The soldiers, now nearby, were motioning for us to move. I took Sam's hand and we started running. By this time, most people had gotten to their feet; that is, those who were not dead or badly injured. We ran with the crowd, stopping only once to help someone who had fallen. After that, we didn't stop running until we got to the Ambassador Hotel several blocks away. The front doors were locked, but people were inside crouching behind chairs and flowerpots.

"Let's try the back!" I shouted.

We ran around to the beach bar. The patio was deserted. The entrance to the interior bar was also locked—of course it would be. I picked up a barstool and raised it to smash the glass door. Just as I got the stool over my head, the back door opened slightly and Joe, the bartender, peeked out from inside.

"Mr. Ken," he said quietly from the partially opened door, "please don' do dat. Ya know, it be expensive to get glass."

I pulled the door fully open with a jerk, nearly yanking Joe out onto the pavement. Sam and I rushed in and closed the door behind us. Joe stayed next to me the whole time and quickly locked it.

"Well, if it isn't 'Set-em-up Joe'!" I exclaimed. "I've never been happier to see anyone in my life! But you don't think these locked doors will keep them out, do you?"

"Yah ah do. For dhey is notin' fo' dem here. Dhey after food. Dhey starving and dhey after Tolbert's head on a stick. Dhey don't wa notin' else. So, why you hee, Mr. Ken. It be almos' ten yee now. You come to fly again?"

"Long story, Joe. Long story."

It was strangely quiet when we got to the hotel lobby. It was dotted with a mixture of Europeans, Americans, some Latin Americans, and Africans—mostly men. Sam was still breathing in gulps of air. Her red hair was wet and clinging to her head and ears.

"What the hell happened out there?" she asked in a raspy voice.

"Somebody started shooting," I said.

"You think it was the soldiers?"

"I don't think so. They seemed to want us to get away. They seemed to be protecting us."

"That's odd. Then who was doing the shooting?" Sam asked.

"De police. Dhey do de shootin'. Dhey be Tolbert's policeman. He personal bodyguard. De Army not his."

It was the hotel desk clerk speaking softly from behind the counter.

An unnatural quiet had settled around us as I looked out on the now empty street. Hotel guests who had been crouching behind the furniture started to stand up. One of the men was an Asian, and from his clothes and appearance I guessed (correctly, as it turned out) that he was Chinese.

He did not seem as concerned or as frightened as the others. Having witnessed our entrance into the lobby and seeing that we were Westerners, he walked toward us and addressed us, bowing slightly.

"You are American?"

"Yes," I said. "And you are?"

"I am Chao Zhan, Assistant Deputy Minister for Agriculture for The People's Republic of China."

He extended his hand. And I took it. It was small and damp.

"Mr. Chao," I said and nodded.

"Ah, so you have been to China?"

"No, why do you ask?"

"You addressed me correctly. In China, the surname is always pronounced first. The opposite from Western culture."

"Let's just say it was a lucky accident and leave it at that."

Sam was standing next to him and I noticed visible discomfort on her face. I put my arm gently around her and introduced myself, and Sam as my wife. I then offered to buy Mr. Chao a drink—Joe had signaled that the bar was now open.

Mr. Chao had all the graciousness of a trained diplomat. His lips smiled and he seemed to nod in agreement at nearly every sentence. We chose one of the tables in the far corner, near the window. Guests were beginning to drift out of the lobby and meander to the hotel bar. Most were laughing grimly as though they had just watched a horror movie and realized with great relief that they were now safe.

Mr. Chao ordered a small bottle of mineral water.

"I never drink alcohol before six," he said, "and even then, I seldom partake except for social purposes. Excessive alcohol consumption is discouraged in The People's Republic."

Sam and I, on the other hand, felt like we had both narrowly escaped death, which we had, so we needed something fortifying—maybe even life affirming.

"So, Mr. Chao," I said, taking a sip of a large gin and tonic, "what happened out there?"

Mr. Chao smiled slightly and poured his mineral water very carefully into a tall glass. "I think it was an old-fashioned food riot. We often experienced them during the Qing Dynasty. In those days, the rich controlled all sources of wealth and production. Workers over the years attempted to march to the estates of the rich, which were surrounded by walls and strong gates, and demand lower prices. Many workers were killed, and some thrown into rivers or dungeons."

"Not like today, huh, Mr. Chao?" Sam said, not bothering to conceal her sarcasm. Mr. Chao continued smiling and sipped his mineral water.

"There are no food riots in China today, madam. The Party sees to it that all workers' needs are cared for."

"But China has had food riots," Sam said.

"Unfortunately, madam, that is true, as I have said, during the Qing dynasty. The workers and peasants wanted only what was rightfully theirs."

"If my memory is correct, Mr. Chao," Sam added, "that was in the seventeenth century, wasn't it?"

Mr. Chao smiled without showing his teeth. "In fact, it was 1644 to 1911."

"Yes," said Sam, "and there was a Royalist attempt to bring the Qing back to power in 1917, but it was aborted and failed."

"Your knowledge is astounding, madam, but in China the past and the present are one. We do not dismiss events which came before as irrelevant. It is all the same to us. The class struggle will always go on."

There was a distant explosion, startling everyone at the bar, but no secondary explosions or gunfire.

"Mr. Chao," I said, "you must know something about this food riot?"

He nodded slightly. "President Tolbert, it seems, is not quite as wily as his predecessor, President Tubman. It is my understanding, I am sure one can get different versions, that President Tolbert's Secretary of Agriculture, Florence Chenoweth, raised the import tax on rice significantly. Some say it was meant to stimulate local rice cultivation, but I think it was to channel more money into the Treasury and into the pockets of the President and other members of his family."

"What do you mean, 'his family'?" I asked.

"His daughter owns considerable rice-growing land; his son is also heavily invested, as is, I believe, his brother, Frank Tolbert, who is also a member of the Senate. I suspect they were not among the rioters." Mr. Chao snickered such that small droplets of mineral water dribbled from his mouth. He went on. "President Tolbert, in his blind ambition to please the Western powers, especially the United States, forgot the power of the workers and peasants. Have you heard of the Progressive Alliance of Liberia?"

"No," I said.

"The acronym is PAL. It was formed a few years ago and is led by one

Gabriel Matthews, an activist who espouses a quasi-Marxist ideology. I would consider it a 'grassroots movement', as you Americans say, to address government corruption and other such abuses of power." He put his hand over his mouth. "I have said too much," he muttered.

"I suspect you're right," Sam said. "What do you think will happen now?"

"I imagine President Tolbert will remove the tax, but, as you Americans say, 'the cat is out of the bag.'"

He turned to look at the ocean and then asked quietly, "What does that mean, I wonder?"

His thoughtful moment was interrupted by renewed bursts of automatic gunfire. A few people ducked beneath the bar, then reemerged, laughing nervously.

I told Mr. Chao about our experience with the soldiers we saw in the street.

"They were acting strangely," I said, "and not shooting at the demonstrators. Some actually helped us get out of the way. But then there were also people who'd been hit and were dying in the street. So, there must have been some soldiers who were shooting."

"The President does not trust his Army. The enlisted ranks are made up of poorly paid and badly treated indigenous people while the officer corps is comprised mostly of the upper class, especially the high-ranking officers. The enlisted men are in sympathy with the struggles of the people and will not fire on them. It is reminiscent of the Russian Revolution, no? Tolbert suspected this, so he asked the President of Guinea for support, who obligingly sent him a detachment of troops. I'm told that they can be particularly ruthless and cruel."

Sam wanted to know how many troops were sent.

"I don't know exactly, but I imagine it's enough to protect Tolbert's Executive Mansion and his home in Bentol City." Mr. Chao shook his head slowly as people do when they believe the outcome is inevitable. "Using foreign troops against your own people can never be justified, but," Mr. Chao shrugged, "he doesn't have to worry about re-election—does he? Did you know he's planning on hosting the Organization of African Unity in a few months? He's already cleared away some small houses on beach property to build acceptable accommodations for the delegates, and I understand he's sparing no expense to house diplomats and other well-placed persons. Quite an expenditure."

"That won't go down well with the workers and peasants," Sam said with a smirk.

"I imagine," Mr. Chao said, "that the struggle is just beginning. This is how all capitalist systems will end—in chaos, confusion, and complete destruction."

"Surely Capitalism can adjust," Sam said. "It has done so in Europe and America."

"Only by much struggle and hardship and by adopting some measure of socialist principals. Take your President Roosevelt and his New Deal. He was criticized as being a socialist by your Wall Street bankers and the opposition party. But had he not done that, America would be arm in arm with the Communist world today."

"Are you saying that President Roosevelt saved Capitalism, Mr. Chao?" Sam asked.

"Madam," Mr. Chao said with a slight smile. "President Roosevelt said so himself."

Sam looked toward the front window of the hotel. The street was littered with the detritus of riot and destruction, but the rioters were gone. Even the bodies of the dead had been removed.

Sam motioned toward the outside. "Do you think those people will embrace Communism as their savior, Mr. Chao?"

Mr. Chao leaned back in his chair, took another sip of his tea. "I think they may have already, madam. They just don't know it."

CHAPTER 2

WINSTON

Shortly after, President Tolbert did, in fact, lower the rice tax but it made little difference in his public image, and though he was an ordained Baptist minister and reputed to be a "decent" man, he was universally hated by all but the Americo-Liberians.

The Liberian Army had, indeed, refused to fire on the rioters, so Tolbert had their ammunition withdrawn and placed in storage, guarded by the police and his personal bodyguards, the SSS. Gradually, life in Monrovia got back to normal, or as normal as it could be in difficult times. There were occasional pockets of unrest, indicated by an explosion or two, but these were quickly suppressed by the police. The press was silent except for its praise of Tolbert's Government and its admiration of his ceremonies and state banquets.

During this time, Sam and I went about the serious business of diamond hunting.

There are many ways to acquire diamonds in Liberia, but Sam and I knew that the best way was to have an agent who was in contact with a reliable source and, if possible, actually get to the diamond mines. This was very difficult, especially in the rainy season. The mines were typically far inside the bush and there were virtually no roads to access them. Iron and ore mining pits, typically owned by foreign countries, had roads leading to them, but these were generally built by the companies themselves.

The De Beers Company did not have a stranglehold on the Liberian mines like they did in South Africa or even Sierra Leone. The Liberian mines simply did not produce enough diamonds to interest them, and the quality, for the most part, was said to be not as high. Even so, with only a few small bags of these diamonds, one could easily clear over a 100,000 USD. And that was what I needed.

I had cleared out my savings for this trip. There would be costs, I knew that. I needed an airplane and something for ground transportation. Sam suggested a motorcycle. She used to ride one to her teaching job in Virginia Beach before she joined the Peace Corps. Despite the wonderful simplicity of it, there just wasn't enough carrying room and I didn't relish the idea of using it on muddy roads in the rain.

After a hotel breakfast of scrambled eggs and some kind of unidentifiable meat, Sam and I went searching for a cab. We found one, as I thought we would, a few steps from the hotel entrance.

"Can you take us to Spriggs-Payne airport?" I asked the driver as we got into the back seat.

"Boss, I take you anywhere you wan' go, oh."

"Good."

He was a man in his thirties, clean shaven and wearing a stained but clean New York Yankees T-shirt and a New York Yankees baseball hat. I liked the way he drove—carefully, cautiously, and with situational awareness—good piloting technique.

"What's your name?" I asked.

"Winston, boss. Like da great Winston Churchill. Only I still don' like cigars!" He laughed.

"That's a good name," I said. "Tell me, Winston, do you know where I can buy a good car?"

"How much you pay, boss?"

"I was thinking as much as a hundred and fifty US"

"A hunded and fitty US! Damn! Boss, I drive you anywhere you wan' till de second comin o' de Lord Jesus Christ fo' a hunded an' fitty."

This sounded like a good offer. It would free me from legal entanglements with the Liberian Government. A vehicle of my own would require maintenance, and expense.

"Okay, Winston, you've got a deal. A hundred and fifty US. I'll pay you half now and the rest when the job is finished. That should be in a few weeks, when we head home."

Winston hesitated. "Why can you not pay me all now? I ha' chillen to feed, a wife to please. I ha' to buy petrol."

"That would not be good business, Winston. You are a man of business. Would you pay all up front before the job is finished?"

"You right, boss. Dhat is da good way o' bidness, oh."

Winston started off on the familiar road to Spriggs-Payne airfield, and right away, I recognized the dilapidated buildings that still had not been improved, the women walking slowly but steadily along the sides of the road, most shabbily dressed, and carrying bundles on their heads. As we arrived, I asked him to stop by the airport bar.

The small building by the side of the orange dirt airstrip was much the same as it was when I worked for Monrovia Airlines. Had I not recognized the dirty concrete structure from my many hours of drinking there in the '60s, I wouldn't have known it was an actual bar open for business. I asked Winston to pull up next to the small doorway on the far side of the building.

"Come in with us, Winston. I'll buy you a beer."

"Da be fine, boss, so fine."

Sam, Winston, and I strode into the airport bar like a trio of successful big game hunters. The place had changed very little, if at all—dimly lit and smelling of stale beer and cigarette smoke. There were fewer patrons than I remembered for the time of day, but my memory of the place gave me a friendly, welcoming feeling.

The reinforcing steel bars protecting the window openings in the shapes of tropical birds and plants were still there, but dusty and in need of repainting. And as evidenced by the amount of guano on them, birds were still happy to fly in and out of the room at will.

"Monsieur Ken! Monsieur Ken!" Madeleine shouted from the opposite end of the bar. She came toward me with her arms outstretched. "How handsome you are, *mon chéri*. You haven't changed at all!"

"And you haven't either," I said, noticing the unfamiliar lines around her eyes and the slightly grayish tint of her hair. "Still as beautiful as ever."

"And this lovely lady? She your latest, *mon ami?*"

Sam glared at me for a second. Then I introduced Sam and made it clear that she was my wife and that Winston was our driver.

"And what brings you back to Liberia? Are you going to fly again?"

"I am looking for an airplane," I said, "but it's for my own use."

"Then you have come to the right place. So many operators are giving up; so much disturbance and unrest. Not like the old days when you were here, *mon cher*, when things were— how do you say—"booming.' My business is no good too—not as many pilots. André is gone, dead, I think. The Germans are mostly gone. There are still a few around but they are too old, or too young, to remember the war. A few Spanish and English—there will always be English everywhere you go."

"Don't people still need to get to the interior? It doesn't look like the roads have improved."

Madeleine shrugged in that special French way as if to say, "I don't know and I don't give a damn."

"The Mandingos, *oui*, the merchants, *oui*, the Peace Corps, *oui*, but the mining companies and most of the other foreign companies have their own aircraft—big helicopters that carry six, maybe ten people. They don't come in here very much."

"Is Honorable Williams still around?" I asked.

"Oh yes. He comes often, like before. All smiles and talks forever about starting an international airline in Liberia, but never seems to get around to doing it."

A very young bartender brought our beers. He set one bottle in front of each of us, opened the cap, and wiped the top with a clean paper towel. I knew from living here before that this was an absolute must—to be sure it was a sealed bottle. By the same token, I never had a gin and tonic with ice. Public water was toxic with bacteria.

"As I said, Madeleine, I need an airplane. Do you know of one for sale?"

"Oh, *mon cher*, everything is for sale here. You know that. For the right price you can have anything you want. But there is a Dutchman at the other end of the field. I hear he's not doing so well. Name of the operation is Omnibus."

I took her hand and kissed it. She smiled and slowly withdrew it.

We finished our drinks and Winston drove us to the far side of the airfield where Omnibus was located. It looked like two outbuildings nailed together with barely room inside for a desk and chair. There were two airplanes parked on what could be considered a dirt ramp next to the shacks. Inside there was a man, red faced with gray stubble on his chin and upper lip. He was sitting in the only chair, smoking a long cigarette. He glanced up at me with indifference.

I asked, "Are you Mr. Van Dick, the owner of this operation?"

He smirked, blowing cigarette smoke and the ash in front of him. "Van Dijk. Please. Pronounced Fan Dyke! De owner? Und yah, yo might could say dat."

"I'm told you have an airplane for sale."

"Yah, yo might could say dat too. Yo might could say de whole damn place is for sale."

"I see you've got a 170A."

"Yah, yah. Ich let you have it for five towsand US."

"I want to look at it first. Where are the logbooks?"

He pointed to a box of cubby shelves nailed to the wall. "De books und keys are in dare."

The logbooks had a thin layer of dust on them, and the pages stuck loosely together as I flipped through them. No recent entries had been made. I asked to look at the airplane. Mr. Van Dijk waved me on.

The airplane was well used, and like most well-used airplanes, it smelled of fuel and burnt oil. However, it was cleaner than I expected and, surprisingly, the engine looked clean and well maintained. I checked to make sure the plane was tied down securely and that the main switch was off, then pulled the propeller through several times. The compression wasn't the greatest but it wasn't bad either.

I walked back into the outhouse of an office. Mr. Van Dijk was there, still chain-smoking.

"I'd like to start the engine," I said.

"Und ich suppose yo vant to fly it too?"

"That would be the usual procedure," I said.

"Goot, den leave a deposit of five towsand US."

I tried not to look surprised.

"I'll leave 2,000 US. If that isn't good enough, then thank you for your time."

After a significant pause, I turned and started to walk out.

"Vate! Vate!" he said, seeming to chew on his tongue slightly.

I stopped and turned back to face him.

"Ya, ya, okay. Leave da money on da desk."

"I'll take the logbooks too," I said.

He nodded, then lit another cigarette from the stub of the previous one. I walked out to the taxi and told Winston and Sam that I would probably take the airplane around the field for a few minutes. Winston had found a shadier place to park, so Sam went back to reading her book and Winston continued humming a plaintive West African song.

I checked the fuel tanks and strainer for contamination. All were clear. The oil was up to the line and reasonably clean. All wires were connected, and nothing was broken, frayed, dripping, or hanging. I untied the airplane, pushed it around to face the runway, and climbed in. I started the engine and all engine gauges jumped into the green arcs, which was very encouraging. The engine ran smoothly with no excessive vibration. I went through the taxi check list, then pushed the throttle in slightly and felt the familiar tremble of the aircraft fuselage. A little more power and the airplane started rolling forward. I held the yoke back against my belt buckle and pushed the rudder pedal, pointing the nose to the end of the runway. Once there, I performed the pre-takeoff check carefully and methodically. I felt a little like a test pilot. The airplane checked out okay, but with an old machine in Liberia one could never be sure. When I convinced myself that the airplane was ready to go, I keyed the mic of the transceiver and asked the tower for permission to take off. The scratchy voice of the air traffic controller, although they were air traffic controller in name only, cackled in the headset. "Yah, yah, go," said the sleepy voice.

It was one of the rare clear days in the West African rainy season. I eased the throttle into full power. The old bird accelerated quickly. As soon as I felt the rudder become aerodynamically effective, I pushed the yoke forward, lifting the tail until the runway appeared over the nose. In a few moments she was ready to fly, so I eased back on the yoke just enough to let her lift off the ground. She was in her element.

The ground fell away as though released from the clutches of my landing gear. The gauges were still functioning normally—all pointers in the green arcs. The engine had not missed a beat. Then all the old familiar sights began to appear—the sprawl of Monrovia, the ocean and the white line of the coast. The distinctive red-orange dirt roadways, so colored by high concentration of iron and aluminum, known as laterite, meandered out from the city until they disappeared into the bush.

At five hundred feet I turned ninety degrees to the left and climbed another five hundred feet before turning downwind. I leveled the airplane out and let it accelerate to cruise speed, then reduced the power to hold that speed while trimming the pitch forward to maintain level flight and speed.

At cruise speed she felt a little out of rig, so I had to hold slight aileron pressure to keep the wings level. Other than that, she performed beautifully. Opposite the end of the runway, I throttled back, trimmed to relieve pressure from the yoke, and did a shallow descending 180 degree turn on to final approach, went to full flaps and retrimmed for approach speed. At slower speed the tendency of the airplane to roll slightly diminished to where it was barely noticeable. I was over the end of the runway and after a short, floating glide I raised the flaps to let the airplane settle onto the runway as smoothly as a goose.

"Vell?" Mr. Van Dijk asked through a cloud of fresh cigarette smoke.

"$2,000," I said, trying to edge my voice with determination.

Mr. Van Dijk shook his head.

"Okay," I said. "Give me my deposit back and I'll go."

He pointed to a white envelope on his desk. I picked it up and checked to see if the money was there. It was. Then I walked out and had almost reached the car door when I heard his voice behind me.

"Alla right! Alla right!" he shouted. "Yo can hab de damn ting vor two towsand. But ya can't keep it here."

I happily agreed and took the keys and logbook outside to meet Winston and Sam.

"Jump in, Sam! I want to taxi this baby over to Monrovia Airlines. Winston, you meet us there with the car."

Monrovia Airlines, my former employer, was under new ownership and management; I knew that. As I taxied onto the dirt ramp and shut the engine down, A familiar figure came toward me from the hangar.

Paterson extended both arms, and with a broad smile, wrapped them around me. He was just as I remembered him, dressed in a white, long-sleeved shirt, pressed khaki trousers, and polished shoes. He had visibly aged, like everyone else I met from the old days.

"Mista Ken, so good to see ya afta so long a time."

"And you too, Paterson. Have you been well?"

"Yes, Mista Ken. All is well, all is well."

"How is it with the airlines?"

"Mista André left some time ago. I hear he went to Cote d'Ivoire. I don't know for sure, but I hear he was killed. De airline now owned by an Israel company and, of course, de Honorable Williams."

Paterson spoke Honorable Williams's name with the kind of reverence shown to high members of the clergy. He was, after all, an Americo-Liberian, one of the "Congo" people, who owned virtually all of Liberia. He was, as all Americos were, referred to as "Honorable."

"All dese Israel pilots be very young like yourself when you was here befo.'"

"Is Honorable Williams in good health, Paterson?"

"Ya. He in de best of health. Only like de rest of us, he gettin' ol.'"

"I need to talk to the new boss. Is he there?" I asked, pointing to the operations office.

"Ya, he dhere. He always dhere."

I thanked Paterson and walked across the orange, muddy road to the operations office. Sam came with me, waving to Winston that we wouldn't be long.

The office had been considerably improved in the last ten years—new windows, paint, newish furniture, and a cleaner smell. I tapped on the door of André's former office.

"Come in," a masculine voice called.

The man was writing something as I entered. He looked up. He was a rather handsome man in his early forties. He had a thin mustache, searching, intelligent eyes, and no indication of thinning hair.

"Yes, can I help you?" he said in a nearly perfect American accent. I told him that I expected to be in Liberia for about a month and wanted to keep my airplane tied down here. He glanced out of the window at the 170A, then nodded and said that it would cost twenty-five US for four weeks.

I didn't mention my past with Monrovia Airlines. He would find out from Paterson anyway, and in Liberia, it was always best not to talk about the past. I paid him the twenty-five.

"Want a receipt?" he said without looking up.

"That won't be necessary," I said.

He nodded and waved his free hand dismissively. Winston drove us back into Monrovia so that I could file the change of title and struggle through the red tape of Liberian bureaucracy to establish ownership of the Cessna, which also meant handing out 'dash' to everyone in the process.

As it was when I was last here in the '60s, bribery, or "dash," was the way of life. It is what greases the wheels of local government, or any establishment for that matter. At the airport, immigration officials require "dash" to get you beyond their desk. Customs officials need their "dash" or "Saturday" if you want to retain all of your bags and their contents. These are not tips. If you don't pay the dash, you don't get the service.

It was late afternoon when all was completed and, while on the way back to the hotel, and for no particular reason, I thought of Heinz and Maria's Restaurant where I had spent many hours with my German pilot friends when I flew along with them for Monrovia Airlines.

"Winston, can you take us to Heinz and Maria's Café? Maybe get a quick beer and a schnitzel."

"Sorry, boss," Winston said. "Heinz and Maria's is closed. Heinz, he wen' back to Germany long time hence, an' Maria, I tink she close de restaurant soon afta."

"Heinz went back to Germany? Why?"

"Well, de story is dhat one day President Tubman was havin' a big party an' he ran outa champagne wine. So he sen' someone to Heinz to get mo' wine. But Heinz, he say no! No, 'cause President Tubman hadn't paid for de las' order o' wine. Or de one befo' dhat. I mean, dhat take cohones, ya know!"

"What happened?"

Winston laughed. "Ha! De next day, Heinz wa' on a plane back to Germany!"

"And Maria?"

"She din' go wid him, but what she did, I don' know. I really don' know."

As long as I was thinking about the '60s, I thought about Mr. Koning and his arts and hobby store. I asked Winston if he was familiar with it and he nodded that he was. When I asked him to drive us there, he seemed puzzled for a moment but made the proper turns through the city streets. The people in Monrovia looked poorer than I remembered. Cheap and temporary repairs had been done to most of the properties. There were a lot of angry and fatigued faces, and many malnourished children whose clothes hung on them like torn rags. Most seemed to wander through the streets aimlessly.

Mr. Koning's shop had changed little, except the bright colors that made up the sign advertising his hobby shop were now sun bleached to the point of indecipherability.

Winston found a parking place near the store and said that he would wait. Sam and I walked the half block through a throng of people desperately trying to sell us anything from glass trinkets to fish. We entered the store half hoping to find a rare, air-conditioned interior, but discovered instead a swirling, out-of-balance ceiling fan stirring the humid air. There was a local woman of late middle age sitting in a metal chair next to a row of primitive style paintings. She was impeccably dressed in a colorful, loose-fitting caftan and equally colorful turban. She smiled at us as we walked past.

The young man behind the glass counter introduced himself as Andrew, a nephew of Mr. Koning.

"And where are Mr. and Mrs. Koning now?" I asked after a short exchange of pleasantries.

"It is very sad," Andrew said, "but Aunt Alide died some years ago. She has been missed by everyone. She was much loved by the arts community here. A couple of years after Aunt Alide's passing, Uncle Geert decided that it was now safe to return to Holland—no more Nazis, he said. And I haven't heard from him since. I suppose he is doing well."

"And you, you don't want to return to Holland?"

"No, I wouldn't be returning. Liberia is all I know. It is my home."

I said that I was looking for an eight-by-eleven sketch pad and a set of graphite drawing pencils. Andrew pointed to shelves and bins against the wall displaying all the art supplies.

"Who is the woman?" I asked.

"She is a local artist. Some of her work has been shown and sold in Europe and America. She comes in when she has a new collection to sell, usually about once a month, sometimes two months.

"What is her name?" Sam asked.

"Her name is Leesai. She is Kpelle but speaks English very well—she went to the Catholic mission school."

I selected a pad of white sketching paper and a box set of twelve drawing pencils. Sam strolled over to where Leesai was sitting and started carefully looking through her paintings. The artist watched her intently. Sam selected one and held it up to the light coming from the large front window.

"Are all of your paintings of women?" Sam asked.

"Ya, most of my work is about woman. I portray all subjects, but most especially women."

"Do you ever paint men, children?"

"I do not know men. I cannot portray what I do not know, but as you will see, I do portray children. I unnerstand children—dehr innocence, dehr endless ability to love. I understand dhem until dhey lose childhood. Dhen dhey know evil and dehr child's love is gone."

Sam stared at her for a moment as though she was thinking about what the woman had said, then she looked through more of the paintings.

"Your women do not look happy," Sam said.

"You must see more close. Dhey are happy. Not movie-star happy or like women in America magazines are happy. Dhey are happy de way Liberian women are happy. Dhey can bear dehr burdens, dhey can care for dehr families, dhey can stand agains' a mighty flood of troubles, and dhey cause no pain. Dhey cause no suffering; dhey struggle to remove dhose tings. Most men do not see dees tings. De women I portray are Madonnas of a diffren' sort."

Sam looked through several more and selected one. It was of a colorfully dressed woman and a man walking along an empty dirt road. The woman cradled something in her arms and had turned to look back. The man, only his back visible, continued down the road. The surrounding colors were muted and seemed to fade into the daylight. Long shadows stretched to a dark thicket of trees beyond.

Sam seemed to be drawn into the painting, studying it for an unusually long time. She put it back in its place and then, still studying it, picked it up again.

"I'd like this one," she sighed softly.

Winston was unimpressed by the picture, and although he didn't actually say so, must have thought it a waste of money. He drove us back to the Ambassador and promised to return the next morning at nine o'clock.

"Do you think we'll ever see him again?" Sam asked.

"I doubt it. I paid him the whole thing. It's probably more money than he'll make in a year. I expect he'll take a Dutchman's holiday."

We took a table at the beach bar. Sam noticed Mr. Chao sitting nearby.

"Ask him if he wants to join us," she said.

I went over to the bar next to Mr. Chao.

"Mr. Chao," I said, "would you care to join us at our table?"

Mr. Chao smiled broadly, showing his yellowing teeth.

"Yes, yes," he said, bobbing his head up and down. He glanced over at Sam, then at the two men at the other side of the bar.

Joe danced up, polishing a whiskey glass with a soft linen cloth. It wasn't necessary for him to ask what I wanted, but I ordered two gins and tonic anyway and a replacement for whatever Mr. Chao was having, which looked like diluted orange juice.

From their clothes, hair, and bulldog expressions I guessed that the two men on the other side of the bar were Eastern Europeans, probably Russians. They pretended to ignore us, but occasionally I would catch them taking a sidelong glance our way. They had muscular arms and thick necks and looked more like soldiers out of uniform than construction workers.

Back at the table, Mr. Chao sipped his drink with unusual zeal.

"Do you know those men?" I asked.

He glanced around slowly.

"They are from the Soviet Union," he said. "They have been shadowing me since I arrived."

"What do they want?" Sam asked.

"I don't know, madam, specifically. It looks like to me they want to know where I go and who I meet with. All Chinese diplomats have their Russian friends tagging along with them." Mr. Chao looked thoughtful for a moment. "But then again, we tag along with them also."

"Should I invite them over for a drink?" I asked.

"No! No!" Mr. Chao said with his eyes growing larger. "That is not the way the game is played. We pretend to ignore one another. We keep up appearances. They don't step over the line and we don't step over the line. It's a rather delicate diplomatic dance, you see."

"Why are the Russians so interested?" Sam asked. "I thought you guys were comrades—Marx and Mao and all that."

"Yes, we do share similar ideologies but theirs was much, shall I say, distorted by Lenin and Stalin."

"And yours by Mao?" Sam added.

"Please, madam, let us not ruin a perfect late afternoon with discussions of politics. Let us enjoy the beautiful golden sunset in this land of plenty."

I wondered where Mr. Chao had gotten his notion that Liberia was a land of plenty. Most people in Liberia lived in conditions of poverty that would not be tolerated in the US or Europe and probably not in China. Ninety-five percent of the wealth and access to wealth was controlled by a relative few who seemed to consider it their birthright.

In one sense it was. Americo-Liberians are the descendants of the American Black freedmen who settled Liberia in the 1800s. They quickly established an American-style society and government and subjugated the indigenous population. Ironically, it was a carbon copy of the antebellum society in the South from which they had fled.

When President Tolbert took office, he further strengthened the hand of the Americo-Liberians in several ways. He had made empty gestures of inclusion to the indigenous groups in a continuing policy of pacification and distraction. However, he openly practiced nepotism as though it was the new norm. He lied fluently as if it were the truth, and he seemed to be completely oblivious to the history of despotism.

"Mr. Chao, what are you doing here?" Sam asked, looking directly at him. Mr. Chao looked as though he was about to say something amusing but decided not to deflect the question.

"You Americans," he said, "always so direct. My Government simply wants to help this country develop to its full potential without interference." He waved his hand as though dismissing any further discussion.

"You realize, Mr. Chao," Sam continued, "that my country is probably not going to just stand by and let you come in here and take control."

"We have no intention of, as you say, taking control. Rice is very important to us, as it is to all of West Africa, and we want to see that Africa is self-sustaining in that staple. Then too, your country is so stunned and demoralized after its total defeat in Vietnam that I doubt whether any of your political leaders have the will to risk such losses again. The Capitalists, who run your country, have already done their cost-benefit analysis and have, no doubt, told their politicians not to get too involved in Africa."

Mr. Chao sat back in his chair with an expression of smug satisfaction, something I imagine the Pope does after speaking ex-cathedra.

"Oh, I don't believe you have to worry about our country, Mr. Chao. You should be more concerned about your Russian friends over there," Sam said, glancing at the two men on the other side of the bar who seemed to be flexing their biceps.

Mr. Chao snickered and sipped his juice. "Our Russian friends are like bulls in a porcelain shop. They blunder about, being very obvious. You know, China was an advanced civilization long before Russia existed. Why, they were still gnawing on bones and eating raw meat while China was producing and exporting fine silks. No, we have nothing to fear from them. In fact, those men should be grateful. I've—inadvertently, of course— introduced them to some of the finest restaurants in this city. Yes, they should be grateful."

CHAPTER 3

BAO

Sam wanted to fly up to Voinjama where she had worked with the Peace Corps as a teacher in a village school. She was still in touch with a few of the teachers who had taught there and wanted to see how the Peace Corps was faring.

I made plans to fly a day trip there and back. I located the best maps I could find, made a list of radio frequencies for directional navigation, and bought a new first aid kit.

To our delight, Winston was waiting for us in front of the hotel the next morning. I asked him if he wanted to accompany us or use the time to make more money. He chose the money. Nevertheless, he assured me that he would be waiting for us at the airfield when we got back.

Sam and I loaded the airplane and, with some excitement, went carefully through the takeoff and departure procedures. As we gained speed and altitude, I once again experienced that magical transition when the airplane rises from the ground and floats on the air. Looking down, I noticed that things had changed very little. All the old landmarks were where they had been ten years ago. The slums of Monrovia were still there, only wider and smokier. We turned up the St. Paul River. I wanted Sam to see where the elite lived and played. Several of the mansions had been expanded and a lot more land cleared. There were a few new sprawling houses built in modern architectural splendor alongside the plantation style mansions that were familiar to me. Sam was duly impressed.

I decided to land on the main road to Voinjama, just outside the village. It wasn't used much and it was within walking distance to the school. I stopped the plane after a short landing. Sam and I jumped out and rolled it, tail first, to the side of the road. Sam gathered a few things she had gotten for the children and we started our trek to the school and Peace Corps office.

We had gotten within a hundred meters of the school when I heard tremendous screaming and shouting coming from between two of the village huts. A small chimpanzee ran out into the light, followed by a group of boys. The chimp was screeching and flinging its arms about and headed for us. The boys, most carrying sticks, were yelling and jumping in glee and trying to run ahead of the chimp to surround it. One of the boys caught the chimp by an arm, but the animal deftly bit it and the boy yelped and dropped the animal.

It ran for us again. We stopped and waited to see what would happen. As the chimp got closer, I could see that it was headed straight for Sam. She noticed it too and instinctively held out her arms. The chimp leaped onto Sam and held her in a tight embrace, looking back at the boys with obvious terror.

The boys quickly surrounded us and demanded their "bush meat." One of the boys grabbed at the animal, which screeched and flailed its free arm at the boy. Sam found herself holding on to the chimp and instinctively drawing away from the boys.

"You wan' buy? Good bush meat. Very fat!" one of the boys shouted.

"How much?" I shouted back.

"Twenny dolla!"

I reached in my pocket and handed him a ten. He smiled broadly, held the $10 bill up as though it was a proud trophy, and ran away, followed by the other boys.

Our newfound friend was, in fact, a bonobo chimp, related to the common chimpanzee but smaller. It had longer legs and seemed to adapt to humans easily. Our little monkey was a juvenile of about three years old. I suspected he jumped to Sam because, in bonobo culture, the female is dominant.

"Do you suppose he belongs to somebody and the boys just took us for ten?" Sam said, the bonobo still clinging to her and nervously scanning the area for his pursuers.

"I don't know," I said, glancing around as quickly as the bonobo, half expecting to see a middle-aged man walking toward us with a glistening and sharpened panga. But no, it was clear, the boys were long gone and most people were in their huts avoiding the sun.

"What are we to do with him?" Sam asked.

"We could always sell him for bush meat or eat him ourselves."

"Don't be ridiculous."

By now we were close to the school.

"He can't come into the school. Why don't you entertain him until I get back?" Sam said, trying to push the bonobo to me. He clung to her with amazing strength and started screeching. I finally managed to pry him away from Sam. He looked at me suspiciously but decided that I was a safe enough bet and climbed onto my chest. He wrapped his legs around my waist and gripped my shoulders with hands that felt like vice clamps. It was clear that Sam and I had acquired a new friend, and since I couldn't speak his language, I had to find a way to keep him occupied until Sam returned.

An old man was selling fruit and palm oil from a cart near the school. Maybe if I fed my little chimp he would relax and calm down. The man glanced at me, then at the chimp, and came up with an expression of mild bewilderment. He was even more bewildered when I bought a handful of bananas, some figs, and a cassava root.

"Ya gwine to feed de bo?" he asked, chortling. I paid the man and thanked him.

"He make good bush meat if yo fatten hi' up," the man said, breaking into open laughter.

I found an empty barrel near the school and used it as a seat. The chimp was still clinging to me like a tenacious vine. I put the fruit on the ground and tore off one of the bananas. The chimp looked at it, then at me, and quickly snatched it out of my hand. He ate the thing, peel and all. I offered him another and he grabbed it, but more slowly this time, more deliberate. Next, I handed him one of the figs. He relaxed his grip both with his hand and legs. I managed to pull him off me except for one hand, which held onto my shirt. He ate the fig. Then, without waiting for me to offer another, he reached down and took the other fig and started to eat it a little more slowly. Several boys from the school walked by and the chimp dropped the half-eaten fig and jumped back onto me, clenching me again in his vice grips. Clearly, we had to get the chimp out of this environment.

Sam returned, stating she was pleased with the progress of the school. The kids, especially the younger kids, were eager to learn and had been excited to show Sam their work. It was a rewarding visit for her.

"We should have a name for him," Sam said as she returned to me and our clinging friend.

I nodded in agreement. "I was thinking of 'Bao.' It means 'protection' in Vietnamese and this little guy looks like he's in need of protection."

Sam agreed and repeated the name to Bao several times, but he did not respond.

Bao was understandably reluctant to crawl into the confined space of the airplane's cabin, but with a little encouragement, he settled comfortably in Sam's lap and did not object too much to the seatbelt. He did, however, figure out, rather quickly, how to open it. Sam refastened the buckle and gripped it with both hands. Bao soon grew bored with the mechanism and preferred to gaze out the window. We took off smoothly and Bao seemed intrigued with the view of the farms and forest moving quickly below him.

Winston was there when we landed back at Spriggs-Payne. He was smiling, as always, and came out to the airplane to help tie it down. When he saw Bao he stepped back, not smiling.

"Boss, ya can buy bush meat in de town oh."

Sam explained that Bao was not bush meat, but the concept of a pet chimp was not something Winston could grasp readily. On the way back to the Ambassador, Winston was emphatic that the hotel would never let us keep "bush meat." He was right, so Sam and I decided to search for a house rental right away. Winston, now feeling like he was in command, smiled triumphantly and gave us the name of an honest rental agency.

"Okay, Winston," I said, "but you have to promise to keep him safe until we can find a house to rent! Keep him in a cage and don't let anyone near him! Understand?"

"Oh yessa, boss but I don' have no cage."

I counted out $5 and handed it to Winston. "You should be able to buy a cage with this and some food for him. He likes fruit, especially figs."

Winston was puzzled. He seemed to want to say something but couldn't get the words out.

"Remember, Winston. He's not bush meat . . . at least not yet."

Winston laughed, a full belly laugh. "I unnastan, boss. He not bush meat . . . yet!" Winston said, still laughing as he drove off with Bao tied to the back seat with a safety belt.

CHAPTER 4

"MINING ENGINEERS"

It was a small place, sparsely furnished, and though not on the beach, within easy walking distance of it. After all, we were not planning on staying long. Bao tended to be more curious than we had expected, so we found it necessary to fasten a leather belt around his waist and attach a line with an eye splice and metal clamp at one end. Bao had learned how to untie every knot I could think of. Sam also wanted to find a couple of pairs of shorts and T-shirts for him to give him some "respectability" when in public. The clothes, hopefully, would also confirm to everyone that he was not bush meat.

"You know," Sam said, "he may have been someone's pet up there after all. He's very friendly with us, and he is actually trained to do his business outdoors."

I had to agree with her. At times, it wasn't necessary to use the leash. Often, he would prefer to hold our hands when we took him to the beach or into the open market. After much coaching we started letting him eat at the table with us, but if he started throwing things (usually food) we would banish him to a corner of the room. He even learned to respond to his new name, but unless there was a reward involved, he would often ignore it.

The house proved to be more comfortable than I expected. That was just as well since we had some free time to spend waiting to hear back from my diamond contacts. The rainy season was wetter than usual with heavy downpours, usually in the afternoon. There were breaks in the weather, however, and we would spend those sunny, delightful hours on the beach reading or trying to teach Bao how to build sandcastles. We would often end up at the Ambassador Beach Bar late in the afternoon where Bao became a favorite among the guests.

Occasionally, someone new would show up but that was to be expected—it was a hotel after all. One evening, two men appeared who looked like they had just gotten off an international flight. Their clothes, though well-tailored, looked as if they had been slept in overnight. They rarely spoke to each other, but when they did, they held their heads close together. It could have been that they were not used to the noise. Nevertheless, Sam and I decided to invite them to join us. We guessed that they were American, so I signaled for them to come to our table. They glanced at one other then got up and walked over.

Once standing, the height difference of the two men became very apparent. The blond had short-cropped hair, was average size but quite muscular, his eyes hidden by wire-rimmed sunglasses. The other man was clearly African American with light skin, had a tall, sinewy build, and handled himself like a former college quarterback.

I introduced myself along with Sam and Bao. They eyed Bao curiously as I gestured to them to have a seat.

"You're American?" I asked.

They looked at each another and smiled.

"Is it that obvious?" the blond said.

"Maybe only to me. We," I pointed to Sam and myself, "are American, and Americans abroad are fairly easy to spot by other Americans."

Both men pulled the chairs out easily, glancing around the room as they did so. The blond extended his hand.

"I'm Craig," he said.

"And I'm Darius," said the other, as if they were about to launch into a vaudeville routine.

Each pulled out two business cards, revealing nothing but their names and a corporate logo, and handed one each to Sam and me.

I found it interesting that they didn't use their surnames. Introductions without surnames was becoming a youthful fashion in the US, but these men were a little too old for 'youth-speak.' Plus, they had the aura of government agent about them—scrubbed clean, eyes always alert, well fed, and with toned muscles from time spent in the gym.

They were a little tight-lipped about what their plans were, so we lapsed into the usual conversation about Liberia, its Government, the weather, and what we were doing here. I told them the truth, that we were here to buy diamonds, legitimately, and that I needed the money to pay debts on my air transport business back in the States.

"What about the chimp?" asked Craig. "You gonna take him with you?"

Sam pulled Bao to her lap, smiled, and caressed his shoulder. "That's on our list of things to investigate. If we leave him here, I'm sure he would be killed for bush meat."

Darius wasn't really interested in Bao's fate but did want to know more about how one goes about buying diamonds. I explained that the best way was to meet with a trusted diamond trader and that I had procured a light aircraft for that purpose. They both seemed fascinated, then said they were mining engineers here to make a study of open-pit mining but, on the side, were also interested in doing some big-game hunting. I mentioned that the best place for that was East Africa, that there was little in the way of that here.

"Maybe I explained it wrong, but the big game we're after is a special kind. Believe me, what we're looking for can only be found right here in Liberia."

They smiled. I understood that was a private joke and decided to leave it at that.

Our casual conversation gradually turned stilted and I began to feel uncomfortable. The questions became too detailed, and Craig had a way of locking his eyes on you so that you felt like you were being interrogated.

After a few minutes, Craig abruptly excused himself, said he had to make a pit stop, and left the table.

I leaned over to Sam and whispered, "Let's make this short. That guy has the eyes of a killer."

Sam nodded in agreement.

Darius was busy scanning the guests—mostly the women. There were a few Liberian women sitting and chatting at a table. They were obviously wealthy Americo-Liberians as they were dressed to the teeth, with spike heels and expensive jewelry. He tried to make eye contact but failed, then spent the rest of the time fidgeting nervously with his beer bottle until Craig returned. With relief on our part, both men then excused themselves.

Sam's eyes followed the two men as they left the bar. "Are you thinkin' what I'm thinkin'?" I said.

A slight smile flickered over her lips. "They positively stink of the clandestine service."

CHAPTER 5

THE CLANDESTINE SERVICE

In every city important and friendly enough to have a US Embassy, the CIA will be there too. It may be a single office with other offices located throughout the city, or it may be a suite of offices. Normally, however, it's a suite of offices in an out-of-the-way section of the Embassy building or grounds. Security is always tight and deadly.

The CIA's offices in Liberia are no different. They are located in a discreet section of the US Embassy, and one cannot gain access except through a system of doors that open remotely from inside after identification is confirmed visually.

Lawrence Green, or Larry as he was known to his coworkers, waited patiently, standing on the designated spot on the floor, as an agent behind the surveillance camera confirmed his identity. Larry's thin, graying hair was cut short and flattened on top. It was a carryover from his time as an Army officer. Larry briefly wondered whether he was that distinguishable in the camera lens from any of his other coworkers. The door opened as it had done many times before, and he slipped inside. He walked briskly down the corridor of offices until he reached the office of Management Officer Ellis. He entered without knocking. Mr. Ellis was expecting him.

"How accurate is this report?" Mr. Ellis asked, not looking up from his desk.

"I would say 95 percent, sir," Larry answered.

"You must trust your sources then?" Mr. Ellis asked.

"I do sir, completely, but as with all sources one has to allow for some margin of error."

"Well, we want to be right about this one," Mr. Ellis said, now looking directly at Larry. "Do we know who Tolbert has been in contact with?"

"Yes sir. He's been in contact with Mr. Anatoly Markov, the Russian liaison; and a Mr. Chao Zhan, who is Chinese Deputy Minister for Agriculture."

Mr. Ellis wrinkled his brow. "I know what he wants from the Chinese—cheap rice, but what does he want from the Russians?"

"We're not sure, sir, but we believe it's arms and material support. I've gotten reasonably good intel that the Tolbert administration is concerned about an insurrection. He can't get arms from us, and it looks like the Guinean Government may pull their troops out, so he's cozying up to the Russians."

"Worried about an uprising among the people? Are you saying your source is a mole within the Tolbert Administration?"

"I wouldn't call him a 'mole' per se. I just know him as a well-connected politician who is against Russian or Asian interference and would like to see a stronger alliance reestablished with the US. If a coup is the only way to do it, so be it."

"Is he part of the Progressive Alliance of Liberia?"

"P.A.L.? At this point, I'm quite sure, but I can't say for certain."

"I can't say I'm surprised," Mr. Ellis said, "after the way Tolbert handled the rice tax concession. I'm told the Army refused to fire on the crowd."

"Yes sir. In fact, some of the soldiers actually protected the crowd from the police and the President's 'Special Security Service,' the SSS."

"Not a good sign for *El Presidente*. We've seen this before."

"There are a few loyal troops, however, and Tolbert has stationed them at locations around the Executive Mansion. The SSS, he's placed around his house and at locations approaching it, plus they cover him wherever he goes."

"What will he have to do to win over the Army?"

"For the Army, he'll have to put more of the indigenous tribal members in the officer class—make them feel privileged, like one of the elite. That would go a long way in winning the Army."

"But he's not going to do that, is he? It wouldn't sit well with the rest of the 'Big Men.'" Mr. Ellis's lips tightened into a scowl.

"By 'Big Men,' I assume you are referring to the Americos. No, you're right, sir. It doesn't look like it, in spite of any suggestions we've made."

"We absolutely cannot let the Russians or the Chinese eclipse us here in Liberia. This is our best foothold in Africa. It's almost like another state in the Union. If they take over here, it'll be as though they've taken over part of the US. Can't let that happen."

"I agree, sir. That's why I wanted to get your permission to bring in a couple of operatives to "encourage an 'event.' I know them well. They've worked for us before in Africa and South America. They're very good, sir—practically invisible, and they'll do the job and leave without a trace."

"You mean back to Langley?" Mr. Ellis asked, attempting to light a cigarette.

"Yes sir, that's exactly what I mean."

"Good then. Do it, and keep me up to speed."

Larry left Mr. Ellis's office like a cat slipping between the door and door frame. He was confident yet wary. Covert operations sometimes had a way of turning sour, and when they did, nothing could make them sweet again.

He had made arrangements to meet the two agents at a small coffee house on Benson Street. He dressed casually, like a European businessman. It was well after dark when the men arrived. There were just a few customers smoking and sipping imported coffee from Sierra Leone. A ceiling fan, turning slowly overhead, did little to relieve the dank heat, but churned the smoke and earthy scent of roasting coffee into a thick, humid, but invisible cloud.

The men arrived on time and made their way quickly over to Larry's table. He held up a trident of fingers signaling the waiter for three coffees. The men sat down opposite Larry, barely noticing the waiter as he brought the coffee and carefully poured it in front of each man. The African American introduced himself as Darius Walker and, gesturing to his blond-headed partner as Craig Miller.

"We believe that something is going to happen," Larry began. "We don't know exactly what, when, or where, but all of the signs are there. Tolbert is very unpopular with the indigenous people, the Army doesn't support him, and we think these Americos are a spent force. How familiar are you with the history of Liberia?"

The two men shrugged.

"The long and the short of it is that the Americos, the Americo-Liberians—that is, they are the elite class, citing the fact that they are direct descendants of the American freed slaves that came over here in the 1800s. They've ruled over the natives with an iron hand for about a hundred and thirty years."

"So, the natives are restless?" Craig said.

"You could say that. So, anyway, I want you two," Larry said, holding up his thumb as a gesture of confidence, "first, to get inside and find out what's happening." He raised his index finger. "Second, find out just how friendly Tolbert is with the Russians and Chinese." Another finger went up. "And Darius, we need intel on the Army. Determine, with accuracy, whether there is a resistance group, who the leader is, how big and how well organized they are, and what are their plans."

He spoke quietly as he ticked each item on a separate digit.

Darius looked like he had been told to swallow a brick.

"We've got time—a couple of months, maybe," Larry continued. "It all depends on how aggressive they and the Russo-Chinese coalition decide to be."

"Are they working together?" Craig asked.

"I don't know."

Craig sipped his coffee.

"We met two Americans when we were at the Ambassador, a man and his wife. They own an airplane. Both know the country very well. They might prove useful."

Darius nodded. "I think so too."

"What's your cover?" Larry asked.

"We're mining engineers for a North American startup."

"Good," Larry said. "That'll give you access to the interior of the country and the Executive Mansion. When you want to make contact in the field use the short wave at 21:00 hours. The call sign is 'Hammer.' Your code name will be 'Nail.'"

Darius looked at Larry. "You shittin' me? Hammer and Nail?"

"No, I'm not *shittin'* you! And when you're in Monrovia, call this number." Larry handed them a phone number scribbled on a torn piece of yellow envelope. "It's a safe number. You can call anytime."

Darius took the piece of paper, carefully folded it, and stuck it into his shirt pocket. "The radio might be more reliable."

"When you're in Monrovia, use the phone first. If that doesn't work, then use the radio," Larry said.

"Do they have Danish pastries in this coffee shop?" Craig asked.

CHAPTER 6

WIESUA

It was a short flight up to Wiesua, but because of the rains, almost inaccessible by ground vehicle. Sam and I loaded up the airplane with canned food and enough water to last for several days. We strapped Bao, much to his displeasure, onto the back seat behind Sam. We couldn't take the chance of him banging me on the head while we were in flight—he was calmer with Sam than he was with me.

We took off from Spriggs-Payne shortly after 08:00. There was a low-lying mist over the ground that had not yet become fog. It had rained the night before, and the runway was dotted with shallow potholes brimming with orange, muddy water. The Cessna splashed through the puddles like a high-speed power boat until she approached takeoff speed. She hydroplaned over the puddles like water skis, but by then she was more aircraft than watercraft.

Once free of the ground, we climbed easily to a thousand feet, when I turned the nose to the northeast toward Wiesua, the heart of the diamond area. The weather improved as we left the coast and flew inland. Bao settled down once we were at cruising altitude and began studying the new toy Sam had bought for him.

I intercepted the Loffa River as planned and followed it, heading to where I knew Wiesua to be. After about twelve minutes the familiar bend in the river appeared where it turns more westerly for a short distance, then resumes its northerly course. Wiesua was there at that bend, right where it was supposed to be.

The airfield in Wiesua was also the main street through the town. It had been widened to accommodate several aircrafts at a time. There was no control tower or even a simple windsock, but there was always smoke curling up from a few huts. The smoke today showed that this would be a crosswind landing regardless of the landing direction. I briefed Sam about the unusual protocol for landing in the middle of town. She smiled and gazed out of the window.

In Wiesua, you didn't have to worry about people in the street. They had learned that the moment they heard an aircraft engine, they would stay clear. A helicopter might have fooled them, but probably only once. However, just to make sure, I circled over the town at eight hundred feet and then did a wide, shallow, descending left turn to line up with the street and brought her in for a muddy landing. I taxied to the side of the street in front of a small vegetable stand and shut down the engine. Sam jumped down and helped me push the plane to a small space out of the way of the shops. Bao was about to jump out, but Sam grabbed him just before he landed in a large mud puddle.

"I think I'll carry him for a while. I can just see him after jumping in and out of the puddles."

Wiesua, because of its proximity to the diamond mines, is home to a large population of Mandingos. Liberia has never allowed foreigners to invest in or own diamond mines, so they became almost exclusively run by the Liberian Mandingos. The Mandingo tribe is native to a large expanse of Africa, originating in various parts of Central and West Africa. They are known for their honesty, business acumen, and largely because of the diamonds, their wealth.

I had made arrangements, not long after we arrived in Monrovia, to meet my old Mandingo friend Al-Haji Tanja Gora and had advised him that we planned to arrive today. His home—or should I say, his principal place of residence—was in Wiesua not far from where we landed.

By the time Sam and I had parked the airplane, Tanja Gora was walking toward us. He had grown a little thinner and a little grayer in the past ten years, and walked a little more slowly. Yet he still held himself erect and was, as always, well dressed in a clean, brightly colored Kaftan and a tight-fitting, brimless cap. He was accompanied by a man equally as tall with a similar air of dignity whom I took to be a son.

Tanja Gora smiled broadly, exposing his perfect teeth and extended his right hand. I touched his fingertips with mine, which was his custom with foreigners, then he put his hand over his heart and said in English, "Peace be with you."

I responded, "And the peace and blessings of the Most High be with you."

He then introduced me to his son, Abdul-Aziz, which means "servant of the Almighty."

Sam, in the meantime, had strapped Bao in our homemade bridle and was holding him securely in her arms. Bao glanced around suspiciously and, except for holding up his arm, kept silent. Tanja and Abdul stared at him, both apparently thinking it curious that we had brought bush meat as an offering. Sam assured them that Bao was not "bush meat," but was now a member of the family. Both men found Sam's explanation very amusing and laughed to the point of guffawing.

Tanja invited us into his home, but Bao had to be tethered to a post outside. We took the places around the low tea table reserved for guests and sat cross-legged on an ornate carpet of red and gold. His wife, Faiha, came into the room and greeted us in a formal way. She then directed two servants to place and serve the tea.

We all chatted politely for a while, as was the custom. Then Tanja asked how he could be of service.

"I have come to buy diamonds," I said.

Tanja nodded, then looked at his son. "Tanja is now an old man," he said, "and spends much time in prayer and thinking on God. My son, Abdul, will serve you in that way."

Abdul had the face of an eager young man anxious to make his mark. I asked Abdul if he was prepared to go with us to the diamond mines in the morning. He indicated with a wave of his hand and a nod of assent and recommended the mines on and near the Gbeya River as being superior.

The mines at Wiesua were not producing as they did ten years ago, and the diamonds found there were not of high quality. The mines on the Gbeya were of higher quality, he assured me.

The problem was that these mines bordered Sierra Leone, and some of the soldiers in the Sierra Leone Army had the lethal practice of slipping over the border, raiding the mines, then dashing back. Nevertheless, Abdul stressed that the risks were worth the rewards and that, if I agreed, arrangements would be made for tomorrow. Sam and I agreed, and we spent the rest of the afternoon discussing the state of the world and the future of Liberia.

We stayed the night in one of Tanja's guest houses. Bao was allowed to share the room. I prepared a makeshift bed for him from bath towels, but he still preferred to hop onto the bed with us. Surprisingly, the three of us had a restful night and in the morning, Sam and I had a good breakfast of bread, goat's milk, and delicious coffee. I refigured my fuel calculation and estimated that I had enough remaining fuel to fly to the mines, return to Wiesua and back to Monrovia with about a fifteen-minute reserve—not much, if anything unexpected happened. I could get fuel at Bella Yella if necessary, but that would put us late getting back to Spriggs-Payne and, although I had done it many times before in the past, I wasn't crazy about doing a night landing on an unlit, uneven runway.

Abdul took the front passenger seat—this gesture of status was highly important. Sam had worked in Africa long enough to understand this, so she strapped herself and the chimp into the back seats. Bao curled his lips back and softly hooted at Abdul. The young Muslim was surprised and a little uneasy. He was clearly a little affronted at traveling on an equal basis with an animal, yet seemed to understand that it was necessary. When it came to matters of wealth acquisition, Mandingos were willing to swallow a little pride.

The diamond area that Abdul had indicated on the map was dotted by pothole mines and alluvial deposits. These deposits were created millions if not billions of years ago from intensive volcanic activity. These diamonds formed deep within the earth at the magma layer when carbon, in some form, was subjected to intense heat and pressure that had accumulated in volcanic eruptions, which then spewed magma and its minerals onto the surface. Millions of years later, natural erosion exposed this blackish rock, bearing its jewels.

We landed on a rough airstrip carved out of the bush near the mines. Mine operators had cut it to transport labor, mining materials, diamonds and any other stones of value. Abdul was well known among the miners and operators, and from the friendly greeting he received, well respected. Sam and I waited near the airplane and watched the miners. Many of them stood in the brown, turbid water up to their knees. Other men dumped shovel loads of river bottom dirt into the large sifters. All the sifters were about the same size, but most of them had different gauge screen bottoms. A number of uniformed guards armed with automatic rifles and handguns patrolled just outside the mining area.

Abdul was talking to two of his Mandingo contacts, animated at times but never submissive. After a short while, he walked back to where Sam and I stood, and held out two stones, one in each hand.

"They are willing to part with twenty-five stones from five to twenty carats for five hundred US," he said. "They will take nothing less."

I did a quick mental calculation and knew that this was fair. Its worth was also close to what I needed for my operation in the States, and perhaps even enough. I didn't want to insult Abdul by trying to negotiate. I knew he had already done that on my part.

"I know you have been honorable, Abdul, and I will take the price."

Abdul bowed slightly and then walked back to the two men, who nodded and walked back to their tent.

"We must wait," Abdul said, "for them to gather the stones."

"How long?" I asked.

"It will not be long," Abdul said, sitting on the ground cross-legged and assuming a position of stoic tolerance. I waited in the airplane trying to shield myself from the growing heat and glare of the sun. Sam walked off in the distance with Bao's hand in hers. Storybook memories from my childhood came to mind as I watched them disappear into the shade of the bush. They would be gone for a while, so I settled into my seat and tried to doze.

I must have fallen asleep because the next thing I was aware of was the sun slowly burning across my face. Abdul was gently shaking me. The two men had returned with two cloth bags and a small scale. It was time to pay the piper.

They were sitting at a small, rusty table shaded by a makeshift canopy. Between them were the bags, both damp and caked with mud and sand. As I sat down, they opened one bag and showed me its contents—all rough diamonds of about the same size. I was allowed to sift through them to confirm that there were no fake stones, a trick sometimes used by miners to cheat buyers. I nodded my consent. We repeated the process with the second bag. Then, very carefully, they placed each bag on the scale to show the weights were correct. They said nothing, but looked straight at me. I nodded.

Next came payment. I walked over the airplane and dug out my attaché case, opened it, and counted out the bank notes, all US bills in hundred-dollar denominations, then handed it to the men. They counted the money slowly, then clasped their hands together and bowed toward me. I bowed in reply.

I was gathering the stones and making sure the bags were tied securely when I heard the sound of raised voices. A foreman was yelling at one of the miners and the worker was yelling back. The mine worker stepped back, then turned and started running. The foreman drew a semi-automatic pistol and fired twice. The worker was a small, underweight man and the bullets took him off his feet. He fell face-first next to the river and rolled onto his back, obviously wounded. He lifted his right arm in a gesture of supplication and raised his right knee. A guard walked slowly up to him, leveled his gun, and shot the man in the head, sending out an explosion of blood and brain tissue. The man's arm and leg dropped into the dirt and did not move again. The guard rolled the body into the river with his foot and then walked slowly away, his attention now fixed on the other mine workers. Some of the miners watched for a moment, then went back to work while the body of the man drifted slowly downriver.

I turned toward the plane to see Sam, wide-eyed, and clutching Bao. Abdul and I boarded, saying nothing.

This is Liberia, I reminded myself. *Life is hard and life is cheap. It doesn't pay to break the rules.*

CHAPTER 7

THE MEETING

The waiting room, though opulent, was not very comfortable. Craig and Darius had been waiting close to an hour at the agreed upon address just outside of Monrovia. It was a two-story house that had been owned by a prominent member of the opposition to the True Whig Party. The Government had confiscated it and it was now a station house for Tolbert's Special Security Service (SSS) and used for every purpose in the SSS's playbook.

"Honorable Wilson will be here soon," a young secretary said to the two Americans.

Craig glanced at his watch, then gestured toward Darius.

"If he's not here in ten minutes, let's go."

Darius nodded. "Hey, I saw a club near the hotel that looked kinda fun. You interested? I mean, later tonight."

"No. And don't you go either. You know better. This is a sensitive assignment."

"There's nothing in the regs that says we can't have some fun. You know what they say, Craig my man: 'All work and no play makes Craig a dull boy.'"

"Okay, okay. I get it." Craig snapped.

Nine minutes later, the door opened and a large man dressed in an expensive business suit walked in, followed by two other men. They were dressed in less formal attire and were constantly glancing around, focusing their attention only long enough to identify a potential threat. The large man spoke to the secretary, then walked over to Craig and Darius and introduced himself as Honorable Wilson. He then invited them into a room, which was bare except for a wooden table and six metal chairs. He motioned for them to sit down and for his two attendants to stand near the door.

Honorable Wilson unbuttoned his jacket, then rested his arms on the table. The musculature of his upper body seemed to expand and stretch the seams of his jacket. His neck was the same width as his head and bulged at his shirt collar. His eyes were coal black and seldom blinked when he spoke. He was one of the rare Americo-Liberians whose complexion was a deep shade of black.

"I'm informed that you are here to help us. Is that correct?" Honorable Wilson asked in a deep, resonating voice.

"Sir," Craig said, "we understand that there may be some unrest between elements of the Army and the Tolbert Administration."

Honorable Wilson continued to stare at them without blinking.

"As you probably know, sir," Craig continued, "the Director is very concerned about your Government's stability. The US has a lot at stake here."

"You go and tell your director that he has nothing to worry about. Liberia has been a stable country for the past one hundred and thirty-three years and will remain so when America has long been forgotten. Our people know how to govern. No one in Liberia suffers. And," Honorable Wilson continued with an increasing tremble in his voice, "what does the US have at stake here? Your Government has repeatedly turned down our requests for assistance. We were not asking the US to give us anything. We were willing to pay, and to pay your Government's price too."

Darius glanced at his partner, then addressed Honorable Wilson. "We have it on good authority that Liberian Government representatives have been negotiating with the Russians and Chinese."

"What is this good authority you speak of?" Wilson interrupted. "Some disgruntled enlisted man? Every army is full of those. These little men from the bush, they're all convinced that they are owed something by the Government. So, what is your good authority?"

"Sir, I can't convey that information to you since it's classified," Darius said.

"You do realize that the Army did not fire on the crowd during the rice riot, but the police did," Craig continued.

"I have heard no such report," Honorable Wilson said. "I cannot tell you anything, gentlemen. So far as we know there is nothing to worry about. The Army is completely loyal to the President, but—" Honorable Wilson hesitated, "if it will ease your anxieties, you may look into the Army, so long as you give us assurances that if you find something amiss, you will inform us first."

Darius assured him that he would. With that, Honorable Wilson rose slowly to his feet and stood like a colossus for a moment, glaring around the room, then gave a hand signal to the two guards who stood by the opened door. Honorable Wilson nodded to the two CIA men and left with his guards.

"If all is peace, love, and prosperity, why does Wilson need two guards?" Craig said, staring at the now empty doorway.

Darius raised an eyebrow. "That, my friend, is what we have come to discover."

CHAPTER 8

HONORABLE WILLIAMS

Although we were running a little behind schedule, there was still a little daylight left when Sam and I arrived back at Spriggs-Payne. We off-loaded our precious cargo and tied the airplane down. Bao had managed to fall asleep in the back seat still holding on to the toy rattle Sam had bought for him in Wiesua.

Incredibly, Winston was waiting, though fast asleep at the steering wheel of his cab, his head resting precariously on the back of the seat. I gave him a little nudge on the shoulder and he jumped awake, glanced around like an old dog trying to remember his surroundings, then looked up at me with an expression of annoyed surprise.

"Thanks for being here," I said.

He smiled slightly. Sam and I gently removed Bao from the airplane and placed him in the back seat of the cab. We were just about to get into the cab when I recognized a familiar figure walking toward me.

"Mr. Spike! Mr. Spike! I was told that you were here."

Only a handful of people still called me by that nickname, and I recognized the voice of Honorable Williams.

"I'm so glad that I waited," he said, extending his right hand. "What brings you back to beautiful Liberia? I'll wager it's a fascinating woman, no?"

"No!" Sam said from behind me.

"Oh, heavens, I was only jesting!" Honorable Williams said, laughing. "It is the way we pilots greet one another, my dear. Don't tell me. Let me guess—you are now husband and wife—yes?"

"Yes," Sam answered, smiling and extending her hand to Honorable Williams.

We exchanged pleasantries for a few more minutes. It was obvious that Honorable Williams was in a hurry—no doubt some state function awaited him. He invited us to dinner the next night at the Ducor Palace Hotel. I explained that I didn't have proper attire—I never expected to need a tie, much less a dinner jacket. He waved my objection aside and said that he would send a car and driver for us at six p.m. We accepted and watched as he hurried to his Mercedes and drove off toward Monrovia.

At six o'clock sharp, there was a soft knock at the door. I opened it to find a man of medium build and height, dressed in a dark blue suit and patent leather shoes. He identified himself as Alfonse, our chauffeur for the evening, in the service of Honorable Williams.

Sam and I didn't know what to expect. We had both been to the Ducor many years before, but I doubted that the dress requirements had changed. Sam, of course, was able to look lovely in a simple cotton dress and something silky she found to wear as a scarf. I, on the other hand, had only a lightweight pair of trousers and a shirt that, fortunately, had a collar. Alfonse, understanding the situation, confirmed the hotel's dress code, but assured us that we would have no trouble. As we drove away, I heard Bao hooting his objections. I hoped that he wouldn't destroy too much before we returned.

As we ascended the hillside that accommodated the five-star hotel, the excessive landscape lighting blinded us to the night beyond. Our car pulled up to the entry and Alfonse stepped out to open the car door for us.

The blast of cold air from the air-conditioned lobby was a delightful relief. Alfonse had proceeded ahead of us to have a few words with the maître d'. The magnificently uniformed man seemed to stiffen a little then quickly nodded. The maître d' then waved to us to follow, which we did, almost trotting to keep up with him.

He showed us to a private dining room a little off to the side of the main dining area. Honorable Williams was there and greeted us with a huge smile and a handshake. He then introduced us to his wife, Antonia. He gestured us to our seats at the table, giving us the full benefit of the view of the city lights below. My memory unexpectedly jumped momentarily back to the magical evening I had spent here nearly seventeen years before with my German girlfriend, Ana. Ana's career in the film industry had placed her on the screen instead of behind it as she had wanted. Her good looks, poise, and femininity were not to be wasted on film editing and production. I had actually seen a couple of her movies, and although the dialogue was in German I could still see that she was a natural. I couldn't resist smiling, thinking of her success.

"Spike, Samantha, I'm so happy to finally meet both of you!" Antonia said.

And in an instant, I was back in the present. Antonia was somewhere in her mid-fifties with very light skin and alert, light blue eyes that did not release you until the conversation ended, no matter how long. She handled everything she touched—her wine glass, her silverware, her food—with deliberate delicacy. I especially appreciated her manner of speaking. She spoke carefully, intending for her hearer to get every word, and pronounced every syllable so that her words came out clearly and precise.

"My dear," Honorable Williams said to his wife, "I have told you about Spike—the way he handled the Commissaire in Guinea. It was brilliant. I could not have done better myself. Spike was one of my best pilots." Honorable Williams said, glancing at us. "And what are you doing now, my friend?" he said, picking up the wine list.

I gestured to my wife. "Sam is teaching English at Montgomery Blair High School in Virginia and I'm trying to sustain a small air carrier business."

"And I have no doubt that you will be a great success, but I know that you have not come to Monrovia as a tourist," Honorable Williams said.

"No sir, I haven't. Truth is, I need some ready cash, substantial cash. I'm hoping to buy enough rough diamonds to do that. And I confess, we both were a little nostalgic of our time in Liberia and wanted to take the opportunity to pay you a visit."

"Yes, yes, thank you, my friend. And the diamonds are a very good plan. You can have them cut in Amsterdam and sell them on the open market. Very good. So, when are you planning to return home?"

"Very soon. We will probably need to make one more trip to Wiesua and that should do it."

"Could you possibly stay a little longer?"

I was a little stunned at the question. "I could probably stay a little longer, but Sam will have to get back to her school."

Honorable Williams waved his hand dismissively. "Oh, never mind about that. I can take care of that," he said.

Just then the sommelier appeared next to our table like a ghost materializing out of thin air. Honorable Williams asked if a bottle of Chateau Margaux would be acceptable. Sam and I glanced at each other, smiled, and agreed. Honorable Williams nodded, then looked up at the sommelier and said, "*Si'l vous plait.*"

The sommelier bowed politely, then turned and seemed to disappear in a mist of smoke.

"Sir," I said, "why do you want us to stay?"

"I want you to manage my flight operation, West African Air Services. The fellow I have working for me is a drunk and a womanizer."

"That pretty much describes most of the pilots I know," I said.

Honorable Williams and his wife laughed. Sam did not.

"That might have been okay, but he is also an incompetent." He leaned toward me, resting both arms on the table. "Look at it this way. It will be great experience for when you return to your own company. Just consider doing it for a few months. That's all I ask. Until I can find someone I can trust and believe in. I know you can do it, Spike. I have no doubt."

He turned to his wife expectantly.

As if on cue, she smiled at me and said, "Robert has told me so much about you and if it is true, and I have no doubt that it is, I'm sure you would do very well."

She was a very elegant woman who handled everything with delicacy, from her napkin to flattery on demand.

"How does $3,000 a month sound, plus perks? I will pay for the use of your airplane and a healthy bonus depending on how profits go. What do you say?"

"Can I have a day to think about it?"

"Of course, of course my friend."

The sommelier arrived with the wine. He partially removed it from the napkin and showed it to Honorable Williams, who nodded his approval. The sommelier removed the cork with a few hard turns and poured a few dollops into Honorable Williams's wine glass. Honorable Williams went through the ritual of checking the cork, the bouquet, and taste, then nodded his approval.

Not long after the wine had been served and distributed and the obligatory toasts made, the waiter appeared. His uniform resembled a Latin American General's more than an obsequious hotel waiter.

The rest of the meal could have been magnificent, but my concentration drifted to Sam's and my immediate future. I just went through the motions of appreciating the evening. I kept thinking about the job Honorable Williams was offering me. We hadn't returned to Liberia to work, to take the same old risks with weather, maintenance, and local palaver. Still, I couldn't shake the feeling that I owed Honorable Williams a debt of gratitude and, of course, as always, we could use the money. It would only be for a few months. We could manage that. My only concern, though barely a conscious thought, was whether the country could hold together long enough.

CHAPTER 9

THE OPPOSITION

Craig and Darius waited in their black Chevrolet sedan in a clearing next to the east bound road, ten miles outside of Monrovia. Craig tapped rhythmically on the worn steering wheel with the fingers of his right hand. A line of thunderstorms was forming along the coast. They could hear the distant thunder building like an ominous drumroll. Occasionally, a lighting flash would illuminate their faces, temporarily blotting out their night vision. "When did you say they would be here?" Craig asked.

Darius glanced at his watch. "They're thirty minutes late now."

Craig unholstered his nine-millimeter Beretta, pulled the slide back, then released it, sending a round into the chamber. The hard, metallic clack of the slide locking into place caused Darius to flinch.

"I told you these men could be trusted," Darius said with some irritation in his voice.

Craig unlocked the safety on his Beretta. "Nobody can be trusted in this country. You'd better realize that. You might live a little longer."

"At least keep the safety on," Darius said.

"No way. That millisecond it takes to unlock the safety could make all the difference in whether you live or die."

"Don't tell me—you were the fastest gun at the Farm," Darius said.

"Make fun if you will. I only hope you never have to find out the hard way."

The headlights of a car came from the direction of Monrovia. He quickly snapped his gun back into its holster. "That might be them," he said.

The car slowed as it approached the clearing, then turned and stopped next to the driver's side of the Chevrolet. Craig rolled down his window. The driver's window of the other car slowly slid down.

A man wearing an army beret stared at Craig for a moment.

"Follow me," he said.

"Where to?" Craig asked.

The man did not answer but drove onto the road. Craig pulled in behind him and followed.

It was a bumpy drive, and at times Craig fell so far behind that he could only make out the red taillights of the car. After about fifteen minutes they entered a heavily wooded area and soon Craig pulled in behind the parked car ahead of him. They had turned into a circular drive and were stopped in front of a large house built in the Greek Revival style reminiscent of the nineteenth century plantation architecture in the American South. Darkness obscured the interior. There were several dim lights inside, some of them moving around.

Craig and Darius followed the two men dressed in army uniforms into the dark house. Signs of decay were everywhere. Water stains streaked the walls. Some of the pictures had fallen to the floor and lay scattered in heaps of broken glass and wooden frames. The two soldiers led Craig and Darius down a short hallway, dimly lit with kerosene lamps. They turned into what appeared to be a library. Books were scattered over the floor, some torn and the pages scattered. The books still on the shelves were covered with cobwebs, dust, and heavy green mold. There were three men sitting at a long table, all wearing army uniforms. The smaller man wore a black beret pulled to the right side of his head. He sat at one end of the table. One of the escorts, a large man with a deep scar on his right cheek, sat at the other end.

The soldier with the black beret motioned for Craig and Darius to sit down. He waited until the room was quiet, then introduced himself as Corporal Pennoh.

"All dis use to belong to a Big Man," he said, motioning around the room with his long arms, "one o' dhe so-called 'Honorables.'" He spat. "He and hees family move all of a sudden to one of hees estates in Europe—wi' no tought to de fate of de staff or o' de house itself. Dhey jus' leff. Don' know why. It wan't 'cause he be corrupt. Everyone in de gove'nment is corrupt!"

He smiled slightly, then continued. "Dhey inform me dhat you de CIA?" he asked, aiming his question straight at Darius. Darius remained silent and stared back at him.

"It don' matter," the Corporal said with a wave of his hand. "My source always accurate. So, you people ha' finally come to help? I ha' tried to contact you so many time, and ha' always been ignored. Do you people tink I am a bush baby? An ignorant man? No! I am educated! I know how many eggs make a dozen!"

He paused.

"And so now you need Corporal Harrison Pennoh's help?"

"Actually, Corporal, it's our understanding that you need our help," Craig said.

Corporal Pennoh wiped the perspiration from his face with a soiled handkerchief. The flickering yellow light from the lantern cast moving shadows over his face and the faces of the men around him.

"We've heard," Craig continued, "that President Tolbert is in contact with the Russians and the Chinese. Is that true?"

"Ya, o' course dhat true. You Americans!" he said with disgust.

"What does he want from them?" Darius asked.

"He wan' what you Americans will not giv' him—guns, money, mo' better trade deals. Dhere is a long list."

"And how do you come by this knowledge?" Darius asked.

"I not de only one who wan' justice. We ha' an important man inside de Executive Mansion. He ha' hees men an' dhey keep us well informed."

"How many of you are there?" Craig asked.

"De Army is wi' me 'cept de officers. Dhey, as usual, know notting. Dhey all be de same; dhose sons o' half-white Congo people. De only thing dhey want from us is slave obedience, like a pack o' dogs."

He slammed his fist down on the table, causing the lamp to jump.

"You don' believe me?" he shouted. "I will show you. Tell me how I can reach you, and when de President has anodder meeting set up, I make sure dhat you see for yourselves."

CHAPTER 10

WEST AFRICAN AIR SERVICE

Bao sat in Sam's lap as we discussed Honorable Williams's offer over a large bottle of Wild Turkey, an extravagance for us, as bourbon was difficult to get in Liberia. There was more at stake here than just the money. Sam and I had been trying to start a family for some time and neither one of us were getting any younger. We had married shortly after returning home from Liberia in 1968, but we had taken our time luxuriating in our new appreciation of the American way of life. We had no bribes to pay, no mosquito netting to worry about, and it was good being back in a society where we understood the subtleties of how things worked. We didn't think getting pregnant would be all that much of a problem. The bourbon gave us an opportunity to discuss our present and our future together. By the time we reached the end of the bottle, we had agreed to accept the offer. We would give it six months. Bao seemed to understand and went comfortably to sleep in Sam's arms.

To sweeten the deal, Honorable Williams offered us the use of his beach house rent free. Knowing Honorable Williams, I knew the house would be elegant, but I had to admit, the offer to gain this type of hands-on experience running an air transport company was invaluable—plus, the money he was willing to pay was better than anywhere else, even in the States. All of that, combined with the money I could make from diamonds, would give me a good start.

The house was located near Ambassador beach, by the hotel. It looked like several glass and concrete boxes joined together at different angles and levels. There were expensive Persian carpets throughout, and even a fireplace that showed no indication of ever having been used. The liquor cabinet was stocked full of the best booze that money could buy. A house boy named

James came with the estate. He was also to be our personal driver for short errands around town. This worked out well as I knew I couldn't really rely on Winston for all of our transportation, so I renegotiated our deal so that he would be on call whenever we needed him.

James wore a starched white waiter's jacket with a clerical-type collar buttoned at the back of the neck, pressed black trousers and polished black shoes. Generally, he stayed out of sight but seemed to anticipate our every need. The house also had one other accommodation that was practically unknown in Liberia at the time—air conditioning. Sam said she felt a little guilty staying there but that she would take it.

James did not approve of Bao at all and was afraid he would mess up the house. Not only that, but I was afraid I'd find Bao missing one day just as I was about to sit down to eat a delicious "casserole" James had prepared. I explained to James, who listened politely, that the chimp would be with us at the airfield every day, and we would take care of him at the house. James nodded with visible relief, only to be shocked once again when I added, "And yes, he would eat at the dinner table with us."

West African Air Service wasn't exactly a total mess. The company employed six pilots and three mechanics plus two "line-boys," supplemented by the mechanics when needed. I hired Paterson, so he would be there to keep the whole maintenance and loading operations running.

The pilots were the biggest problem. Two Spaniards who mourned the death of General Franco with bottles of Russian Vodka every chance they had, one South African who was constantly reading the Bible, two Brits who really did not like flying and always demanded more money, and one Irishman who constantly railed against the Catholic Church and the Christian Brothers.

I met with the pilots separately and, as my father would say, laid down the law. They squirmed and smoked and glared at me, but I made it clear that there was to be no drinking eight hours before a flight. And no one was to refuse a flight for any reason other than sickness or severe weather. Any violation of these rules and that man would get severance pay and "walking papers."

"And try to look like professionals and not like a bunch of pirates," I shouted at them as they left the room. There was a lot of sighing and grumbling, but they got the message.

I next met with the mechanics and line-boys. I praised the work they were doing and told them to keep it up, and if we could get profits up, they would get a pay increase. They cheered and danced.

This approach seemed to work—a little praise, a little fear—a bit like parenting, I'm told. Sam eagerly took to handling the office work, which meant keeping records, scheduling trips, and collecting fees. I would fly some trips, assign pilots, schedule maintenance, handle contracts, and make sure that all wheels turned smoothly in the right direction.

There were several Cessna 180s and two Tripacers. I ordered all the planes to be cleaned and polished, and the hangar to be swept and reorganized. I got on the phone to former customers, got some ad time on Monrovia's commercial radio station, and put ads in the newspaper. We couldn't afford to advertise on television but relatively few people in Liberia had television, so I didn't consider it much of a loss. Nevertheless, I bought a black-and-white television to keep Bao entertained when he stayed with us in the office. He was happy, so long as he was with Sam and he could roam around inside without any restraints, but when we took him outside for exercise, we had to fasten the harness on him. He never realized that if he really wanted to, he could easily have pulled the lead out of our hands. He never quite realized how strong he was.

After about a month of this, Sam and I felt that we were getting bogged down. I had spent over seven years here in the 1960s and did not want to get too complacent and spend another seven years. Sam had arranged a year off from her high school in Virginia and Honorable Williams had offered her a salary commensurate to her teaching job. She had settled into the routine fairly well, but I had to correct my course. I was here to make enough money to finance my own air transport operation stateside. I had to keep telling myself that. I could not lose focus.

I found that flying an occasional trip helped me do that. West African Air Service was now making a profit, the machinery of running the airline was working smoothly, and most importantly, Honorable Williams was happy.

I would occasionally fly with one of the pilots if the load permitted. This time it was the Irish lad's turn, Cian McNerney. Cian had been trained in the United Kingdom as a civilian. He had, like most civilian pilots, a checkered career as an air transport pilot, then as a crop duster in the US, until he underestimated a turn at the end of a run and ended up in a pile of twisted aluminum covered in insecticide. He spent a month in the hospital and still had difficulty keeping his hands and feet from trembling.

We were transporting a Catholic priest, Father O'Brian, up country to a mission near Gbarnga. The mission, like most missions in Liberia, had its own airstrip—nothing fancy, just a dirt strip cut out of the forest with a small clearing on the side where you could park off the runway. This mission had a wind sock, which was unusual in itself. However, the wind sock was generally useless since the surrounding forests did a good job of blanketing the wind. Nevertheless, the tops of the trees were light and pliable, and it was fairly easy to determine the wind direction from the orientation they were bending relative to the runway.

"Do you support the Irish language, Father?" Cian asked the priest. Silence.

"Do you support the Irish language?" he asked again.

"You'd better answer him, Father, or he'll never let it go," I said.

"I don't know," the priest said. "I suppose I do. You see, I'm not Irish."

"With a name like O'Brian, Father, how could you be anything else?" Cian asked.

"My family emigrated from Ireland over a hundred years ago. I'm American. I've never been to Ireland," the priest protested.

"Nonsense, Father! Once an Irishman always an Irishman. Eventually they all return to the emerald green island in search of their sacred roots."

The priest seemed puzzled and a little concerned. We were over the airfield, and Cian did a tight left turn to check the field for obstructions and holes, then lined us up on a left downwind leg. The tops of the trees, bending slightly with the wind, showed a slight right crosswind on final approach. The priest was hanging on to his shoulder strap with both hands.

Cian made a flawless landing, touching the wheels gently on the orange laterite surface. The drum-like rumbling sound they made was oddly comforting.

"Well, Father," Cian said. "Were you saying the rosary, or did you only need three Our Fathers and three Hail Marys to get you through?"

The priest ignored him and stared out of the side window as though he expected to see someone. Cian swung the airplane into the clearing next to the runway and shut the engine down. I eased myself out of the passenger side with as much alacrity as I could and opened the door to the back seat passenger and cargo area. The priest climbed out like a nocturnal creature emerging from its cave. He brushed the dust off his shirt and trousers, then brushed his hair back and adjusted his Roman collar. Cian pulled the priest's bags out of the cargo area and dropped them in front of him. The priest glanced at him then at me.

"In this country," Cian said, "people carry their own bags. Even priests."

"How long will you be staying, Father?" I asked.

"About two months, I believe. I'll get in touch with you when I'm ready to return."

I nodded. "We'll be waiting for your call."

Just as I said this, a white Land Rover pulled to a stop next to us with two nuns in the front seat. The older nun was driving. The younger nun got out of the vehicle and started struggling with the priest's bags. Cian rushed over and picked the bags up and dumped them into the back seat. The young nun smiled and thanked him. Cian smiled and stepped back as the nun reentered the Land Rover. Father O'Brian got into the back seat with as much dignity as he could muster.

"Did you have a good journey, Father?" the older nun asked as they roared away toward the mission.

"'Tis a fucking waste, I tell you, a fucking waste!" Cian almost shouted toward the dust trail of the Land Rover.

"What's a fucking waste?" I asked.

"That sweet young creature covered up in a nun's habit. That's what."

"She chose that life, Cian."

"No, she didn't. She was brainwashed into it. I know. I come from one of those Catholic families that regarded the clergy as near divine, and pray for at least one of their children to have "The Calling." My father has never forgiven me for rejecting the priesthood and leaving the tyranny of the Church. The whole business is a con, I tell you. They try to convince you that they have these magical powers, like any witch doctor practicing juju. They want you to believe that they've been chosen by God himself, which in the minds of the rest of us suckers, makes them God's personal friend. You see the power it gives them over the fearful and gullible?"

"They're not all bad, Cian. Certainly, there are sincere ones?" I said.

"Maybe, but they all like the power. They all like it when the rest of us kiss their rings or asses."

"You may be right," I said. "But for the moment, let's find something to eat at the mission and then head back."

"That's fine with me, boss. Nothin' would give me greater pleasure than to shake the accursed dust of this place from my feet." Cian hesitated for a moment then added, "Except for a smooth pint of Guinness sliding down past the old tonsils."

CHAPTER 11

THE ARMED FORCES OF LIBERIA

After being generously served a tasty lunch by the good sisters, Cian and I walked leisurely back to the plane. The sound of an unmufflered vehicle rumbled down the road. A military truck was raising a red, dusty cloud in its wake. It was traveling at a good speed for a truck that size. It skidded to a stop in front of the airplane. A man wearing clean army fatigues jumped out and hurried toward us. I could see by the insignia on his collar that he was a Liberian officer. A captain.

"Stop! Is this your aircraft?" he shouted from a distance.

I said that it was. He was a young man, possibly, in his mid-twenties, rather tall with curly brown hair and light brown skin. He introduced himself as Captain Roberts.

"I have two prisoners that I need to transport to Monrovia as quickly as possible."

I glanced over his shoulder. Two men were sitting in the back of the open truck. Their hands were shackled behind their backs, and they had been beaten rather badly.

"Are you taking those men to a hospital?" I asked.

He looked for a moment like I had told him his fly was open. "This is a Government matter and Army business. Now, will you consent to fly us to Monrovia or not?"

"Who's paying for the trip?" I asked.

"You realize that I have the authority to confiscate this aircraft and take you into custody."

He put his hand on his gun, a 1911 .45 caliber, attached to the web belt around his waist.

"Then how would you get your prisoners to Monrovia?" I asked.

"Wait here," he said, turning around and returning to the truck. He opened the door and got in, leaving the door ajar. I could see that he was writing on a slip of paper. He jumped out of the truck and returned, handing me the piece of paper about the size of a bank check.

"Give this to the sergeant at army Headquarters downtown. It's a field requisition for transportation. I trust you will not overcharge the Government."

I read through the paper. It was what he said it was, and he had signed it and left a space blank for the amount.

"Okay, Captain."

I looked at Cian and said, "Put those men in the cargo area and make sure they are well restrained."

Cian, seemingly unaffected by the Captain's threatening demeanor, nodded and walked toward the truck. The Captain seemed calmer now and very satisfied with himself.

The driver of the truck got out, walked around to the rear, and pulled the two men out. Both fell onto the hard ground with a thud, and for a moment I thought one had been knocked unconscious. The Captain motioned for the Sergeant to get the men up and put them in the airplane. The Sergeant grabbed each man by his torn and bloody shirt, and without giving the men a chance to get to their feet, dragged them over to the Cessna and pushed them into the cargo bay.

"They need to be strapped in!" I said.

The Captain nodded to the Sergeant, and the soldier began tying the men down with the cargo restraints. One of the men grimaced in pain but did not make a sound.

I motioned for the Captain to get into the back seat. He did and immediately put his seat belt on as though from habit. Cian completed a preflight check and we both climbed into the front seats, checked to make sure the area around the airplane was clear, and started the engine.

The airplane was heavily loaded and used up most of the short mission runway. The ninety-degree heat severely reduced the airplane's performance, and we barely missed the tops of the trees at the end of the airstrip. Even Cian was a little tight-lipped. The Captain, however, seemed unperturbed. He sat, leisurely gazing out of the window, until the restrained men in the cargo bay started thrashing around.

The Captain pulled out his gun and pointing it down at the men. He shouted, "Ya stop dhat, oh! Or I shoot ya! Do ya hee!"

The thrashing and movement stopped, and the Captain holstered his gun.

"What did these men do?" I asked, not really expecting an answer.

"These men are subversives. They were caught plotting against the Government. They are Krahn people, not to be trusted."

"What will happen to them in Monrovia?" I asked.

"They will be given a court martial, found guilty, and publicly executed as an example," the Captain said, resuming his casual gaze out of the window.

"Captain, you speak very well. Were you educated in Europe?"

"No, in the US. I graduated from the University of Pennsylvania with a degree in political science."

"So I imagine you'll be going into government," I said.

"When my tour is over next year. I will take over my family's businesses, and when the time is right, I plan to follow my grandfather into the Senate." The Captain paused for a moment. "I am a descendant of Joseph Jenkins Roberts. You might know that he was the first president of Liberia."

"Yes, I did know that, and also the seventh president. Congratulations. It's always good to have such lineage."

The Captain's smug profile was silhouetted in the window. His head tilted back a little. He was very conscious of his regular features and prominent profile. It reminded me of Houdon's marble busts of King Louis XVI and members of his family that I once saw in the Washington National Gallery, all with their heads turned slightly upward.

"What kind of subversive activity were these men up to?" I asked.

"They were trying to stir up their fellow kinsmen against the Government, and I believe they are smuggling arms across the border. They are ignorant men. They believe the Government should give them everything. They know nothing and they can learn nothing. In my opinion, they are less than human and should be treated as such."

"Do you mean 'Untermensch,' Captain?"

"I'm sorry, but I don't know what that means," he said.

"It's just a phrase I learned from my German pilot friends when I was here before. It means 'underclass,' but when they said it, is seemed to imply so much more."

The Captain said nothing but regained his stony composure.

We landed back at Spriggs-Payne in a light rain. There were two soldiers there to meet us. They ran up to the airplane before Cian could get the engine stopped, and opened the back door. The Captain got out and the two soldiers snapped to attention and saluted. The Captain returned the salute in a casual manner, then motioned toward the cargo bay and gave the men an order. They dragged the two prisoners out onto the ramp, kicked them a few times, and ordered them to their feet. The men got to their feet as best as they could. Their knees were bleeding. Both men kept their heads lowered and their eyes cast down.

"Take them to the truck. I'll be along in a minute," the Captain said.

Then, he momentarily glared at me. "As I said before, take your receipt to Headquarters, give it to the sergeant at the desk, and he will see to it that you are paid."

The Captain turned as though he was doing a formal, military about face and strode toward the truck.

CHAPTER 12

THE BIG MEETING

Darius and Craig had been told to wait in the church parking lot for a Sergeant Doe. They had no information on him. Langley also had nothing. They could only guess at what part he was to play. This time they had been waiting in the car for over an hour.

"I don't think the son of a bitch is coming," Craig said with nervous impatience. "I need a cigarette. Do you mind?" Without waiting for an answer, Craig reached in his shirt pocket for his half-empty pack of cigarettes.

"Yes, I do mind. Please don't light up one of those things in here. It's difficult enough to breathe in this damp, filthy air."

"I could roll down the windows."

"It wouldn't matter. The stink would still get all over me—in my nostrils, in my lungs. It takes forever to get rid of it. I don't see why or how you can do it. Besides, I have a date later tonight and I don't want to smell like an ashtray."

"What?" Craig said. "Don't tell me you messed up again and got another girlfriend."

"I'm going stir-crazy here. I'm gonna go check out that club I told you about."

"It's against protocol," Craig said, smiling.

Just then a black Chevrolet with its lights off pulled up next to them. Two soldiers in starched Liberian army uniforms waited in the front seat. The driver's window slid down. Craig did not recognize the driver in the sergeant's uniform.

"Get in," the Sergeant said.

The back seat reeked with the stench of stale cigar smoke and the faint odor of spilled beer.

"Are you Doe?" Darius asked.

The Sergeant corrected him. "Master Sergeant Doe."

Sergeant Doe drove off with the car's headlights on dim and at high speed. He skidded around two of the turns in the road but corrected without slowing down. He ran over a small animal scurrying to cross the road and continued without noticing. The soldier in the passenger seat continued to stare at Craig and Darius as though he expected them to reach for a gun.

After about half an hour Sergeant Doe pulled the car off the road and close into the bushes.

"We must go on foot from here," he said. "Be very quiet. They have highly trained guards and dogs."

Craig slapped at mosquitos on his arms and face several times before one of the soldiers grabbed his arm and signaled him to be quiet. They followed Sergeant Doe and his companion in single file through the bush until they came to a building in a small clearing in the dense growth where they crouched out of sight.

It was a large, modern house—single story residence, minimalist in design with floor-to-ceiling windows. Outside, the garden at the entrance was lit with floodlights, engulfed in a cloud of insects, and the exterior glass walls shone with the interior luminescence reminiscent of an Eero Saarinen design. Darius could easily see people moving around from room to room. Some were domestic servants, others were well-dressed men and women that the two CIA men assumed to be Americo-Liberians. A few minutes later, a black limousine pulled up to the front door. The driver got out and opened the rear door.

"Who is that?" Darius whispered to Sergeant Doe.

"He's the Russian KGB man that work in dhere embassy."

"Can we get closer?" Craig asked.

"No, it not safe," Sergeant Doe said.

"We have to get closer," Craig insisted. "We need to positively identify the man."

"Then follow me. Do not make a sound."

Sergeant Doe signaled for the soldier, a corporal, to take the rear. Then, slowly drawing a combat knife from this belt, he carefully and quietly crept through the bush toward the house. They stopped at the edge of the tree line.

"Dhere no way we can get across that clearing wit'out bein' seen," the Sergeant said. "But here, see if dhese help."

The Sergeant handed Craig a small pair of binoculars. Craig slowly scanned the house, then passed them to Darius.

"This shouldn't surprise you. It's our old friend, Honorable Wilson."

Darius took the binoculars.

"So it is. I can't believe such an 'Honorable' would have lied to you," Darius said mockingly. "I've got the Russian in my head. I'll recognize him."

"Then let's go," the Sergeant said, motioning to the Corporal to start back.

They had almost reached the car but were still pushing their way through thick bush when there was a sudden rustle of small twigs and branches followed by a muffled cry from the Corporal. One of the guard dogs, a Rottweiler, had been stalking them. He was trained to track silently and attack without barking. They were especially good at getting their prey to the ground then going for the throat. They had exceptionally strong jaws and long teeth.

Sergeant Doe knew instantly what had happened, and before the dog could wrestle the Corporal to the ground, Doe rushed forward, grabbed the dog by the snout, and cut his throat with a single, swift movement of his knife. He opened the trunk of the car and threw the body of the dog into it.

"Let's go!" he muttered with urgency. All four men jumped into the car, and Sergeant Doe, backing it out onto the road, turned and drove toward Monrovia. After about twenty minutes he pulled off the road, got out of the car, dragged the dog's sodden body out of the trunk, and threw it into the bush.

"They'll find the blood back there," Darius said.

"Not afta the rain. The hyenas will take care o' de dog," the Sergeant said. "It will all be gone afta de rain and it gonna rain before mornin'. Have you seen enough?"

"Yes, but we need to know what was discussed," Craig said.

"No worry. I get you that, but it will cost," the Sergeant said.

CHAPTER 13

MILITARY SECRETS

I had no luck with the Sergeant at the desk, and even though I knew better, I wasn't going to pay the dash.

"Do you know Honorable Williams?" I said to the Sergeant. His eyes lost their half-asleep drowsiness. He sat up more erect. It was obvious that he did. I persisted.

"He is the owner of this airline, and I would hate to have to tell him of this breach."

"I no believe you," he said in a deep, resonating voice.

"Then hand me the phone and I will call him. I know his number."

The Sergeant trembled as though he'd had a sudden chill and bit his lower lip.

"Wait here," he said while getting to his feet and carefully brushing breadcrumbs from the front of his uniform. He disappeared down a short, dimly lit hallway and into a room near the end.

About fifteen minutes later the Sergeant emerged, followed by Captain Roberts. The Captain came directly up to me with his hand extended. We did an American handshake since the Captain appeared not to want to shake hands Liberian style with a foreigner. The "Liberian handshake" was unique to this part of Africa. Done properly, it always ended with a loud click with the snapping of the two men's fingers. It was a symbol of comradery, which clearly was not present here.

"I am sorry for the difficulty, Mr. Varrier," he said, deliberately mispronouncing my name and looking accusingly at the Sergeant. "The Sergeant will take care of it right now."

He flung the receipt on the desk in front of the Sergeant. "Take care of this immediately," he commanded. The Sergeant disappeared with the receipt.

"There is a matter I would like to discuss with you, Mr. Verrier," the Captain said, softening his tone as though he were speaking with one of his fellow officers. I thought of suggesting a first-name relationship, as in, "Call me Ken," but no matter how friendly he seemed at this moment, my sense of caution told me to keep it formal with this man. He motioned for me to follow him into his office.

He had a large map of Liberia tacked to the wall with the international borders clearly drawn in red ink.

"As I suspected," he said, "we confirmed from the two rebels that you transported for us, it's true—illegal arms and drugs are being smuggled across our borders with Guinea and Sierra Leone. Based on the information we received from the two prisoners, most of the activity occurs here." He pointed to the northwestern border between Liberia and Guinea and to a short section of the western border with Sierra Leone. "I have convinced my superiors that the best way to interdict this supply is from the air, and they agree. We want to contract with West African Air Service to do this work." He held up his hand as if to silence me before I could speak. "I have already spoken with Honorable Williams and he agrees wholeheartedly."

I walked over to the map and studied the border.

"How long of a stretch are we talking about?" I asked.

"For the moment, we are not too concerned about the Cote D'Ivoire, but," he paused, "I expect we will have trouble with them at some point. So right now, we are concentrating on this border along Guinea and Sierra Leone."

"How often do you want these patrols to take place?"

"Once during daylight and once at night—all at differing times—no schedules. They will catch on to that quickly."

"What are we looking for?" I asked.

The Captain shrugged. "Arms, equipment, logistic supplies—anything transported across the border that's not at a check point, and as you know, there are very few of those. The smugglers are probably using camouflaged trucks or vans."

"How can this be verified? Or does that concern you?"

The Captain knitted his brow, resembling a football coach whose play has been questioned by one of the players. "The aircraft will be fitted with a surveillance camera for daylight operations and an infrared camera for night. It'll take two men, one to fly the plane, of course, and one to operate the camera."

"Who in the name of Beelzebub came up with that crazy idea?" I said.

"I can assure you that the plan is sound, Mr. Verrier, and that Honorable Williams is aware of it."

"Does Honorable Williams know how much this is going to cost?"

"The money is no problem, I can attest to you sir," the Captain said with a smile of confidence. "That the Government is fully behind this action and is prepared to fund it whatever the costs. We do have the right to protect our borders, Mr. Verrier."

I couldn't convince myself that Honorable Williams would have agreed with this risky adventure unless he had been under pressure from above. The Captain did seem to have influence in high places, and this seemed like the perfect scheme, if successful, to gain a quick promotion.

"We may have to hire more people," I said. "Will my men be considered a part of the military?"

"Certainly not. You will be contract employees just the same as a construction company hired to build an office building."

"If Honorable Williams has given the go-ahead then that is enough for me. However, I will need to talk to him as soon as possible."

The Captain picked up the phone handset on his desk, and after a few moments said, "I need to speak to Honorable Williams immediately."

It was only a few blocks to the Executive Mansion, so I walked. I felt the exercise would do me good. Although the rain had let up, it remained very humid, and by the time I got to the guard house at the entrance to the driveway I was sweating profusely. I showed the guard my passport and told him that I had an appointment with Honorable Williams. The guard picked up his intercom handset, nodded a few times, then handed me a visitor pass with instructions to return it to him upon my departure.

The Executive Mansion was a complex affair littered with offices for seemingly every function of the State. Honorable Williams's office was near the end of a curved hallway on the third floor. He greeted me with an extended hand and his usual joviality.

"Thank you for what you did, Spike, bringing those saboteurs back. I— or should I say *we*, if I can speak for the President—are grateful. Captain Roberts tells me that you are willing to perform the other service." He looked at me knowingly.

"Sir," I said, "it's your company. I work for you. As I may have said, I'll do anything that isn't illegal, immoral, or—"

"Yes, yes," he interrupted, laughing. "I know, or fattening." There was an uncomfortable moment of silence when he stopped. His expression hardened.

"I would prefer that you not talk to anyone about this. Think of it as a military secret." This made me immediately uncomfortable, like being exposed to cold weather that you're not dressed for. I never liked the idea of state secrets, especially military ones. It always seemed to me as if something unclean was being covered up. I'd heard the arguments before—we don't want the enemy to know what we are doing. But I kept asking myself on the drive back to Spriggs-Payne, who is the enemy here?

CHAPTER 14

ALL THE PROOF YOU NEED

Larry accompanied Craig and Darius down the corridor that led to Mr. Ellis's office. Their report was sitting on the desk directly in front of Mr. Ellis. Larry in-troduced the two men as Agent Craig Miller and Agent Darius Walker, and stood erect as the senior officer nodded in recognition. Mr. Ellis continued perusing the last page of their report and finished by gently putting the pages back into the brown envelope. He quickly tied the retaining cords into a careful and precise bow.

"This is pretty damning evidence," he said, glaring at both of them. "How confident are you about the validity of this source?"

"Very confident," Darius said. "On a percentage basis, I'd say 90 percent."

"The question remains, what is the Tolbert Government negotiating with Communists for? And why do they need these kinds of arms and equipment?

"It's my suspicion, sir, that the Liberian Government is worried about a coup from within the military, and they're keeping it quiet so as not to frighten foreign investors. The Russians are being very cooperative now, thinking they can edge out American influence in the future," Larry said.

Darius nodded in agreement.

"Can you guys get me something more definitive regarding any internal military action?"

"Yes sir," Craig said. "We can."

"Good! Gentlemen, very good! As you both know, the Administration is becoming increasingly concerned about outside interference in our affairs, both foreign and domestic, and word is already coming down that Russian and Chinese inroads into our interests will no longer be tolerated.

I'm informed that the Administration is taking a hard line on Communist aggression."

"We understand, sir," Craig said.

This had the joy of a new day for Craig and Darius. This was the kind of news that they had been hoping for. The Agency Bureau Chief had just given them the green light. No more Mr. Nice guy, no more negotiating—it was go-for-the-throat time.

Darius looked at Craig. "This is why I joined the Agency, Craig! It seems, to me, that Ellis and the Agency will back a coup."

"Yes," Craig answered. "We can straighten this place out once and for all."

They walked hurriedly to their car, both men barely able to suppress a smile.

There were only a few people at the Ambassador Beach Bar that evening. Joe had taken the day off and a tall, slender Liberian woman had taken his place. Efficient and reticent, she seemed to have a slight snarl on the left side of her mouth. She was careful to avoid eye contact when she served the drinks.

"Twenty bucks says she's Mossad," Craig said.

"She doesn't look Jewish to me," Darius said.

"Maybe she's a mercenary," Craig countered.

Darius covered his mouth with his hand to suppress a smile.

Sergeant Doe appeared at the bar with Corporal Pennoh. Craig realized that he had never seen the Sergeant smile. Even now he seemed devoid of any mirth. After speaking with the waitress, the two men came over to Craig and Darius's table, pulled up chairs, and sat down.

The Sergeant was dressed in a clean, immaculately pressed uniform; nothing was soiled or out of alignment. His black beret was pulled neatly to the right side and his face was masked with large aviator sunglasses.

"Do you have it?" Darius asked. The Sergeant looked over at Corporal Pennoh and nodded. The Corporal produced a large envelope.

"This did not come cheaply," Sergeant Doe said. Darius smiled and reached inside his jacket pocket and handed a letter-sized envelope to him. The Sergeant, taking out the money, thumbed quickly through the bills, then handed the envelope, with the money, to the Corporal.

"That is all the proof you need," Sergeant Doe said, sliding the large manila envelope slowly across the table from Pennoh to Darius. Darius dutifully placed his hand on the envelope, glanced in to see the photographs and cassettes, then looked up, expressionless, and did not move. Everyone sat for a moment, not speaking or moving. Then Sergeant Doe made a signal to Corporal Pennoh with his left hand, and both men rose quickly from the table and left.

Several moments passed.

"That was like a meeting with the devil himself, wasn't it?" Craig said.

Darius said nothing but gently placed the envelope in his attaché case.

"Let's get out of here," Craig said.

Just then Darius noticed a tall, rather light-complected Liberian woman, somewhere in her mid-thirties, enter the Ambassador bar accompanied by another, older, woman.

"You go ahead," he said to Craig, unable to keep his eyes off the woman. "Here, take the tapes. I'll see you back at the office."

Craig noticed his distraction and smiled slightly. "You see something?"

"Indeed I do. Over there by the window. They just walked in."

"Hmm nice. But I'd be careful if I were you. The rules might not be the same here as back home. She seems pretty classy to me. I don't imagine you can just sashay up to their table and say, 'Hi! Ya live around here? What's your name?'"

Darius looked at Craig and nodded. "You have any suggestions?"

"Why don't you wait until she goes to the 'sandbox' and just hang around within eyesight of the door. Then, when she comes out, arrange an accidental meeting. I know a guy who did that and he ended up marrying the girl. So you see, it works some of the time."

Shortly after Craig left, the woman got up from her seat and walked into the hotel lobby. Darius waited for a few minutes then left, hoping it wasn't too obvious, and waited in the lobby. In a few minutes, the woman came out of the restroom and started to walk past him.

"Excuse me," Darius said in his most polite voice. "But is that a Louis Vitton scarf you're wearing? Did you buy it at Bloomingdale's in New York?"

The woman, startled, touched her scarf with her left hand. "You're American?"

"Yes, how did I give myself away?"

"You mentioned New York and Bloomingdale's. I'm familiar with both. But it's your accent too—very American," she said, visibly relaxing and giving him a bright smile.

"You could pass for an American also—an upscale American, that is. The way you dress, the way you move, and your accent, also more American than British." Darius moved his left hand as though drawing a picture in the air.

"Thank you," she said, "I do have relatives there, and I did buy the scarf there, but it was at Nordstrom in DC."

"So, you're an Americo?" Darius said with mock surprise.

"Yes, my great-grandparents, several numbers back, came here just before the American Civil War." Darius noticed a tone of pride in her voice, the same tone he had noticed in white Americans when talking about their wealthy ancestors.

"Christ, I would love to hear about that," Darius said, hoping she would not detect the insincerity in his voice. "Would you join me for a drink, or anything else you'd like?"

"I would, but I'm with an old friend and she's waiting."

"Then have her join us. That would be fantastic," Darius said.

The woman hesitated for a moment. "Why don't you join us? I'm sure she would be delighted, but first I need to know your name—can't introduce you as 'some guy.'" She flashed him another big smile.

"Darius, Darius Walker. I'm attached to the US Embassy."

"Very impressive, Darius. I'm Piers. Piers Davis. Come. I'll introduce you to Pauline."

Darius followed her to her table, and Piers introduced him to the older woman.

"And what do you do at the Embassy?" Pauline asked.

"Oh, I spy on people, and when I'm not doing that I suborn governments and, in my spare time, I arrange coups d'état."

Both women laughed, with Pauline sloshing some of her martini onto the table.

"Very funny, Mr. Walker, but what do you really do?" Piers asked.

"I advise the Embassy's staff on technical matters."

"Then you're a lawyer?" Piers said.

Darius shook his head. "An Engineer."

"What school?" Pauline asked.

"University of Virginia School of Engineering," Darius said.

"And what are you engineering here in Liberia?" Piers asked.

"We want to see what we can do to improve the roads and bridges here—very important for the development of infrastructure which, of course, further develops the economy."

After a few more minutes of light conversation, Pauline excused herself. Darius then leaned closer to Piers and said that he had to go but could he see her again. Piers withdrew a calling card from her purse and handed it to him.

"You'll have to call," she said.

"The phones aren't all that reliable in Monrovia," Darius said.

"Well then," Piers said with a slight smile, "you're a smart man. I'm sure you can figure it out."

CHAPTER 15

IN TOO DEEP

Sam did not like the idea of using a civilian flying service for military-type operations. I tried to explain that it was for a limited time and that using civilian aircraft for this type of operation is not uncommon in small countries. I gently reminded her of Air America and its clandestine role as a civilian air carrier.

"And do you want to be one of those assholes?" she shouted.

"No," I said, "but Honorable Williams has asked for my help, and I think he's in some kind of political jam. And he assured me that it will only be for a few months. And here, he offered us a bottle of Jack."

Sam didn't look convinced. There was a long silence. I poured each of us a glass of Jack Daniels. Finally, she stared at me over the rim of her glass. "You know," she said, "I'm not that old, but I don't know of a time when there wasn't an armed conflict somewhere in the world. Remember the Cuban missile crisis? We came within a hair's breadth of blowing up the entire world. I'm beginning to believe that deadly conflict is natural to the human species just like hunting and killing are natural to a lion. We are, after all, predators. Our survival depends on it, but then again, maybe the Calvinists are right—human beings are just basically evil."

After a long interval and several more ounces of Jack Daniels, she settled down to quiet acquiescence.

Honorable Williams's beach house was large, open, and airy. We walked out onto a vast stone porch overlooking the beach. Bao was curled up on the settee, asleep. A gentle, humid breeze was blowing in from the ocean, and we could just hear the murmuring of a tumbling surf.

"Such a beautiful place," Sam said, "but I have an uneasy feeling. It's like we are playing house in someone else's life. Look at Bao. He's like the child we've been hoping for. But he's not. He's a monkey. And this house. It's gorgeous! But it's not ours. We're treading water here. I'm hoping we can go home to Virginia soon and get back to our own life—the life I love! And there's something else. I feel like bad things are coming. I can feel it. Normally I dismiss premonitions but I can't dismiss this. I just can't get over the feeling that something terrible is about to happen here."

I put my arm around her waist and she gently laid her head on my shoulder.

"Of course you would feel that. This is West Africa. You've seen a lot of bad things here, but keep in mind—it's only a feeling."

"Well," she said, with a slight smile. "So is love. Are we to dismiss that?"

"Not in a million years," I said.

Our mission was to fly a hundred-mile stretch of the Guinean border two days and two nights a week. Captain Roberts had both Cessnas fitted with a high-resolution camera for daytime and an infrared camera for night. The team consisted of two German technicians recruited from the optical companies that made the equipment. One technician was to accompany the pilot, and maintain and operate the cameras during flight. The techs were young men who knew little about airplanes but were very knowledgeable about optics and cameras. Their knowledge of English seemed restricted to the limits of their occupation.

We decided to base the airplanes at an airstrip near Kolahun, close to the Guinea-Sierra Leone border. The topography was fairly flat there, so our visibility would be decent. It would also allow for short flying time to the border and yet far enough away, we hoped, to discourage sabotage. Radio contact was restricted to essential use only, so we flew back and forth to Monrovia and Spriggs-Payne on a regular basis.

The problem was supplying the small base with fuel and maintenance. Also, I insisted on safe, comfortable accommodations for the crews on site.

Honorable Williams took care of all these issues. He leased a fuel truck from a service operator on Monrovia's main airport, Robertsfield, and had the locals erect a temporary structure next to the field for the crews, complete with a water supply, kerosene lights and stoves, and safe waste disposal system. We were ready to go.

Cian volunteered to take the first tour of duty. We figured each crew would do about a two-week stint, then rotate with the pilots back at Spriggs-Payne. We also sent a mechanic, fully equipped with tools and as many spare parts as we could afford. The weather, of course, was always a problem. We needed reasonably clear visibility—not too difficult during the dry season but much tougher during the wet season. We were experiencing the "middle dries" during August, so setting up the operation was able to proceed. But come September, we would just have to wait it out for a month or two for the dry season to be upon us. Fortunately, along most of the border, the terrain was a challenge, being hilly to mountainous and covered with thick vegetation. Captain Roberts told us that he suspected most, if not all, of the illegal shipments were coming across the Guinea border where the land was a rolling plateau and low hills. Smuggling heavy arms through the mountains would be too difficult and too expensive. There were several small rivers lined with tree canopies we had to consider, but Cian didn't believe that would provide enough cover for vehicles, except at night.

I was on site for the first reconnaissance flight. Cian had with him one of the German technicians who specialized in daylight photography. The other technician's specialty was the infrared camera for nighttime operation. Much to Cian's displeasure, Captain Roberts insisted on riding along on this first flight. He was sure that he would see a caravan of smugglers crossing the border just where he imagined them to be. I had the impression that this was all a great adventure to him.

I waited until they had departed, then made a cup of coffee in the makeshift base and tried to relax. Two hours later, they returned. The Captain was pleased with the flight and was sure he had "outfoxed the enemy." We did not have photographic processing facilities in Kolahun, so the Captain would have to fly back to Monrovia with the film. He wasn't happy about this, but his superior officers, apparently, wanted it right away.

I was a little curious, maybe even suspicious, because as far as I could see, there was really no tactical urgency. My understanding was that the Army only wanted to prove that arms were being smuggled across the border and identify the routes.

Cian was to make another run that night, so I flew the Captain and the film to Spriggs-Payne. He could take a cab back to his headquarters from there.

A routine developed and I didn't hear from the Captain for several weeks. Film continued to come in from the day and night missions and was flown to Monrovia daily. Wiesau was on the path between Kalahun and Monrovia, so during one trip I was able to take the opportunity to acquire more diamonds from Tanja Gora.

There were, fortunately, no aerial accidents, close calls or, much to the disappointment of Captain Roberts, no obviously incriminating information. I rotated pilots and the two techs on a regular basis. The men seemed to like the duty. The Government continued to pay handsomely and on time and everyone seemed happy.

Then, unexpectedly, the Captain appeared in my office with a new plan. He laid the charts, the photographs, including the infrared, and a dossier onto my desk.

"As you can see, these are mules and small vehicles transporting arms into Liberia," he said, pointing to several fuzzy images that seemed to be in the middle of a forest.

"It's all pretty blurry How do you know it's arms?" I asked.

"We know this from an independent source," he said dismissively. "The photographs help us to identify the routes." He paused. "What we are going to do is arm two of your planes and send them to block this traffic."

"What do you mean, arm our planes?"

"We plan to attach rocket pods to the underside of the wings with three ARS-57 rockets in each pod."

"That is the most insane idea I've ever heard," I said, almost shouting. "These are civilian, light airplanes. They can be used for reconnaissance, yes, but they were not built nor intended for hard military use. And my pilots are not military pilots. They don't do this job to kill people and blow up their things."

"Mr. Verrier, Mr. Verrier," the Captain answered in a raised voice. "As you know, Liberia does not have an adequate air force. Of the three aircraft we have, only one is serviceable, and it is required for other vital government tasks. This action is only meant to discourage arms deliveries. It is not intended to deliberately kill people." He hesitated and added quietly, "Although that is a risk, which must be taken in this kind of work."

"I seriously doubt that Honorable Williams goes along with this," I said.

"I must admit, he did show some reluctance at first, which is understandable, but in the end, he agreed. Even he has his superiors." He paused and did something that I had never seen him do before. He lit a cigarette and blew the smoke out nervously. "Feel free to call him. I think you should."

I thought this question was too important to be settled with a phone call. I ran to the company truck, drove to the Executive Mansion front gate, and insisted on seeing Honorable Williams. To my relief, the guard, after a short intercom conversation, passed me through.

"I expected to see you, my friend," Honorable Williams said, looking up from his desk. "It is not something I want to do, and I even protested all the way up to the President, but to no avail. The President wants to do this. He has been convinced that this kind of interdiction will help and will be cheaper and, shall we say, less politically damaging than hiring mercenaries. And it will only be for a short while."

"Help what, sir? Why are arms being smuggled across the border?" I asked.

Honorable Williams threw up his hands.

"There is nothing I can do. I am sorry," he said.

And I knew the conversation was over.

After that, I did something that I hadn't done in quite a while. I drove straight to the Ambassador Hotel to get a drink. I walked through the lobby, waving to the people that I recognized, then straight out to the beach bar. Joe was tending bar and smiled broadly when he saw me. I took a seat on a stool and ordered a double gin and tonic.

"Rough day, Mr. Ken?" Joe said.

"I think so, Joe, but I'm hoping the G and T will ease some of the pain."

"It sometime works, Mr. Ken. And where is the Mrs., or should I have no ask that?"

"The Mrs. is just fine. We are just fine. But honestly, Joe, I can't talk about what isn't fine."

"Juss as you say, Mr. Ken. Juss as you say."

He brought the gin and tonic and, against all my better judgement, I gulped it down and ordered another one.

I was well into the second one when I sensed a vague presence, like someone was standing next to me. I turned my head toward the seat next to me.

He was staring straight at me. "You look familiar, mate. Where have we met before?"

I've always been a little wary of this kind of introduction. It could be anybody claiming anything, followed by threats. I prepared myself to say, "I didn't do it."

He was a man in his mid-forties, sunburned except for the top of his head where his bush hat shaded it and part of his face. His light, thinning red hair was matted down with sweat where his hat had been, and he had a red, well-trimmed beard. He had hunter's eyes, clear and steady.

"I don't think so," I said, hoping to discourage any further conversation.

"It was a long time ago, during President Tubman's time. The name's Trevor. You were one of the pilots with Monrovia Airlines. I used to see you at the airport bar a lot. I was much younger then, or so it seemed."

"I know. I did go there then, but I wouldn't say 'a lot'. I'm sorry," I said, "I don't remember meeting you."

"We never met back then, although I don't know why. I was a mate of Colin's. You remember him?"

Hearing Colin's name did bring back an avalanche of memories. "Yes, I remember Colin well. Do you know anything about him?"

"Oh yeah, sure. I'm told he's living in the UK now, Manchester. Runs a pub called the Red Gazelle. Doing well. Has no intention of ever returning to Africa."

"Good for him," I said.

"I agree. I get the feeling things are about to happen here, and soon."

"What do you mean 'happen here'?" I asked.

"You haven't noticed? There's a lot of unrest here. Prices are high, nobody has any money—at least the poor people here don't, and that includes practically everybody except the elite, the Congo people."

I shrugged. "If you want to see it like that, there's a lot of unrest everywhere in Africa."

"Yeah, well, here it's all coming to a head. Were you here during the rice riots?

"Rice riots? Is that what they're calling it? My wife and I were swept away by an angry mob when we first got here. Fortunately, we found sanctuary right here at the Ambassador. Word here was that it was all about the price hike in rice. So, yes, I guess we were. I have also since heard that some of the soldiers were Guinean, not Liberian."

Trevor nodded.

"The Government doesn't trust their own army, especially not to fire on their own people. They don't even give them bullets. When they send 'em off on peace-keeping missions to other places in Africa, their guns are old and out of date. They have almost nothing in the way of heavy firepower— no big guns, no mortars or tanks, nothing. The Government keeps them poor and dispersed throughout the country. I've heard rumors, you know."

"You can't trust rumors," I said.

"I know that, mate, so I did some checking, and it's true. Everything I've told you is the bleedin' truth. I swear on me old mum's grave."

"So, what do you think is going to happen?" I asked.

"I'm willing to bet there is going to be some kind of purge, kinda like what old Grandad Stalin did after the war."

"Stalin killed his top-ranking officers. Tolbert's top-ranking officers are mostly America-Liberians, and all are loyal to him. Why would he purge them?"

"Oh, he ain't after the officers, mate, he's after the enlisted ranks—kick 'em all out and replace 'em with mercenaries."

"Mercenaries cost a lot of money and they tend to alienate the citizenry," I said.

"Tolbert and his friends have a lot of money," Trevor said, rubbing his thumb and index fingers together. "And employing mercenaries won't alienate his supporters. In fact, it will, I suspect, increase their support; and he and his supporters don't give a rotten apple for the country people."

When you meet someone in Liberia, it's always best not to ask what they do for a living. That information will usually slip out at some point if the person wants it to. If it doesn't, it's prudent to, as my grandfather use to say, "Let sleeping dogs lie."

Trevor had a pervasive scent of the bush about him, and my impression was that he could handle himself as well as a variety of weapons.

"How would you like to do some work for me?" I asked.

CHAPTER 16

"ONE PICTURE IS WORTH
A THOUSAND WORDS"

Craig and Darius spread the pictures out on Larry's desk. The photographs were in black and white and enlarged to 8 x 11 inches. They clearly showed a Russian agent conversing with their Americo-Liberian contact, Honorable Wilson. The other pictures showed the same agent in a different location conversing with Mr. Chao. They gave Larry time to examine the photos. Then Craig produced a small cassette tape recorder.

"This is a recording of most of the conversations. The Russian agrees to supply a limited number of automatic rifles and other small arms if Liberia agrees to stay out of African conflicts involving Russian interests."

"And what do the Chinese want?" Larry asked.

"They want a lot," Darius said. "They want to compete against American companies in Liberia and eventually supplant them; and they want to limit Russian influence in Africa."

"That is a lot. And what are they offering in return?" Larry asked.

"Not much," Craig said, "but at the moment it's important—cheap rice."

"Yes, it's amazing what people will sell their souls for," Larry said, hesitating for a moment. "Have you shown any of this to Ellis?"

"No sir. We wanted to run it by you first."

"Good! I'll set up a meeting with him ASAP, and hopefully we'll get something moving on this." Larry picked up his interoffice phone and punched in a number. He waited for a moment, then Mr. Ellis answered.

"He wants to meet with you right away," Larry said.

Mr. Ellis studied the pictures carefully and listened to the recordings as the three men stood and watched. He stopped to rewind occasionally. He glanced up. A look of satisfaction came over his face and he shoved himself deeper into his high-backed leather chair and twirled his thumbs around one another. After a moment, he sat up.

"Okay, I've seen enough. It's obvious what Tolbert intends to do, and we can't risk losing our best foothold in Africa. I want you two boys," Mr. Ellis pointed at Craig and Darius, "to find out what this Sergeant Doe really has in mind. If it's a coup that's in our favor, then do what you can to assist. But find out if he has any Communist connections. We don't want another sneaky Castro-type takeover."

Mr. Ellis leaned back in his chair and carefully put his feet up on the desk, crossing them comfortably at the ankles. He was as contented as one who had enjoyed a satisfying meal.

"I can help," he continued. "But if it comes down to it, you both know that nothing material can be laid on us. Larry, I want you to work with these boys, give them what they need and keep me informed. We have to maintain a certain amount of deniability. You understand that?"

"I do," Larry said. He motioned for Craig and Darius to follow him out.

Once out in the hall, he turned to the two men and asked, "What are your plans?"

"We will meet with Doe tonight," Darius said.

"And do what?" Larry asked.

Darius glanced over at Craig and said, "We'll dangle a carrot in front of his face and see if he'll bite."

"And what if he doesn't bite?" Larry said.

"He will," Craig said. "But in the unlikely event he doesn't, we've got more carrots in the bag, and I know he's a hungry man."

"You see, boss," Darius said, leaning toward Larry as though whispering in his ear. "Once he takes a bite of our carrot, he is ours."

Craig snickered and tried to cover his mouth.

"God! Don't you just love this Agency?" Larry said.

Then Larry, smiling, dismissed the two men and walked quickly back to his office. He had that familiar feeling, the one he got every time he climbed into his F-4 during the latter years of the Vietnam War. He could feel goosebumps popping up on his arms and a kind of mental clarity known only to a hunter who has a target in his gun sights. This was why he loved the Agency. He had the chance to get things done—to make, as he once heard his first boss say, "a difference."

Craig and Darius met Sergeant Doe in the abandoned house of the departed Americo-Liberian. They sat facing each other around a once elegant wood inlayed table in the library of the derelict mansion. The oil lamps threw dancing shadows across the shelves of books. The Sergeant had the same men with him, and the big corporal, Harrison Pennoh, stayed close by him at all times. Doe was drinking a bottle of beer, some of it trickling down the corners of his mouth. He casually wiped it away with the back of his hand. "So, now you ready to help?" Doe said. "What will you do fo' us?"

"How many men do you have and can you count on them?" Darius asked.

"I can ha' de whole Army if I wan' it. All I ha' to do is call fo' them, but there not enough guns an' no ammunition. We ha' made deals wit odder people, but it is not enough."

"If we could get you more guns and ammo, how would you use them?" Craig asked.

"When de time is right, we would attack de Executive Building an' de radio station an' de SSS force all together. Dhen, when our victory is complete, we will announce it to de world that all of Liberia is free."

"*Sic semper tyrannis*, huh?" Darius said with a smile.

Doe made a confused face. "What do he mean? Why do he smile, oh?"

"*Sic semper tyrannis* means "thus always to tyrants," said Darius. "It's what John Wilkes Booth is supposed to have yelled after he shot President Lincoln."

"Dhat's good! I like that!" Doe said, laughing loudly, spilling part of his beer. "Sick semplar tyrantus. Dhat is what I will say when de tyrant William Tolbert and all his kind are out from office."

Doe's men all laughed. Corporal Pennoh's eyes glistened as he laughed maniacally. The lamps illuminating their faces from below reminded the agents of grotesque carnival masks.

Craig and Darius stood up and shook hands with the Sergeant.

"We'll be in touch soon," Craig said.

Sergeant Doe rocked back in his battered chair and watched as the two Americans started to leave the room. He picked up a copy of one of the damaged library books, leafed through the crumbling pages, then threw it across the room where it fluttered to the floor like a dead bird.

"You tink you dealin' wit an ignorant man, a man from de bush. You tink I am lying—dhat I did not speak de truth. You tink I would not tell you my plan."

The two agents stood motionless for a moment. Craig's lips moved slightly as though he was mouthing what he was thinking, but no audible words came out. Then both men turned and hurried out the door.

Sergeant Doe looked up at Pennoh. "Dhere are times when one mus' lie by telling de truth. I will show them how a man, unjustly treated by these Congo people, deals wit tyrants."

On the way back to the Ambassador Hotel, it started to rain heavily. Both men rode in silence, Craig leaning slightly forward and squinting through the obscured, rain-spattered windshield.

Finally, Darius asked, "Do you think he can be trusted?"

"Not for one second," Craig said.

"Then how can we control him?" Darius asked.

"We keep him hungry. We keep just enough coming out of the tap to feed him, but not enough to satisfy him. If things don't go our way, we turn off the tap until they do. It works every time."

By the time they reached the hotel, the rain had slackened. The night sky was illuminated with complex and momentary webs of lightning that seemed to jump from one dark cloud to another, then unite to snake their way to some unseen place on the horizon.

CHAPTER 17

GUNS

"I can't believe this!" Sam shouted. "You're going to do what?"

I told her for the third time about the rockets and what West African Air Service was being required to do.

"Shit! Ken, we didn't come here to get involved in this kind of crap. Using these airplanes for military surveillance is bad enough, but this makes you a combatant, and responsible for God-knows-what kind of war crime this Government may commit. You have either got to stop this, or let's take what we've got so far and get the hell out of here. I can't believe Honorable Williams wants to do this shit."

"He doesn't," I protested. "He's doing what he was told to do."

"By Tolbert?" Sam asked.

"Probably. It's a joke, Sam. Something out of a sick comedy. My biggest concern is that the damn things might explode while attached to the airplanes."

"Do they even know who these smugglers are?" Sam asked.

"My understanding is that they believe arms are coming across the border. That's all they've told me. I suspect it's some tribal thing. Tolbert never did fully succeed in bringing the various indigenous groups into the Government, and some of the tribes, the Krahn in particular, are thought to have started gaining some strength. He's made a lot of wrong moves since he's been in office. One indication of that was last April during the rice riot that we got caught up in. If he balanced the government to reflect the real population of this country, his fellow Americo-Liberians would consider him a traitor and probably have him removed. The Americo-Liberians are simply not going to give up what they have. There's too much history here, and they don't trust the tribes."

Sam walked over to the bar and poured two tall bourbons. She handed me one. "So, I'm beginning to see. If, in fact, there is a tribe or two dissatisfied with the way this government had been essentially ignoring them, and they're making a move to gain their freedom, you will try to prevent that?"

I sat stunned. Sam's point was dead on. She took Bao by the arm and walked out onto the wide porch. I followed her, and the three of us sat together on the steps. She tethered Bao onto a long lead and let him wander and explore the property a little bit. A stiff breeze was blowing in from the ocean. It was slightly damp and smelled of the sea. I took a swig of bourbon.

"If I find out that's the reason, and not some group of thugs or outlaws, then I'll quit," I said.

She sipped her bourbon. "You know," she said, "maybe we'd better get some guns of our own."

I knew she was right. I didn't want to admit it, but I knew she was right. Maybe I was just getting old, but the thought of carrying a gun again somehow made me uncomfortable. And yet, I knew that here in Liberia, it could be a necessary option.

Buying a gun in Liberia wasn't exactly easy anymore. If you bought it from a dealer it had to be registered, and I seriously doubted that a legitimate dealer would or could sell to a non-citizen. On the other hand, TIA (this is Africa). You can get most anything in this country with enough money. However, I did not want to take the chance of offering dash to an honest gun dealer.

I thought about the various people I had met at the Ambassador Beach Bar. There was potential. If I didn't have any luck there, I would go back to my old haunts on Gurley Street, assuming they were still there.

My luck was still heads up. I hadn't been at the Beach Bar more than thirty minutes when Trevor sauntered in and dropped into the seat next to me.

"I need something, Trevor," I said.

"I thought you were happily married, mate," he said with a smile.

"I don't mean that," I said.

"Good," Trevor said, "because, judging from the look of your wife, mate, I'd say she would make you a soprano before you could shout 'no' in your best baritone."

I thought of asking him how he knew Sam but stopped before I could get it out of my mouth. Trevor was, among other things, an observer, and despite his appearance, a man who preferred staying in the background.

"I need a gun."

Trevor looked at me, expecting more—an explanation, a reason.

"Actually, I need two. One for me and one for Sam."

"Can't disagree with you there, mate. Everybody in Liberia needs a gun or some other way out."

"I don't mean to use it on myself."

Trevor laughed.

"I've gotten unintentionally involved in something that gives me the willies."

"What are you looking for?" Trevor asked.

"Something light, concealable, maybe 9 mm. Can you do it?"

"You know an unregistered handgun in Liberia is now illegal," Trevor said.

"I'll pay the cost of the inconvenience," I said.

Trevor hesitated for a few moments, then nodded. "Shall we order a couple of drinks to celebrate?" he asked, motioning for Joe.

Trevor was as good as his word. A few days later, he showed up at my operations office. He was carrying a small case.

"Do you want to do it here?" he asked.

"Here is as good a place as any," I said.

He put the case on my desk and motioned for me to open it. Inside, two semi-automatic handguns were neatly packed in brown wrapping paper.

"Go ahead, mate," he said.

I unwrapped the top one and held it up to the light.

"It's a Sauer 38H," he told me. "Thirty-two caliber, lightweight and very easy to conceal. Made a year before the war. Imagine the things that little baby can do—just the tool Sam would want to discourage uninvited guests."

After some hesitation, he seemed to read my mind. "You could say it was a gift from one of our German friends."

I unwrapped the other one and held it up also.

"A gift from our Russian friends, a Makarov 9 mm, although you can use a thirty-eight slug in it if you need to."

I popped out the magazine. It was empty. I looked up at Trevor, but again he anticipated my question. He pulled out two bags from his bush jacket.

"This should be enough ammo for your concerns."

I was surprised to see that the ammo was fairly new, with little or no signs of corrosion.

"What do I owe you for your efforts?" I asked.

"Two hundred and fifty US ought to do it," he said.

"Sounds like a bargain to me, and I'll tell you what. You can have it all back when we leave. Sam and I are planning on staying only a few more months."

"I don't blame you, mate. This place is like a tinder box. Anything could set it off, but if it does blow, an enterprising guy could make himself quite a few bob, don't you know."

I counted out the money. "Have you thought about that job I offered?"

"I have, but I can't fly an airplane, mate, nor do I work on them—don't like getting me hands dirty in that way."

"We're doing some special work for the Government, and I might need someone of your skills."

The right corner of his mouth curled up. "Sounds like it might involve killing."

"It's more like protection. I might want you to ride shotgun on a few of our missions."

"Missions? Sounds very cloak-and-dagger. What kind of 'missions' are you running?"

"Uh, surveillance. Just surveillance."

"So what do you need me for?"

"Well, you know the country better than anyone I know, and yes, you can handle a gun."

"And what are you offering as an incentive?"

"I was thinking $150 a mission."

This time he twisted the left corner of his mouth and looked to one side, then at me.

"Make it $200 and I'll do it."

"Okay," I said. "I'll get in touch with you. By the way, how do I get in touch with you?"

He took a pen out of his pocket and wrote a number down on a scrap of paper lying on the desk.

"Call this number and ask for Trevor."

Sam wasn't very pleased with the Sauer. It was too light, a 'lady's gun,' she said. And she complained that there wasn't enough ammunition to allow her to practice shooting. I promised that I would get more. She wanted to try it out, so I set up an unopened can of beer on a pole in the ground facing the ocean. Sam counted off fifteen paces, took aim, and fired. The can remained unmoved. She fired again; the can remained mockingly still. She fired a third time. The can jumped from its place on the pole and lay on the ground, spurting foaming beer from its wound.

I retrieved the can, which was now nearly empty. The bullet hole was to the left of center and low. I showed it to Sam, who motioned for me to replace it. She aimed and fired again. This time the hole was almost dead center. She wanted to try again, and again I replaced the can. She barely waited for me to get out of the way before firing a fifth time. This time the bullet missed. I looked at her, and before I could do anything she fired again, knocking the can up into the air where it tumbled, end over end, to the ground.

"I think you can handle it!" I shouted, picking up the can, which was now a twisted chunk of metal.

I took the results back to her. She bounced the gun in her hand as though feeling its balance.

"Ya know," she said, "I rather like this pea shooter after all. It's more accurate than I thought. The recoil's not bad. It's no Uzi but," she looked at me, "thank you."

Bao was jumping up and down and running through the house, flailing his arms around. He knew nothing of guns, but the loud popping sound was all the danger he needed.

Sam had to console him with mumblings, "It's okay, Bao Bao. Don't be afraid, baby. It's just Mommy having a little fun. Here, have a banana. That's a good boy!" She stroked him on top of his head and lifted him to her lap.

CHAPTER 18

STEPHENS & COE & CO.

Craig and Darius walked out onto the balcony of their penthouse room atop the Hotel Palm Camayenne. They stood for a moment surveying Guinea's capital city of Conakry and the nearby Atlantic Ocean. A faint stench of garbage rose from the city mingled with sea air and faint sounds of traffic and human voices.

Darius looked at his watch and then at Craig.

"They're late," Darius said.

At that moment there was a knock at the door. Craig went to the door and looked through the peep hole.

"It's them," he said, opening the door.

In walked two young men who looked like American college students. Both Craig and Darius stood semi-paralyzed, staring at the fledgling arms dealers, unaware that their mouths had dropped open.

"Are you guys Stephens and Coe?" Craig asked.

"Yah, that's us. I'm Stephens, he's Coe." Stephens pointed to his partner.

Stephens was an American, dark hair, somewhere in his early twenties, and wearing baggy shorts and a red tee-shirt with FUCKED UP printed across the front. Coe was also American with tousled red hair and smokey blue eyes. He wore faded blue jeans with holes in the knees and a collared pullover shirt with a marijuana cigarette printed on the back. Stephens was the talker, and Darius got the feeling that Coe was the enforcer.

"Frankly, we were expecting someone—"

"Older," Coe said. "Maybe wearing a bush hat and shooting jacket."

"Something like that," Craig said.

"Yah, everybody makes that mistake," Stephens said, his voice cracking and straining. "As far as anyone is concerned, we're just a couple of pothead college dropouts." Stephens was interrupted by a fit of coughing, which ended when he pulled out a small bottle of water from his back pocket and took several long swallows.

"We don't have much time," Stephens said. "Shall we get down to business?"

Craig and Darius nodded and took seats on the plastic-covered sofa in the room. Stephens and Coe sat down on the remaining two chairs.

"What do you want?" Stephens asked in a raspy voice.

"Five hundred AK-47s, equal number of Russian or Czech pistols, as many RPGs as you can get," Darius said.

Stephens and Coe looked at one another.

"We can do that," Stephens said. "When do you want them?"

"How soon can you supply them?" Craig asked.

"Two weeks. Maybe three weeks tops," Coe said.

"How much?" Darius asked.

"$500,000," Stephens's raspy voice said without hesitation.

"That's a lot of money," Craig said.

"We have other customers," Coe said.

"We have other contacts," Craig said shaking his head. "We'll get back to you."

Coe and Stephens stood up and started for the door but stopped just short of opening it.

"All right, all right," Stephens said, turning around to face them. "$350,000."

"Including the ammo?" Darius asked.

Stephens hesitated, working his mouth as though he was chewing his lips. "All right, all right, you're taking advantage of a couple of poor boys just trying to work their way through college, but . . . it's a deal."

Stephens and Coe returned to their seats.

"No US marking of any kind on the weapons, ammo, or packaging!" Darius said.

"Got it," Coe said.

"I'm goddamn serious, man!" Darius said, his voice clear and elevated. "You do know who you're dealing with here, don't you?"

"Yah man, y'all's got spook stamped all over you," Stephens said.

"If that were so, then you know not to cross us," Darius said.

"Chill out, man. We're not going to stiff you. We want your repeat business. The goods will have USSR all over them. Trust me on that."

Darius looked the two men up and down, then nodded in approval.

"Transfer the money to this account number and the goods will start flowing," Stephens said, handing Craig a small business card with the transfer and contact information on it.

Craig took the card and put it in his shirt pocket. "We want to see samples before we give you any money."

"Whoa!" Coe said. "Where do you think you are, the U.S. of A?"

"Again, let me remind you who you're dealing with here. If you guys don't come through, you will be hunted down like animals."

"Okay, okay. I can have one sample crate of product, with proper markings, dropped off next week."

"Good. Send the stuff to this address." He handed Coe a scrap of paper with the address of a warehouse in Conakry. "We will contact you in the usual way. When can we expect the full delivery?"

"As I said, in about two to three weeks," Coe said. "We'll send it in lots of a hundred and fifty."

Darius nodded, "That's good."

The men shook hands and Craig and Darius watched as the two young arms dealers left the room.

"Did you get everything?" Darius asked.

"Every word," Craig said.

"Can we trust 'em?" Darius asked.

"Oh, I think so. They know who we are, and if they don't deliver or they spill the beans, they've probably figured out that they'll find themselves locked up in the worst place on earth for the rest of their short lives."

CHAPTER 19

TREVOR

Mr. Ellis was late returning from lunch, and Larry found himself trying not to pace in front of his office door. He wanted to smoke a cigarette but resisted the urge. He heard the hall door unlock and swing open and recognized the figure of Mr. Ellis trudging down the hallway.

"Sorry I'm late, Larry. You know how it is once you start talking golf."

Larry smiled and barely nodded in agreement.

Mr. Ellis unlocked his office door and opened it, motioning with his free hand for Larry to enter first.

"Take a seat." Mr. Ellis said, pointing to the bare wooden chair in front of his desk. Mr. Ellis walked around his desk and dropped into his heavy-cushioned, leather-upholstered chair. He leaned forward and placed his two index fingers together, forming the outline of a small church steeple.

"Larry," he said, knitting his thin eyebrows together. "When will your two case workers be back from Guinea?"

"I'm expecting them back today, sir."

"And did you say they have an asset working for them?"

"Yes sir, a Brit named Trevor. We've given him the code name of 'Boom.'"

Mr. Ellis laughed and sat back in his chair.

"Really, Larry. Couldn't you guys come up with something less explosive—something like Zoom or Zowie?" Both men laughed.

"Have we worked with this asset before?" Mr. Ellis asked.

"I used him in the Congo a few years ago. He's very reliable, and he's a survivor."

"Where is he now?"

"He's made contact with the American guy who's managing West African

Air Service at the moment. He's an old acquaintance of Honorable Williams who owns most of the flight operation. Boom is supposed to find out how thick the Tolbert Administration is with the Russians and Chinese."

"And how is he doing so far?" Mr. Ellis asked.

"We don't know. We've had no report, but it's early yet. We expect to know something soon," Larry said.

"Good, then. Keep me informed," Mr. Ellis said, making a gesture of dismissal to Larry.

When Larry got back to his office, there was a message on his phone recorder.

"Stop by the store on your way home." It was a female voice—the usual courier that Trevor used—probably one of his prostitutes.

Larry left the office at the usual time, carrying his attaché case. He drove to within a block of the Randall Street coffee house. The owner behind the counter, Mr. Aristi, recognized him and waved him through to the back.

Trevor was sitting at a table littered with papers and coffee stains.

"What do you have for me?" Larry asked.

Trevor looked directly into his eyes. "Something's happening at Spriggs-Payne."

"Yesss!" Larry said, dragging the word out.

"The Government is arming some of West African Air Service's planes."

"Go on," Larry said.

"They're mounting rockets to the wings. It looks like a cheap, sloppy attempt to stop smuggling across the border."

"Do you know what they're after?"

"I heard rumors of guns and explosives. Whatever it is, they are serious about stopping it. The manager, a guy named Ken Verrier, has asked me to help them out. I'm not quite sure what he wants me to do. I'll let you know as soon as I can."

On the way out, Larry gave Mr. Aristi an envelope with the usual $100 in it. The owner acknowledged with a slight wave of his hand.

Larry knew that the first thing he had to do was contact Craig and

Darius, but he would have to wait until they returned from Guinea, which he hoped would be some time that day.

When Larry reached his apartment, the phone was ringing. The phone service had gotten better in Monrovia in the last five years. The system worked most of the time now instead of occasionally.

"What's up? I called your office earlier but couldn't reach you," said the voice on the other end that Larry recognized as Craig's.

"Call me on the secure line. It's important," Larry said, "It can't wait."

"When?"

"As soon as possible." Larry hung up the phone and in less than a minute the red phone rang. "What's missing from history?"

This was a secure code and Larry would wait no less than five seconds for a reply.

"Forgotten Leaders," said the voice at the other end of the line that Larry recognized as Craig's. "Now what's so important?"

"It seems as though our ambitious Captain Roberts has gotten a wild hair up his ass and has organized an interdiction plan. They're going hunting for arms smuggling, probably with the intention of blowing them away. They'll be using rockets fired from single-engine airplanes they've contracted from West African Air Services. Let your people know so they can plan accordingly."

"Roger that," Craig said and disconnected the communication.

CHAPTER 20

ARS-57

It took over two weeks for the Russian-trained weapons techs hired by the Government to make the necessary wing modifications to attach the rockets. First, they tried to fabricate a pylon-mounted launcher, but that turned out to be more difficult and costly than they had expected. They then decided to fasten rails under the wings so that the weapons could slide onto them and rest against metal stops. This proved to be much more efficient and lighter weight.

Then the electrical system had to be wired to the rails and a switch selector box installed in the cockpit. Although simpler than the pylon, it was still a nerve-racking process and Captain Roberts was at the airfield hangar every day supervising the project.

The Captain was able to acquire the Soviet-built ARS-57 rockets, which were a little over four feet in length and weighed eleven pounds. That would be over twenty pounds per side. The airplane could handle that easily. I had some concerns about the rocket motor possibly damaging the wing or even burning a hole in the wing's aluminum skin. As a result, I made the technicians, much to their annoyance, install a deflector plate between the wing and the rails.

Honorable Williams came out to see the completed work. He inspected the work for some time. I noticed a look of horror on his face. Then he asked us to join him in the operations office.

He looked directly at Captain Roberts.

"You do realize how dangerous this is, Captain?"

The Captain clearly did not like being challenged, not even by a superior. His eyes glistened, and for a moment, moved rapidly from side to side.

"One mistake—if you stray over the Guinea border—if you kill somebody on that side of the border, even if that person isn't a Guinean citizen, you could bring down serious reprisals, even war. And do I need to tell you what that would mean?"

"No sir," the Captain said through tight lips. "I understand fully, sir. I assure you, sir, that we will not violate international borders nor create unnecessary casualties. But sir, as I'm sure you are aware, we have an international right to protect our borders as well as resist insurgents that may wish to destabilize our Government."

"Don't give me that college political science bullshit, Captain!" Honorable Williams shouted. "We're on the razor's edge of chaos now. You screw this up and I will personally hang your ass out to dry! Do you understand me?"

"Yes sir, I do," the Captain said, looking as though he had been backhanded across the face.

Honorable Williams glanced at me, his nostrils flaring. He took a deep breath in an overt attempt to calm himself, then turned to me and said, "Why don't you and Sam join us at our house for dinner tonight, say about six for cocktails?"

"Yes sir. Thank you. We will. See you then."

And at that, Honorable Williams turned and left.

The Captain flopped down into one of the stuffed chairs and exhaled audibly. He'd had the wind knocked out of him and he knew it. He looked at me and slowly regained his air of contempt.

"There are a lot of things Honorable Williams doesn't understand. In the Army, I hear things. I hear rumblings. I see discontent. I see jealousy and envy. I see reluctance to obey orders. I hear rumors, bad rumors. Honorable Williams doesn't know those things sitting up in his paneled office in the Executive Mansion. Like the rest of them, he only hears what he wants to and sees what he wants too. They are way too self-satisfied." The Captain shook his head in despair.

"You sound like you are about to join the other side," I said.

"You watch yourself," he said, glaring at me.

I let a moment go by.

"All we have to do," I said, "is to not stray into Guinean airspace and to not shoot at anyone or anything on that side of the border." I took a deep breath. "That's all we have to do."

"That's easier said than done, Mr. Verrier," the Captain said.

"Maybe it isn't," I suggested. "Why don't you go along on the flights? They plan to do two or three a week, and there are only a couple of pilots who will fly these missions. You could make sure the pilots know what the limits are, and when you're convinced they do, you can fly with them periodically."

The Captain's eyes brightened. "Yes, yes, that might do. I can arrange the time away from the office. If I'm to take the blame for anything that goes wrong, I sure as hell want know what it's for."

With that, the Captain vigorously shook my hand and rushed out of the operations office, bounding to his car like an excited cat and roared out of the parking area.

CHAPTER 21

PRECAUTIONS TAKEN

Honorable Williams's principal residence, his family home, was located on the St. Paul River along with many other Americo-Liberians of inherited wealth. His city house, however, was in Congo Town where many of these same Americo-Liberians lived when they weren't in their vacation homes or traveling in Europe or North America. The Congo townhouse was on the beach side, and although modest by wealthy European standards, it was well furnished, tastefully decorated, sturdy, and comfortable.

Honorable Williams had a dog, Maximum, a Labrador retriever. Maximum greeted us at the front door by jumping up on his hind legs and placing his forepaws on my chest. He was panting heavily and made gentle humming noises.

"Down, Max, down! I think he smells Bao on you. He likes chimps too," Honorable Williams said.

Honorable Williams would take the dog with him to swim in the ocean. Maximum had the run of the house and was probably not as well trained as he should have been. Honorable Williams had installed dog doors in the entrance and the back door of the house so that Maximum had unobstructed passage to race outside when he spied something he wanted to chase.

He took to Sam right away and hardly left her side the whole time we were there. We walked out onto the veranda and stood gazing at the ocean. Then Honorable Williams raised his hand slightly, and a young man dressed in white with a black bow tie materialized instantly.

"How about a drink?"

He turned to the young man and ordered three gins and tonic.

Honorable Williams had a small household staff—a cook, two maids, and a sort of butler/servant whom he called Leo.

"Would you all like a chair?" he asked, motioning to an empty chair nearby. "Antonia will join us in a few minutes."

"Thank you sir, but the view is better standing," I said.

"You're quite right, quite right. I forget sometimes how beautiful it is here," he said, turning toward Sam and me. "I'm sending Antonia to the States," he said quietly. "I'm beginning to be concerned for her safety."

"How is she not safe?" Sam asked.

Honorable Williams wrinkled his brow.

"I can't put my finger on it, but somehow things aren't progressing well in the Government. There's a lot of secrecy, a lot of talking behind your back. We might take a simple ride into town, you know, to pick up something at the market, and out of nowhere a rotten piece of fruit or an egg will hit the car. That hasn't happened before in my memory. I know that times are a little rough but we, as a nation, have gone through it before. Then there is the ambitious Captain. He's managed to convince the President that we are practically under attack. I'd like to trim him down a little if I could, but he comes from an influential family and it would not be wise to turn them against me just now. There is something going on, I'm sure of it, and I want Antonia safe so I can give the situation my full concentration."

Leo brought the drinks, served each one of us, then bowed politely and asked if there was anything else. His face was expressionless and he avoided eye contact.

"Leo is of the Krahn tribe," Honorable Williams explained. "I sent him to the UK for training. It took nearly a whole year. He's done very well—as good as any English butler—but somehow, I still get the feeling there's a bit of the bush lurking in him. He keeps it well suppressed. Yes, and I have two Bassa girls also, and a Kru woman. They all get along very well, just like a family. All these tribal people living together in harmony. It could be a good lesson for the nation, don't you think?"

I agreed but wondered inwardly if this was standard propaganda or whether he was just naïve. Nonetheless, I could see Sam was impressed with Honorable Williams's positive outlook and global view.

Leo came out onto the veranda and announced that dinner was ready. Antonia joined us in the dining room and motioned to Sam and I where we were to sit. The table, long and oval shaped, was made of a rather rare, dark wenge wood native to Southern and West Africa. It was highly polished and could easily seat eight. The chairs, also of wenge wood, were custom made and looked similar in style to Queen Anne.

Everything was done very properly; even the imported beeswax candles on the table burned evenly. Soon the two Bassa women came in with a rolling tray and began serving the first course. It was shark steak, medium rare, with new potatoes and chickpeas with a green salad.

Antonia noticed Sam's reluctance and said, "It's okay, Samantha; the salad is safe. I grow the greens myself and rinse them thoroughly in filtered water before serving."

Sam smiled but could not stop the blush that came over her cheeks. To change the conversation as quickly as she could, she asked about Honorable Williams's sons.

"Eugene is still living in the US. He is flying as first officer for a regional airline. We are hoping that he will get on with one of the majors soon, but as you know, it takes time and the accumulation of many flying hours, but we are confident that he will get there. Anthony is teaching at a small college in California and hoping for tenure.

"I dearly miss them. When we sent them abroad for schooling, we truly expected them to come home and either get into politics or get involved with Robert's dream, building up a national airline in Liberia. But now with the successes they've had in their respective jobs, I fear we will only be seeing them on family visits either here or there."

The rest of the dinner conversation turned more thoughtful. I had forgotten how much I admired Honorable Williams and how close our friendship had been ten years ago. He had been like a father to me. After a dessert consisting of an elegant chocolate and strawberry ice cream parfait concoction, we were offered a "digestif" in the form of a Courvoisier VSOP. Eventually, when the conversation returned to questions about family and the air transport business, it seemed that then it was time to go. Honorable Williams walked us to the front door. Pausing and glancing around briefly, he said he wanted me to fly Antonia to Robertsfield International Airport the next day at 09:00. He did not want to trust her safety to road travel. He didn't say why.

That morning a rather plain sedan rolled slowly into the parking area of West African Air Service at precisely at 08:30. Two men got out, one a uniformed policeman and the other an SSS agent carrying a holstered sidearm on his hip. The policeman opened the passenger door and helped Mrs. Williams out of the car while the SSS agent stood by looking around like someone expecting an explosion. The policeman then hurried around to the trunk, threw it open, and started removing Mrs. Williams' set of matching valises.

Paterson appeared and helped the officer cart the bags to the ramp where his workmen would load them.

"Would you like to come into the office?" I suggested.

Mrs. Williams looked at the gray, concrete, metal-roofed office for a few moments like one who discovers rotten meat on their dinner plate.

"No thank you," she said. "If it's all right with you, I'drather we get to Robertsfield as soon as possible."

"Yes ma'am," I said. "The airplane is ready except for loading, so if you would like to come with me, I'll get you seated and secure and we'll be on our way to Robertsfield."

Paterson's loaders finished stacking the bags and strapping them down. Mrs. Williams took the right front seat next to me. She seemed interested in the procedures for flight, so I explained the use of the pre-flight checklist and its importance.

The SSS agent and policeman climbed into the back seat and waited patiently for departure. Due to their extra weight, the takeoff was longer than I had expected but it was, nevertheless, uneventful. As I continued to explain the functions of the aircraft, Mrs. Williams's ' mood abruptly became serious, as it was evident she had been aware of the reason for this trip all along and now lost all interest in the workings of the airplane or in the miniaturized world below. The security men, however, couldn't stop looking around and smiling.

The flight from Spriggs-Payne to Robertsfield takes about fifteen minutes with no delays. I taxied up to the main terminal and parked well away from the heavy, four-engine Pan Am B707 sitting there.

The officers unloaded Mrs. Williams's bags and carried them to the base of the metal stairway leading up to the airplane's passenger hatchway. There was some discussion with a uniformed guard there, but Mrs. Williams continued up the steps followed by the SSS agent and policeman. Her bags were left to be stowed in the cargo bay.

In a few minutes, the SSS agent and policeman returned and climbed in the plane with me. I started to make preparations to depart when the SSS agent reached over and put his hand on mine.

"Let us wait until the airplane leaves," he said, looking me straight in the eyes.

The other passengers were led out of the terminal building and onto the waiting B707. Twenty minutes later and slightly behind schedule, the engines on the 707 spooled up and the big jet moved slowly from the ramp to the cracked and under-strength taxiway. We continued waiting until the airplane took off and turned on course, leaving only four black trails of jet exhaust in its wake. The SSS agent nodded and I started the engine.

CHAPTER 22

THE FISHING TRIP

Craig tapped lightly on Larry's office door. Then, without waiting for a reply, he stuck his head inside the office. Cigarette smoke was rising from an ashtray, but the room was empty. Rather than wait, he decided to buck protocol and go straight to Mr. Ellis. As he knocked, he heard both of them talking.

"Enter!" Mr. Ellis said.

Craig slipped in, looked at both men, and said, "It's happening this week."

Larry looked up. "When will you know?"

"The dealer will make contact by radio. Darius has decided to stay in Conakry and come with the first shipment just to see how things will go. But there may be a problem." Craig hesitated, grimaced slightly, and looked at Mr. Ellis. "I am assuming Larry told you about the Liberian government's plans to stop the shipments. They're arming a couple of Cessna 180 airplanes. That's serious."

"I wouldn't worry about it." Larry said. "I've heard from Trevor and he tells me that it's more like a silly, comic opera. I very seriously doubt that they know anything. They have no intel. I suspect that it's more of an attempt by Captain Roberts to gain a promotion. And it appears that Tolbert has bought his line of shit."

"What if they get lucky? What if they actually spot a shipment?"

"Then they spot the shipment and shoot a couple of rockets off. They have no telemetry, no command and control. All they can do is hose one or two off the rails without a chance in hell of hitting anything except a few trees and a bunch of wild monkeys. Hah! Maybe they'll even shoot themselves down."

"Nevertheless," Mr. Ellis said, "Darius should be advised. History turns on lucky chances just as it does on planning."

Larry looked at him quizzically, then shrugged and pretended to read a document on his desk.

"Okay," Mr. Ellis said with an air of authority. "Do what is necessary to get that supply through."

Darius had managed to purchase three used GMC vans, and per Coe's instructions, had them each painted a different color: one blue, one green, and one red—all colors that would be difficult to see at night. He met with Coe and Stephens at the designated place in the warehouse district. The wooden boxes containing the arms were marked as farm tools and machinery.

"Farm machinery!" Darius said. "You've got to be kidding me."

"You have to admit, man, it's better than Beecher's Bibles." Coe and Stephens laughed and slapped their hands together, and then each other's. "Farm machinery attracts no attention here, man, so chill. Your guys will get the stuff."

"What is the plan, if you have one?" Darius asked.

"As you can see," Stephens said, "the rides are different colors, so as they say in the US Government, in the unlikely event that one gets hit, it'll reduce the chances of the others getting nailed. We'll send them on different routes and different times with a rendezvous point across the border at Voinjama. Trust me, man. This ain't our first ro-day-o!" Coe was laughing and spinning slowly around in his chair with his hand on the top of his head.

"And what about the border guards?" Darius asked.

Stephens and Coe looked at one another and laughed, slapping their knees as they did so.

"All taken care of. Noooo problemo," Coe said, still laughing and spinning.

"Would you guys take this seriously?" said Darius, his face hard as dark marble. "When will they get there?"

"It'll be several days, man. You know the fucked-up roads in this country. But they'll get there, man. Everything is cool," Stephens said.

Later that night, Darius contacted Craig using his radio.

"You want to go fishing with me. The fish are biting," he said. "I'm leaving for Voinjama tomorrow morning. Plan to catch some fish there in a few days . . ."

Craig replied with an "affirmative" and said he would join him in Voinjama with his fishing equipment, but that there were other fishermen in the water, and they would use dynamite rather than fishing line and tackle. Darius knew what this meant. They had used this code exchange before, and he also knew that the most likely place for interdiction would be along the border inside Liberia. They would have to somehow cross the border without being seen.

The next morning, at first light, Darius tossed his duffel bag into the Series III Land Rover. He sat for a while in the driver's seat mentally going over his departure checklist. He was convinced he had left nothing behind, not even a toothbrush. He had hidden his nine-millimeter in a green metal box marked "First Aid" that was attached to the side panel in front of the passenger seat. He had burned all of the paperwork and flushed the ash. There was nothing that he could think of that would link him to the job. He and Craig had used cover names for the hotel and booked it with one of their many false passports.

"Good to go," he said to himself.

The bright African sun was beginning to lighten the dark streets and illuminate the buildings of Conakry. He said his final goodbye to the city and started on the long, muddy road to Voinjama. The rainy season was slowly coming to an end, but in some ways it made driving even more unpredictable. Mud, potholes, and dust were all in the equation now. The country roads in Guinea, as in Liberia, were narrow, yellow-red strips of rocky dirt. Once the surface was disturbed, the dust seemed to swirl and hang in the air like a permanent gritty cloud. Safety was an issue too, as there was little to nothing in the way of overnight accommodation along the way.

He had brought forty liters of extra fuel in twenty-liter jerry cans, several liters of bottled water, and a sleeping bag with mosquito netting. He planned to drive all night if he had to. Nevertheless, there was always the possibility of making a wrong turn.

CHAPTER 23

SKRU UP

The surveillance flights had gone well; that is to say, there had been no shots fired and no accidents. The planes performed well enough with the added weight and drag of the rockets. Captain Roberts was beginning to exhibit symptoms of anxiety and self-doubt. Nothing was happening. He wanted something to show for the investment. He had put his reputation on the line and was now seeing his promotion fading with the sunset.

I had started to relax, thinking that all the intrigue was in the Captain's imagination, when Sam came into the office with a message. Her hair and clothes were wet from the rain. She had a stack of papers cradled in one arm, and with her other arm completely outstretched she was being pulled by Bao on his leash.

"Here, take the papers; I have to deal with Bao. He's a mess. He did his best to jump in every puddle on the airfield!"

Bao calmed down instantly as if he understood every word. He looked up at me with innocent eyes. I decided to stay out of it and let Sam be the disciplinarian. She rubbed the mud off each of Bao's feet then sat him rather forcibly on a clean pile of towels.

"What was the message?" I asked.

"James drove me over from the house and said that Honorable Williams wanted to meet you at the airport bar today at noon."

He was there when I arrived, sipping a bottle of beer and studying some papers. He quickly beckoned me to join him at his table.

"Look at these," he said, dropping a folder of photographs in front of me. I examined the file and saw nothing but forest vegetation and the spots of what could be an unpaved road. "What do you make of them?"

I looked them over again. "Nothing. I don't see anything but trees, shrubs, and parts of an unpaved road."

"That's right, nothing. I've heard no reports of arms transiting the border. And we have other sources more reliable than this as well." He pointed to the photographs shaking his finger. "All of this is unnecessary."

"Do you want me to shut it down?" I asked.

"We can't do that yet. Captain Roberts, it seems, has President Tolbert's ear. The President wants to give the boy some more time. He believes he has a lot of promise. I think he wants to groom him for high office." He hesitated, then looked up at me. "When is the next flight?"

"Today, in about two hours," I said.

Honorable Williams wiped the perspiration from his forehead with his handkerchief and finished his beer.

"Watch him for me, please. Let me know immediately if anything goes wrong."

I assured him that I would. We stood, shook hands, and parted. Honorable Williams seemed to be sweating blood. As I jogged back across the mud-caked airfield, I wondered what it was that I was missing. It was usually what you didn't know in Liberia that got you killed.

Before reaching the operations office, I noticed that the Cessna 180 was on the ramp with the doors open. Inside the office, Sam sat at her desk and looked at me silently. She had restrained Boa to the leg of the desk, and he was fidgeting and murmuring hooting sounds.

Cian had flopped in one of the chairs with Captain Roberts pacing back and forth across the room. Cian glanced at me then looked away. He was still holding his chart and looking very pale.

"What's up? I asked.

"Let Napoleon here tell ya," Cian said. "Me thinks we have fucked up royally."

Bao started jumping up and down and hooting loudly.

"There's no problem!" Captain Roberts exclaimed, "and get that bloody ape out of here!"

With that, Bao let out an ear-piercing screech. Sam took him in her arms but stayed in the office, curious to know what had happened.

The Captain was still waiting patiently for an explanation.

"Okay then," Cian said, "I'll start. The Captain here decides to not make the scheduled flight as planned. He wants to go earlier. He's convinced that his alleged enemies know when we're scheduled to fly. So, since he's paying the bills, I agreed to go. We had been up for over an hour and somewhere near the village of Mendecoma, following a dirt road not used very much, when he spots a vehicle. He shouts, 'That's it! That's it!' Well, I tell him that's not bloody likely. It was too small to be a proper transport vehicle and there were no markings on it."

"It was painted camouflage green," the Captain interrupted. "Typical smuggle tactic."

"But the young Captain here knows better. He wanted to get lower and closer. So I did. Then, quick as you can say 'Flanagan is your uncle,' he grabs the controls, points the airplane at the vehicle, and fires two of them bleedin' rockets. I'm thinking, surely they ain't got a chance in the house of the devil of hitting anything. One of the damn things hits the road in front of the van and doesn't even explode, but sure as there are no virgins in a cat house, the other one hits square in the center of the roof of the van. It penetrates the roof and explodes inside. And then, as Beelzebub is my witness, two people get out—one is a white woman and the other a white man. His shirt's on fire. No secondary explosions, nothing. The Captain here fucked up in good fashion. I seriously doubt the man lived."

The Captain glared at Cian.

"He knows damn good and well that there could have been arms in that van!" the Captain shouted. "Just because he saw two white people doesn't mean a damn thing." He paused then said, as though discovering a new truth,

"They should not have been on that road in the first place. It's nothing but a ganga road used by smugglers and thieves. If they were not transporting arms, they were probably transporting other contraband."

"I'm considering suspending all flights until we find out," I said.

"You do not decide what to do here! I decide what to do here!" the Captain said, with a shrill tone of authority. "And I say flights will continue until the threat to our country is eliminated."

Having said that, the Captain adjusted his officer's cap and marched out, shoulders back and chest out.

Cian followed him with his eyes.

"Of such is the kingdom of heaven," he said proverbially.

I asked him what he meant by that.

"Well," said Cian, "he's nothin' but a child, isn't he? And that's what you have to be in order to enter heaven, or so the good sisters told me. Could never figure that one out until, maybe, now." Then Cian said in a quiet voice that seemed to be more of a distilled thought, "He's a child playing war but with real guns. That's what he is—a very dangerous child."

"Was Trevor with you?" I asked.

"I'll say he was, but instead of holding his gun, he was holding a camera and snapping pictures like one of them photojournalists."

"Where is he now?"

"Search me," Cian said. "He jumped out of the aircraft as soon as the prop stopped turning and took off in that beat-up Chevy pick-up truck of his."

"And you're sure they were civilians?" Sam asked.

He crossed his arms. "As sure as I am that the Pope is Catholic. The two I saw were white and one was a woman."

White gun runners didn't usually run their own guns. They usually paid locals to do the dangerous work and take the physical risks. I told Cian to secure the airplane and, if anyone asked, we were suspending surveillance flights until further notice.

I knew I had to get back to Honorable Williams immediately before he got the news from an unfriendly source.

"Cian," I said, "is your car here?"

Cian stared at me, puzzled for a second, then correctly assumed why I was asking him.

"It's a little low on petrol," he said.

"I'll buy you some more. Will you drive me to the Executive Mansion?"

"Just let me bleed a lizard and I'll be right with you in a flash."

While Cian was attending to his bodily functions, I told Sam to stop scheduling the flights until I discussed it with Honorable Williams.

"I thought something like this would happen," she said. "Yes, get it straight with Williams and let's end this insanity."

Fortunately, Cian was not squeamish about violating traffic regulations. After all, very few drivers observed them and those who did were often the targets of verbal abuse and vulgar hand signals.

Naturally, I had some trouble getting past the guard, but after calling Honorable Williams, he quickly waved us through. We walked hurriedly through the building and jumped on the elevator. Elevators or lifts never move fast enough when you need them to. We breezed by Honorable Williams's aging secretary just as she was starting to object. Honorable Williams was at his desk and looked up. Our expressions of alarm alerted him, and he reacted by placing his pen down and motioning for us to sit down.

"You men look as though you're being chased by a pack of mad dogs," he said, smiling slightly.

"It's more like the very hounds of hell, sir!" Cian exclaimed.

Before Honorable Williams could comment, I started explaining what had happened.

"Cian flew the mission, sir. He can give you a firsthand account."

Honorable Williams looked at Cian and nodded. Cian then launched into a seemingly inexhaustible stream of religious and Irish mythical similes and metaphors. Honorable Williams leaned back in his chair, somewhat amused and somewhat puzzled. I helped him decipher some of the information lost in translation.

Honorable Williams, annoyed, said, "You're sure the people you saw were white, and there was no indication of explosives or arms?"

"As sure as a pint of Guinness will make the hairs grow on your chest like roses in a summer rain," Cian said.

At that point, Honorable Williams' phone rang. He looked startled, then picked up the handset. He listened intently for a while, staring down at his desk blotter. He toyed nervously with his pen.

"Are you absolutely sure about this?" he asked over the phone. "I don't care. You need to verify it beyond a shadow of a doubt," he continued, then replaced the handset with the gentleness of an explosives expert defusing a bomb.

"That was the Attorney General," he said with gravity. "In spite of the fact that there has been no confirmation as of yet, it seems as though an attack was made on a van transporting Peace Corps volunteers near the border town of Guéckédou. In addition, the Attorney General believes it occurred on the Guinean side of the border. Five Peace Corps personnel and the driver were killed. There was one survivor, a woman."

"When do you expect to have confirmation, sir?"

Honorable Williams shrugged. "I have no idea. But soon, I hope."

"Assuming it's true, what would you like us to do?" I asked.

"Well, certainly we'll have to close down those operations."

"I've already put a temporary hold on them," I said.

"Good, good," Honorable Williams said. He looked like a victim of an accident suffering from temporary amnesia. "Do either of you know where Captain Roberts is?"

"No sir," I said. "He left the operations office in a hurry. I thought he might be coming here."

"No, no, I haven't seen him," Honorable Williams said.

Just then the phone rang again. Honorable Williams hesitated before picking it up. He stared at it for a long moment and then, biting his lower lip, picked up the handset and listened.

"Okay, yes, I see. I'll do something about it," he said into the phone, then slowly, with an expression of inner pain, replaced the receiver back into its cradle.

"I'm afraid it's confirmed. We killed four Peace Corps Volunteers and a Guinean driver. And to make matters worse, if it can get any worse, it actually did happen on the Guinean side of the border. A lousy ten feet into Guinean territory, but into their territory nonetheless."

"Jesus, Mary, Joseph, and all the Holy Martyrs!" Cian blurted out. "We gone and done it now—started freaking World War III."

CHAPTER 24

VOINJAMA

The place where Darius was supposed to meet the vans and Sergeant Doe's man was a mile or so outside of Voinjama on the right side of the road. The sun had been up for several hours when Darius got to the town. The heat was beginning to hit him in the face like an intense fever. The milling crowds and small shops that usually filled the dirt streets by day had not yet awakened. A few dogs loped along the streets, panting in anticipation of rising heat.

At the intended meeting point, Darius found an abandoned one-room concrete building with a rusty, corrugated roof. It looked like any number of typical modest village houses surrounded by grass and weeds. It had once been painted white and blue, but those colors had long since faded, exposing patches of hard, gray concrete. Darius drove onto the overgrown driveway, parked, and stayed in his car on the shaded side of the unwelcoming house. He had been driving all night without a stop. The long road had been full of potholes and debris, and now that he had arrived, he felt the heavy weight of sleep closing his eyes with a gentle but assertive hand.

He was awakened by what seemed like a faraway voice speaking to him from inside a furnace. His shirt was soaked through and sweat was running down his face.

"It's not healthy to sleep in your car in this country. It could dehydrate you to the point of looking like, and probably feeling like, a chunk of beef jerky. And you can count yourself lucky to wake up with your wallet and clothes still on."

He perked up. "How long have you been here, Larry?"

"Lucky for you, I've just arrived."

"What about Craig? I thought he was coming."

"I told him to go with one of the shipments. I'm more familiar with the countryside around here than either of you guys. Besides, I'm the one who found this place. It's a site we picked up cheap. Not the most elegant, I admit, but adequate. Let's go inside."

Larry pushed the front door open, scraping it on the cement floor below. The two men stood in the small space in silence. The place was furnished with a metal card table and four metal chairs. There was an old army cot against one wall and a camping stove, still in its box, stacked against the wall along with some rudimentary provisions. There was no electricity. The bathroom door was missing, exposing an open toilet with no lavatory or bathing facility. A faint odor of feces, urine, and dirt permeated the dark, damp air in the house.

"Is it remotely possible to get a cup of coffee in this dump site?" Darius asked.

"Over there." Larry pointed to the other end of the room by the stacked boxes, where a percolator and some tin mugs were sitting on a stone ledge.

"Any chance of getting some potable water?"

Larry again pointed to a blue plastic bucket at the other end of the ledge. It was about half full of water. The water had several small insects swimming around in it and an oily sheen on the surface.

"You'd better boil that for a few minutes first," Larry said.

"Really, Larry. I had hoped for better from the CIA."

Larry shrugged, took a lighter out of his pocket and lit one of the Coleman gas lanterns.

"The Government has to cut expenses somewhere."

Darius went out to his car and retrieved a clean handkerchief from his duffle bag. He folded it in layers and placed it inside the percolator cup that normally held the coffee and carefully poured the water from the bucket through the handkerchief to filter the water.

"I was the only Black kid in my scout troop."

"And I bet you made Eagle Scout too," Larry said.

"As a matter of fact, I did."

When Darius had finished filtering the water—he had filtered enough for two cups—he lit the gas and waited for the water to boil. It was necessary to let the water boil for at least five minutes to kill any of the little single cell beasts that may have gotten through the cloth filter.

When the coffee was ready, Darius poured himself a cup and held the pot out for Larry, who nodded and pointed to an empty cup on the table. Darius looked at him as if to say, *I'm not your boy,* then poured the coffee. The coffee was, as always, good even without sugar. Darius especially enjoyed the first swallow.

"Who will we be meeting with?" Darius asked.

"It'll be either Sergeant Doe or one of his lieutenants, or should I say corporals."

"When?"

"According to the last message I received, it'll be sometime this afternoon, but I expect that we won't see them until tonight. Doe is no dummy. He never does things when he says he will, just in case someone is listening, and he always does important things at night."

Darius finished his coffee and went out to his Land Rover to get his sleeping bag. He walked over to the cot, brushed it off with his hand, and spread out the sleeping bag. He stretched out on it, lying on his back.

"I've been awake all night so I'm going to catch some Zs. Wake me if you need me."

Shortly after midnight the loud, metallic noises of a heavy vehicle woke Darius to full consciousness. The intense beam of its headlights burst through the front windows and lit up the interior of the small house with a diffuse but angular light. Darius felt for his gun. It was there on the floor, next to his shoes where he had put it. He quickly felt inside his shoes for one of a million nocturnal bugs that crawled around inside and outside of the house. His shoes were clear. He slipped them on and picked up his gun, placing it in his back pocket, then proceeded carefully to the door.

The vehicle's engine switched off. An intense silence followed, broken only by the loud hum of insects outside. He drew his gun but held it behind him. Larry had come quietly in the dark shadows next to him. His rumpled clothes indicated he'd been asleep too, but his quick movements confirmed he was entirely alert. Larry also had his gun out.

"I think it's our contact," Larry whispered.

The vehicle's headlights blinked off, and both Darius and Larry squinted from the sudden loss of night vision. They could hear movement outside and the sound of footsteps.

"Who goes there?" Larry shouted.

"Is that what they taught you to say in Marine boot camp?" Darius asked in a whispered tone.

"Identify yourselves, goddammit!" Larry shouted again.

"We hee from de Massa Sergeant!" a heavy male voice answered.

The door burst open and the intense beams of two powerful flashlights hit Darius and Larry in the face. Darius raised his gun with every intention of using it.

"Put ya guns down," the heavy male voice demanded. Darius and Larry held firm.

"We hee fo' Sergeant Doe."

The two agents slowly lowered their guns and pointed them toward the floor.

"Ya put on some light," the voice said again. The flashlight searched the room until it settled on the Coleman gas lantern. Larry found his cigarette lighter and lit the gas under the lantern's lens. A dim, white light filled the room along with the sound of hissing gas.

"Ah am Corporal Thomas Quiwonkpa and dis Corporal Pennoh. We hee representing de new Progressive Alliance of Liberia. Whae har de goods?"

Darius recognized Corporal Pennoh from the meeting in the abandoned house near Monrovia. "Where is Master Sergeant Doe?" Darius asked.

"He in Monrovia. Dat all ya nee ta know. Now, whae har de goods?" the Corporal asked more emphatically.

"We expect them any time," Larry said, "but you know the roads in this country."

"Ma country's roads be good. It is you who delay!"

Larry noticed Corporal Pennoh putting his hand on his side arm. "Does he ever talk?" he asked, gesturing toward Corporal Pennoh.

"He speak only wid hes gun an' knife," Quiwonkpa said. "Han when he speak so, he speak loud." Quiwonkpa smiled, showing most of his yellow teeth.

Pennoh continued to stare at Larry as though he would pounce on him at any moment and tear out his throat with his teeth. Larry looked away and, trying to defuse the tension, suggested that they all have a beer and wait for the shipment to arrive. Knowing the Liberian's taste for beer, Larry had brought along a case of American Budweiser and had packed it in expensive ice. He opened the plastic cooler and distributed the cans around. Corporal Pennoh let his hand slide off the handle of his pistol and took the beer, not taking his eyes off Larry.

There were enough tattered chairs for everyone and each man chose a seat, Corporal Pennoh inspecting the seat carefully before sitting down. Once seated, he placed his hand back on his pistol and shifted his eyes from Larry to Darius. Under these circumstances it was difficult to try to sleep but it wasn't too long before everyone, except Corporal Pennoh, began nodding and slowly, but eventually, slumping down in their chairs to doze.

They were awakened several hours later by the rumble of motorized vehicles and the beams of their headlights. Corporal Pennoh was first on his feet, followed by Larry, and Darius who yawned and shook his head. Corporal Quiwonkpa struggled to his feet, checked his side arm to make sure it was there, yawned, and motioned for everyone to follow him.

The three vans hired by Larry and Darius had arrived. They were in surprisingly good condition with only a few dents and mud spray. Quiwonkpa and Pennoh moved the beams of their flashlights over the vans like two extraterrestrial eyes exploring new and unfamiliar objects. The passenger door of the first van popped open and Craig jumped out, his clothes and hair a little disheveled, with streaks of dirty sweat running down his face and neck. He removed his baseball cap and slapped the dust out of it on the side of his worn and faded blue jeans, then replaced it on his head.

He looked over at Corporal Pennoh. "I know you. You were with Sergeant Doe at our last meeting. Where is the Sergeant?"

Pennoh was tight-lipped and seemed to snort.

"Sergeant Doe sent this guy as an envoy. He has credentials," Darius said.

"It's all here," Craig said. "The boys have been going non-stop. They need something to eat and a few hours of sleep." Craig signaled to his drivers to get out of the vans and go into the house. The men stepped out, carrying paper bags of what Darius presumed to be food.

"Find what you can to sleep on," Craig said to them in a loud whisper.

"What's your plan, Craig?" Darius asked.

"I'm riding with them," Craig gestured with his hand toward the drivers, "back to Guinea to make sure the vans get back to the station; then, fly back to Monrovia. Shouldn't take more than a few days."

Meanwhile, Quiwonkpa walked over to the rear of his army truck and pounded sharply on the metal fender. He opened the tailgate and shouted something to the men inside in Kru dialect. In a moment, four young soldiers jumped out of the truck and began unloading the van and transferring the arms to their truck.

This was done with a sense of urgency. The noise of the work was more like the continuous muffled roar of a lion hidden in the darkness. Darius and Craig knew that this was it, the hard reality of impending death and general destruction, and it wasn't likely to be stopped.

CHAPTER 25

BINJI

The representative from the Guinean Embassy slammed his fist down on Honorable Williams's desk so that the object on the desk seemed to jump as though they were alive and startled. He called it an unforgivable infraction of international borders as he strode around Honorable Williams's office, gesticulating in the air and at one point tearing his suit jacket open, ripping the buttons out. He further shouted to Honorable Williams that his country might consider it as an act of war, and threatened to withdraw the Guinean Army forces that had been loaned to Liberia for its protection.

Honorable Williams, in his most honed diplomatic skills, explained that the Peace Corps killings had been a tragic military mistake made during a training exercise and that Liberia would make any and all satisfactory restitutions. At that, the representative of Guinea seemed to calm down. It was really a lesson in stage acting—Honorable Williams seeming to grovel just enough and make agreements that he knew would never be honored, and the representative feigning personal insult and outrage, and seeming to be mollified with the promise of rewards that he knew would not be forthcoming.

It soon became clear that Captain Roberts had not thoroughly studied his military history. In every military, when a mistake occurs, the blame always falls on the officer in charge, and if the mistake is big enough, blame goes even higher up the chain of command. In politics, it's just the opposite—blame usually starts at the top and goes down to someone who's expendable.

Captain Roberts was at the Kolahun airfield location inspecting the new shipment of rockets and mounting rails when an army truck came screeching to a halt next to the launch airplane. Two Liberian soldiers and a lieutenant jumped out. Without saying a word, they approached Captain Roberts, threw him head-first against the plane, and quickly cuffed his hands behind his back.

"What the hell are you doing?" the Captain shouted. "Do you know who I am? Do you know who my father is? You will pay for this! You will pay for this! I promise you!" He continued shouting as they hauled him away.

I later learned that Captain Roberts was spared the firing squad and was given the choice of resigning his commission from the Army or accepting a demotion to private. He, of course, chose resignation.

After this, the arms interdiction effort from the air was canceled and operations at Kolahun were shut down. The modifications made to the two aircraft to carry rockets were removed, the planes returned to commercial service, and we got back to our routine tasks of transportation at Spriggs-Payne.

By this point the dry season only had a few months to go. It was still cold in the States and Sam was beginning to miss skiing in the mountains of Pennsylvania. We had acquired enough rough diamonds to solve our financial problem back home. Our problem now was getting diamonds back to the States safely. Sam had a friend in New York who was in the diamond business, and he had assured her before we left for Liberia that the diamond cutters he knew in New York were every bit as good as the craftsmen in Amsterdam. Her idea was that we mail the rough diamonds to him and ask him to hold them for us until we arrived and, naturally, offer him a percentage.

I had justifiable concerns about the Liberian mail service, especially for overseas mailing. Sam thought that the old tried-and-true method of finding a book that nobody would want to read, much less possess, and cutting out a section to conceal the diamonds would work, provided there was generous padding for concealment. It was corny enough to work. After all, this was not South Africa. Diamond smuggling wasn't a national obsession—de Beers didn't dictate the rules in Liberia.

Sam suggested an odd book: *The Complete Ronald Firbank*. It had been required reading for her in college and she could still recite the quote on the back cover from W.H. Auden: "A person who dislikes Ronald Firbank may, for all I know, possess some admirable quality, but I do not wish to ever see him again." She was still not quite sure what it meant.

Where in Liberia could one find a copy of *The Complete Ronald Firbank* or the like? The task wasn't as difficult as I thought it would be. Cian, as it turned out, was a great reader, especially of James Joyce and Sean O'Casey. He told me about a shop operated by a Lebanese man named Bazif Karam. Mr. Karam sold just about everything from old radios to used clothes with the blood stains barely washed out. He boasted that if he didn't have it, he could get it.

Winston was free that afternoon and he drove Sam and me over to Mr. Karam's shop on Camp Johnson Street. It was a small affair crammed in between a vegetable market on one side and an abandoned hardware store with broken front windows on the other. When I asked Mr. Karam if he had ever heard of Ronald Firbank his eyes went totally blank, but when I asked him if he could find it, his expression changed to that of a happy hunter.

"Of course, of course," he said. "How much are you willing to pay?"

"As much as is reasonable," I said.

"Very good, very good. I will contact my friends in London, and I should have something for you within a week. Check by Tuesday next."

I thanked Mr. Karam and glanced around at the oddities in his shop. As I turned and started to leave, someone called out to me in a voice that I vaguely recognized. It was a man, a Liberian, somewhere in his mid to late twenties, smiling and walking toward me. Sam glanced at me, wondering if we should expect trouble.

"Mista. Ken, Mista Ken, you don't recognize me, do you?" He must have seen the expression of mild shock and bewilderment on my face because he smiled slightly. Still, his face did not gel into something that I could clearly recognize. Nothing, not even his voice was familiar enough to clarify the memory cells.

"I'm very sorry," I said. "You look familiar, but—"

"Binji!" he said, taking my right hand and shaking it with both of his. Slowly, the face of the mature man in front of me melded into the face of the house boy that I had known back in the sixties, then reverse again into its present form. He had lost that look of teenage wonderment, that gazelle-like energy. His eyes seemed to portray strength and intelligence, yet indefinable wounds of disappointment and betrayals.

"Binji," I said, feeling a little ridiculous. "It's good to see you. You look so different! Sam, you remember Binji, don't you? He was our houseboy when I shared a house with Deiter. Binji, my God, what have you been doing with yourself? How's your cousin Ku?"

"Oh, Mista Ken! Ku is jus' okay. After the German pilots left, he went to work for the Firestone Company. Very hard work. Very, very hard. And not much pay. But at least he's workin'. Not many people workin' these days. He lives over there now, so I don't see him much."

Sam caught his eye. "Oh, and look'a here; is this your fine, fine woman, Miss Sam? Oh, yeah, she is still *buku buku* fine!"

Sam extended her hand to shake his in the Liberian manner.

"But what about you, Binji?" I asked. "You're so well dressed and you're talking almost like a Congo man. Have you been to school?"

"Oh yes, yes, Mista Ken, I have. And I have you to thank for that!"

"Me!" I said. "Why, how did I do this?"

"I guess you must'a said good things about me to Honorable Williams, 'cause one day he tells Ku that he wants to see me.

"Ku? Why Ku?"

"Well, when you and Miss Sam left, I went back home to my village in the bush, not doin' much at all. But when Honorable Williams came lookin' for me, Ku knew where to find me."

At this point, Sam and I took a seat in the bookstore. There were no other customers in the shop, so Mr. Karam didn't mind Binji giving all his attention to us.

"You want some coffee?"

To my knowledge, Liberian coffee is the best in the world, so Sam and I eagerly accepted.

"What did Honorable Williams want?" I asked.

"He had a friend, Honorable Clement, who was looking for a houseboy. Well, more than a houseboy really, more like an adopted boy. He had a son my age, Solomon, an' 'cause they lived in this big house on the beach wit nobody around, he wanted a frien' for his son to hang around wit. It sounded too good to be true. He would sen' me to high school and everything."

"Well, was it too good to be true?" Sam asked.

"Hmm. Let's jus' say, I think they really did only wan' a houseboy. The kid, Solomon, was a bully and beat me up all de time. He treated me like his own personal boy, all the while, I did cleanin' and fetchin' for the whole family. An' when I didn't make good grades at school, I got a beatin'!"

There was a long moment of awkward silence. Then I spoke.

"I'm sorry to hear that, Binji. I feel somewhat to blame for all of this."

"Oh, no, no Mista Ken! Don' say that! If it had not been for de Honorable Clement, I'd not know how to read, how to talk, or how to dress! Look'a me here, I am workin' at a bookstore! No, if it had not been for Honorable Clement, I'd be livin' in the street. That's what it like here, ya know. Lotsa my friends are livin' in the street! Nobody has money to buy food! No money to buy rice! No, Mista Ken, I'm the lucky one, an' I'm hopin' soon to go to law school here in Monrovia and be a lawyer someday."

"I have no doubt that you will, Binji. I know you'll make a fine lawyer," Sam said. "You are what this country needs."

We shook hands with Binji in the Liberian manner and left the store.

"You see," I said to Sam. "There are happy endings here."

CHAPTER 26

MR. CHAO

Sam and I finally left and had Winston drive us over to the Ambassador Beach Bar. I told him he could come back for us in about an hour, which gave him the opportunity to make a little extra money. Joe was there, at his usual place behind the bar, not as happy as I remember. Gone was the toothy smile, the open and friendly eyes. His face had some uncharacteristic worry lines and he no longer handled the drinking glasses like a skilled juggler.

Sam and I decided to sit at the bar. There was a pleasant, cooling breeze blowing from the ocean—just enough to blow Sam's auburn hair back, framing her face. She had let it grow longer during the past couple of years and though she had initially cut it short for the trip, it was growing back, and I have to say, it became her very well. She never seemed to grow older with the passing of time. Back in Africa again, it seemed like we were back on our first great adventure. It was tempting to take her with me on another giant leap in this wild country.

"So, good for Binji," Sam said. "His life doesn't seem all bad and he has a good attitude. I hope we run into him again."

"Mista Ken," Joe said, returning to his former geniality. "An' de so pretty lady; wha' can Joe do for ya?"

We both ordered gins and tonic. Joe was the best creator of that delightful mixture of anyone I had known. We sat for a while enjoying the caresses of the gentle ocean breeze and the soothing sounds of waves breaking on the beach. I must have assumed a serene and pleased expression.

"Don't be fooled again, Ken," Sam said, looking at me knowingly. "Remember why we left. Don't forget the Malaria, don't forget the rainy season, and for God's sake, don't forget the Guinea worm that crawled out of your knee!" She paused. "And for some reason, I'm not feeling all that great, and I'd like to get home where there is decent medical facilities."

Sam was right, amenable as she was to this whole enterprise, daring as she was to fly with me over shaky ground. She was right about two things: Africa stirs up your blood like a vague but ancient genetic memory, and I knew that if we stayed, it would be the death of us—literally.

"When do you want to leave?" I asked.

"How are you planning to transport the diamonds?" she asked.

I had given this problem considerable thought and had decided to put half of the rough diamonds in Ronald Firbank's hollowed-out book, something I was sure he would approve of, and impose upon Honorable Williams to take it to the American Embassy and send it through a diplomatic pouch. The other half I would simply sew into our clothes when we traveled. Robertsfield was usually either in complete pandemonium with mobs of travelers or it was empty with only a few security soldiers or policemen, usually asleep, watching the terminal building.

Sam thought the risk of losing one or both packages was too risky and suggested that we acquire more diamonds. That was a sensible suggestion. The more I could accumulate, the better the chances were that enough would get through to solve our financial problems at home. I would have to meet with Tanja Gora or his son one more time, and soon.

We were about to finish our drinks when Sam noticed Mr. Chao take a seat at an empty table.

"Why don't you ask him to join us?" Sam said.

I thought it was a good idea. Rather than wave him over, as I would have done in the States, I walked over to his table, hoping this would show proper respect, and invited him to join us. He smiled and nodded, seeming to genuinely appreciate the friendly gesture.

There was something calming about Mr. Chao's company. Maybe it was his completely non-threatening manner or his seeming deference and acute politeness. I never knew why, but we enjoyed his company, even though I knew it was probably misplaced. I couldn't help but feel an odd sense of protectiveness toward him.

"I was hoping I would see you again," he said in his slight Mandarin accent. He noticed our puzzled expressions and continued. "I am returning to China," he said, glancing over his shoulder.

"Looking for your two Russian friends?" I asked.

He smiled. "I'm so accustomed to them being with me that I thought of asking them over for a drink," he said with a humorless snort. "I shall miss them."

"Are you leaving for good, Mr. Chao?" Sam asked.

"Regrettably, yes, and I tell you this, at some risk, but for your own good: my Government believes this Government will collapse soon. Look at what the President has done this past year. Yes, he did reluctantly lower the price of rice after the riots, but then he spent at least twice the national budget on preparations for the OAU Conference just three months later. He built several expensive houses on the beach for visiting African heads of state to stay in. He rented an ocean liner, the USS America, as accommodations for the world press and foreign staff members. All of that in addition to the large conference center he built for the occasion. And what has this done for public confidence in his government? Nothing. In fact, it has undermined what little confidence the people had in him. Why do they always make the same mistakes—these little tyrants?"

I resisted the nearly overpowering urge to ask him whether it was different for big tyrants. Instead, I asked him if China intended to withdraw their embassy.

"I don't believe so," he said. "My Government has taken—how do you Americans say it—a wait-and-see attitude. They are trusting in the diplomatic inviolability of the Embassy. A critical mistake, I think. Consider what happened to your embassy in Iran last November. Not even your elite Marine Corps troops could protect it."

"When will you be leaving?" Sam asked.

"Soon," he said. "My Government is sending a plane for those of us who will be reassigned. It's just as well. I cannot get anywhere with these barbarians." Mr. Chao finished the remainder of his drink in one gulp and looked around at the bar. "I see my Russian friends have arrived. I suppose it's time for me to lead them elsewhere." Mr. Chao dabbed his mouth with a cloth napkin and stood up.

"Mr. Chao," Sam said. "I suppose there are no Asian barbarians?"

"Oh yes," Mr. Chao said. "The Japanese—they are barbarians despite their elaborate tea ceremony, their kabuki, and their exterior politeness. It is all merely a surface gloss, a thick polish. Underneath, below that surface, they are barbarians to the core."

He smiled broadly, the way he had done when he first arrived at the table, then turned and with a glance at his two Russian followers, left the Ambassador.

"Do you think he's right?" Sam asked.

I tapped at my glass thoughtfully. "The Chinese Government knows a great deal about what's happening in the world, despite what our State Department would have us believe. I suspect he is right."

She seemed to shiver. "Then we have to start making serious arrangements."

"Can it wait for another hour or so? Let's enjoy this pleasant place and the wonderful ocean breeze while we can."

We ordered another drink. Then Sam did something entirely unexpected; she slowly took my hand in hers and held it softly and quietly for a long time. Something I don't ever remember her doing.

CHAPTER 27

ADOPTION OR BONDAGE?

It was the beginning of December by the time Darius finalized the smuggling mission in Conakry and drove back down to Monrovia. He wanted to regroup with Craig and Larry in the clandestine offices of the CIA in the American Embassy. The dry season had gotten underway with a vengeance and the smallest outdoor task seemed to take hours' worth of energy. The Embassy's offices were air-conditioned, so tedious paperwork was now actually considered a pleasure.

Shortly after arriving back in Monrovia, Darius went straight to Larry's office.

"Did you wrap things up in Guinea?" Larry asked, looking up from the document he had been reading.

Craig walked in the room. Darius nodded an affirmative to Larry.

"Did you confirm that the goods got delivered to Doe?"

"I did," Larry said. "Now let's let human nature take its course."

"I noticed some unrest in town on the way here," Darius said. "What do you think it means?"

"It means that there will probably be another anti-government demonstration," said Larry. "An organization known as the Progressive Alliance of Liberia, or PAL for short, is stirring up trouble. It's been around since 1974 but they are starting to get more powerful. They were the ones responsible for the rice riots, and now they've gotten some new blood—a guy named Baccus Matthews and a bloodthirsty lawyer from the wrong side of the tracks named Cheapoo. Che Cheapoo to be exact. It seems that Cheapoo is the adopted son of Joseph Chessons, who happens to be Attorney General."

"What do you mean 'adopted son'?" Craig asked.

"These Americo-Liberians have the practice of taking in native kids from poor families as wards—at least that's what they call them. The deal is that the Americos will take care of them, send them to school, and see to it that they get a grown-up job. The indigenous families fall for it, hoping that just being associated with the 'Big Men' will pay off. But the reality for most of these kids is that they are usually little more than household servants. Some families even take these kids in just so their kids can have a playmate. Then, when their usefulness is over, they dump 'em back out into the world they came from."

Larry reached into his desk drawer and withdrew a box of cigars. He opened the box and offered a cigar to Craig and Darius. They both shook their heads, then Larry took out one of the cigars, a Montecristo, and lit it from a small butane lighter. He drew the smoke in with a few quick breaths and slowly let it out, forming miniature cumulus clouds above his head.

"Yah know," he said, gazing with satisfaction at the cigar, "I use to hate these things. It's kinda like that girl in high school that you couldn't stand. Then one day you look at her and it's as though she had been transformed overnight. You see, now, that she is supremely beautiful. Then you talk to her and know that she is super intelligent, and you wonder how you could have been so wrong."

Larry took a long pull on the cigar, blew the smoke out under higher pressure. He was again ready to "get down to business." He placed the cigar on the edge of his desk and continued.

"In young Chesson's case, however, it did work to his advantage. He was a belligerent kid and alienated his first adoptive family. But Chesson Sr. saw potential in him. He sent him to university in the US, and after returning to Liberia, he worked in government ministries for the True Whig Party.

"This Cheapoo, he's changed his name several times, went by the name of Chesson after he was adopted, but he and his Americo father had it out and they've hated each other ever since. That's when he changed his name too. He's one of the extremely smart ones—worked his way through law school, knows how to operate. We need to keep an eye on him. He's probably got Marxist leanings, the way they all have.

"Chesson has always resented the settler class and has proven it over the years by repeatedly antagonizing his superiors. He was even impeached from his Senate seat a couple of years ago when he provoked Tolbert's brother, Frank.

"Matthews too. He was a ward of a Congo family and was equally pissed off at his father's generation. So when Chesson, a.k.a. Cheapoo, rebelled, Matthews was there to welcome him to PAL.

"There's talk of Tolbert actually permitting the PAL to become a registered party, registered under the name of the Progressive People's Party, the PPP."

"So, PAL and PPP are the same?" Craig asked.

"Virtually, for our purposes, yes."

There was a long silence, then Darius said, "What do you want us to do?"

"I've heard there is going to be a meeting with Tolbert and the PAL. It could be about the future of the PPP, but I don't believe so. Tensions are too high. I want you to find out what's discussed. If it's about what I think it is, I want some hard data—something we can use."

"Sir," Darius said, "if PAL has Marxist leanings, I seriously doubt that they would welcome us."

"Of course not," Larry said, showing some irritation. "I don't expect you to join the damn organization. Just find someone who's vulnerable and pay the dash to get them there."

CHAPTER 28

A SENSE OF HONOR

Darius and Craig arrived at Honorable Williams's office on time. He was just finishing an overseas call, and the two men were asked to sit in the waiting area outside his office.

Honorable Williams could not be considered vulnerable, but he did have a strong sense of right and wrong, self-professed duty to country, and a sense of honor. Both Craig and Darius had heard this about him and asked Larry to get Mr. Ellis to set up a meeting. They had planned to appeal to this sense of honor and twist it if necessary. Threats and promises would not work with Honorable Williams.

Craig and Darius were used to playing the waiting game. It was expected when you made a formal appointment to meet with one of the Big Men. Finally, after the customary delay, the door to Honorable Williams's office opened, and he appeared at the doorway to beckon them in. There was one chair in front of Honorable Williams's desk facing him and several more along the walls.

Darius sat in the chair facing Honorable Williams, and Craig pulled up another to sit next to Darius. Honorable Williams leaned forward, placing his arms on the desk.

"I received a call from your station chief," he said. "What do you want to see me about?"

"Sir," Darius began. "We have good reason to believe that PAL is a closet Marxist organization. We know that they are meeting with the President soon to discuss their grievances. We need to know who will be at that meeting and what will be discussed."

Honorable Williams pushed back from his desk and crossed his legs. "So, what is it again that you want from me?"

"Sir," Craig said. "We want you to attend the meeting."

"And spy for you?" Honorable Williams asked.

"No sir. You see, we can't attend for obvious reasons, but we need someone to confirm or disprove our suspicions of PAL."

"And you think they are going to present Marxist ideology to the President?"

"We don't know what they are planning to do, sir."

"You mean that you haven't already bugged their offices, their homes, their phones, or their cars? Really, gentlemen, the CIA couldn't be that inept."

"Sir," Darius said, ignoring the slight. "Will you help us? It would be helping Liberia and all of West Africa. Communist ideology is sweeping over this continent like the proverbial plague."

Honorable Williams was silent for an uncomfortable period of time. Craig noticed the rapidity of his eye movement from side to side as though a string of thoughts were flashing through his brain.

"All right, gentlemen," he said. "I will find a way to be present at the meeting, but keep in mind I am under no obligation to you, and I will not do anything to harm my country."

"Fair enough," Darius said.

"That went well," Craig said as the two men got back into their car and started the engine. "Did you notice he said that he would not do anything to harm his country? He didn't say anything about harming the present government."

"Appeal to his sense of honor, duty, and country. That's how you get these aristocrats," Darius said as he drove away.

Darius dropped off Craig at the Embassy and continued on to pick up Piers Davis at her house in Sinkor. He had not been in contact with her since meeting her at the Ambassador and was anxious to see her. As he approached her address, he noticed that the surrounding neighborhood was resplendent with flowering vines, manicured gardens, and beautifully maintained houses hiding behind protective concrete walls and decorative iron gates. The hordes of pedestrians walking with parcels on their heads were nowhere to be seen. The few cars that were parked on the street (and not within a courtyard) were late German and American models.

As he turned off Tubman Blvd, he could see Piers standing in front of her house's courtyard, waiting for him. She was immaculately dressed in a pale linen suit and another designer scarf draped elegantly around her neck. She waved as he approached.

"You're right on time," she said with an easy smile.

"Hey, I'm a government official. And an American. We are always on time. But you. You're Liberian. Why are you ready on time? I thought when a Liberian said 'soon,' it could mean anywhere from a couple of minutes to three days."

"Well, you're right there. But as you know, I have family in the States. I also got my degree there too, so I was there long enough to learn your ways."

"Wonderful. Because, as it happens, we're returning to Virginia!"

"I beg your pardon?"

"Yeah, I've made reservations at Hotel Africa. It is located in the suburb of Virginia."

"Hotel Africa? Great! I've wanted to see that place since they held the OAU there last July. It's huge. Very new and up to date."

The Hotel Africa was meant to impress, and it was very impressive. Built on the North side of the Saint Paul River on a point of land near the Atlantic Ocean and the mouth of the river, it was one of the biggest, if not the biggest, hotel in Africa. It was minimalist in style built of concrete and glass with an elegant interior. Many of the rooms had balconies where the cooling breeze from the Atlantic could be enjoyed.

The opulent Christmas decorations, the luxury and the latest in all things architectural transported Darius to another world.

Just think, Darius said to himself. *Less than two weeks ago I was sleeping with cockroaches in an abandoned hut!*

"I don't want you to think this is the way I live," Piers said. "Yes, I have a nice house in a nice neighborhood, but I spend all of my time and money trying to help the people you see in the streets."

"Oh really, how?" Darius tried to cover the tone of sarcasm in his voice.

"I work with the women mostly." Piers said, ignoring Darius's tone. "I try to empower them. They are the ones who do all the work. They are the ones who earn money in the street markets. But they have no power. Men have all the power here and they are the lazy ones. They are the corrupt ones. They ask for 'dash' for everything. They ask for 'dash' without doing anything."

"It sounds like you learned more in the States than just 'book learning.' What was your major?"

"Sociology."

From out of nowhere an immaculately dressed waiter appeared, nodded his head slightly, and handed out two enormous menus.

"May I get you a cocktail while you decide?"

"Just the wine list, thanks."

In what seemed like an instant, the waiter produced a wine list from some unseen hiding place, and placed it before Darius as though it were a prized possession. Darius noticed Piers's look of concern—she would glance at him then at the wine list.

"Would you like to choose?" Darius said, sliding the wine list slowly over to her. Piers smiled slightly and gently picked up the list. Darius knew from the change of light in her eyes that he had done the right thing.

Piers knew her wines. It took her only a moment, then she handed the list to Darius and said in a quiet voice, "I would suggest the Chateau Pauillac."

"That's fine with me." Darius said, closing the wine list and handing it to the waiter. The waiter smiled and turned to leave, but not without a curious glance at Piers.

To begin a conversation, Darius mentioned the unrest in the capitol. He was curious to know what she thought of it.

"I don't see what they've got to be so unhappy about," she said. "My people have done wonders for this country. Before we arrived, these country people were little more than tribal savages killing one another out of habit. We've civilized them. Well, almost." She rolled her eyes upward. "They don't want to work. They seem to want something for nothing. They're irresponsible, generally untrustworthy, and will steal anything they can get their hands on."

"Wow," Darius said. "I've heard that before."

Piers smiled slightly.

Just then, the waiter brought the wine and did his ceremonial opening of removing the cork. He poured a taste in Darius's glass and waited for the result. Darius handed the glass to Piers.

"You chose it. I think it only fair that you decide."

The waiter did his best to cover his shock and disapproval, but he could not stop his lower lip from trembling slightly.

When Darius drove up to Piers's house later that evening, he decided to take the 'friendly approach' to saying good night. Playing the perfect gentleman, he hopped out of the car, ran around to open Piers's door, and escorted her to the front door.

Bowing slightly, he said, "It was a lovely evening, and I look forward to seeing you again." With a quick kiss on the cheek, he turned and made a hasty retreat.

CHAPTER 29

WE MUST MOVE ON TO OUR DESTINY

I found Honorable Williams in an agitated state. I know this because as he was staring out the window, he was unconsciously scratching his left forearm raw.

"Ah! You're here. Let's go to the airport bar," he said, hurrying past me out of his office. "Let's go in your cab. I don't want to take a government car."

Winston drove us in silence. Honorable Williams sat back, immersed in thought. When we arrived at the airport bar, he did not move, still lost in thought.

"Sir," Winston said. "We hee."

Honorable Williams looked up as though awaking from a deep sleep.

"So we are. So we are." He opened the door and stepped out of the cab. I followed and told Winston to come back for us in an hour.

Madeleine was there looking very fresh. She had hired a new bartender, an older man with graying hair and a gray mustache. His complexion was quite dark and I had him pegged as a Bassa. He was eager to serve but not as skilled as Madeleine's usual bartenders.

Honorable Williams and I sat down at the last empty table, and I signaled the Bassa man for two beers. He acknowledged with a military type salute.

"Were you in the Army, my good man?" Honorable Williams asked as the bartender placed the beers on the table.

"Aie sa. I wa' in de AFL foo fie yee. I made de rank of corporal oh."

"Why did you leave the Army?" Honorable Williams asked.

"De AFL ee no good place for Bassa man, oh. No food, no house, no money, no nottin' sa. Only sure death, oh. Army no good place." With that he bowed slightly toward Honorable Williams and returned to his place behind the bar.

"That's the perennial problem here—the Army. I've tried to initiate reforms—increased pay, better housing, and all of that, but the Senate, all True Whigs, will not have it. They will do precious little to improve the lot of these indigenous people, and that's going to be the mad dog that bites them." Honorable Williams took a long pull from his beer. "God!" he said, "but this is good stuff."

"Sir," I said, "The time is coming for Sam and I to leave Liberia."

Honorable Williams leaned back in his chair and took another swallow of beer.

"I know," he said with disappointment. "I've been expecting this. I wish things were different, but I'm happy you stayed as long as you did. You did a great job. And my compliments to Sam. Tell her so, for sticking it out as long as she did."

"Do you have anybody else in mind, sir?"

"No, not at the moment. With the exception of you, my friend, pilots make truly poor managers. I don't know whether you are aware of it, but I adopted a Krahn boy years ago. He was only nine or ten at the time. His name is Togba but we called him Toby. He lived with us when my sons were in school here. He would be my natural choice but he has become very distant lately. I sometimes feel that I hardly know him. I don't even know where he is. But I can't concern myself with it right now. We all have to get through this next year somehow, then I'll worry about it. When will you be leaving?" Honorable Williams said with a look of resignation.

"I was thinking in a month or two, sir. I want to make sure the operation is running smoothly."

"We shall all be sad to see you go. But alas, this is not your home."

"It feels like my second home, sir. I shall always see it that way."

"Good, good, that makes me happy. When you get back to the States, would you mind stopping by to see Antonia? I have a few small things to give her and I know she would want to see you."

"Of course, sir. I'd be more than happy to."

Honorable Williams smiled and jotted his wife's address and phone number on the back of one of his business cards and handed it to me.

"Tomorrow, the PAL leadership will be meeting with the President, and I plan to be there. Personally, I'd rather take a beating. Oh well," he said with a wave of his hand. "We must move on to our destiny."

Winston came back as expected and we rode back to the Executive Mansion in silence. When Honorable Williams got out of the car, he looked straight at me and shook my hand with both of his. This type of gesture has never been a good sign. It only means one of two things: *I sympathize with your situation but there is nothing I can do.* Or, *this is goodbye.*

CHAPTER 30

TOLBERT AND PAL

President Tolbert kept the delegations from PAL waiting for over an hour. Albert, the President's secretary, watched with increasing concern as Baccus Matthews twisted in his seat, doing little to disguise his growing impatience. "It won't be long now, Mr. Matthews," he said with a ringing voice. "The President is a busy man these days," he added, glancing nervously toward the door of the President's office.

Matthews huffed and looked skeptical.

"This is just another Big Man's game," he mumbled. "Always keep you waiting just to let you know who's running the show, who's in control."

When they finally were admitted, Matthews, Amos Sawyer and Che Cheapoo brushed by the secretary with enough force to disturb several loose papers, which fluttered to the floor.

Cheapoo was surprised to see his estranged father, Honorable Chesson, the Attorney General sitting near President Tolbert. Honorable Williams was sitting in a chair against the wall next to President Tolbert's son-in-law, Honorable Shad Tubman, Jr. Honorable Wilson was sitting with the President, facing them.

President Tolbert, dressed in a tailored beige suit, seemed flushed. His eyes, magnified by his glasses, were focused on the men as they entered. He alternately squeezed and toyed with a pen in his right hand. Although there were enough chairs, he did not ask the men to sit down.

"You boys asked for this meeting and you know everyone here. I've asked Honorable Williams to attend in his capacity as liaison to the US Embassy." He took a deep breath and glared. "So, why are you here? What is this meeting supposed to be about?" he asked in a strained voice.

"I'm sure you know the answer to that, Mr. President," Matthews said.

Tolbert was silent, but his thick-rimmed glasses stared at Matthews—the reflection was such that one could no longer see his eyes.

"We represent the Progressive Alliance of Liberia," Matthews said, "and we have come to demand that you lower the price of rice to what it was before."

"You demand?" Tolbert shouted as visible tremors ran through his body. "You demand! Who are you and what is the Progressive Alliance to demand anything?"

"We represent the people, sir! The people!" Matthews shouted.

"What people! What people! I represent the True Whig Party. They are the people. They are the people who built this country. They are the people who allow you—all of you—the freedom to do such as this."

"Allow? You and your oppressors in the True Whig don't 'allow' anything. We are free by right. It is a human right to be free!" Cheapoo shouted.

"I see that American education you have has filled your head with romantic idealism." Matthews looked at Honorable Chesson, then back at Cheapoo. "I hope your father is proud!

"And you! Mr. Sawyer! You come from a prominent family! Has your foreign education turned you against us also?"

"Not against you, sir. We are simply asking you to listen to reason. And it is Dr. Sawyer to you."

"Mr. President," Matthews injected. "These philosophical arguments are a waste of time. The fact is, sir, that our organization knows the will of the people."

President Tolbert began fidgeting nervously in his seat.

Dr. Sawyer continued, "They may be poor, and as you might believe, an uncivilized people, but I assure you there will be consequences if you don't do something as simple as lower the price of rice. I know for a fact that a hundred-pound bag of rice costs a little over 9 US dollars to ship from America, and your government is allowing it to be sold here at $26 a bag."

"I have lowered the price once. I can't do anything more. The price is necessary to encourage more local production of rice and free us from imports."

"That tactic, if it was meant to do that, and I doubt very much that it was, is not working," Sawyer said.

"You must give it time," Tolbert answered. "Nothing that significant happens quickly."

"I promise you, sir, if you don't lower the price of rice at least another 20 percent, there will be trouble."

President Tolbert slammed his right fist down on the desk so hard that the small bell in his telephone tinkled and his ball point pen twirled out of his hand, landing at the feet of Matthews, who pretended not to notice it.

"Are you threatening me?" The President shouted. "Are you threatening the Government? I'll have every one of you locked up and charged with treason."

"I have a better alternative, Mr. President," Matthews said calmly, his face not showing a flicker of emotion. "PAL is prepared to donate 20,000 US dollars to help subsidize the price of rice for this year."

President Tolbert leaned back in his chair. The springs in the chair creaked under his weight. Then he let out a short, harsh laugh which sounded more like a cough.

"Do you think $20,000 is going to make a difference? How can you be so naïve? It would take nearly two hundred times that amount to even make a dent in the rice economy."

"You see how unrealistic they are?" Tolbert said to Honorable Wilson, who was sitting next to him. Honorable Wilson nodded in agreement without taking his eyes off Matthews.

"No!" Tolbert said. "The Liberian people will have to trust their president. They must be made to realize that I have only their best interest at heart. The way I see it, it is your responsibility to see to it that they understand that."

The three men looked at one another, then Matthews said, "Then sir, I request a permit to assemble."

"Assemble!" Tolbert shouted. "I will not permit these weighty issues to be decided in the streets. No! I will not give you a permit to assemble, and if you do organize such a thing, I will have the army put it down."

"What army?" Cheapoo shouted. "You have no army. What you call your army refused to fire on the people. And in any case, you have had their ammunition taken away."

"That was because you and the devil and the PAL have poisoned their minds against me. You have worked bad juju. I know it when I see it." Tolbert said, then hesitating for a moment, picked up his pen and began tapping the top of the desk with it. "My good friend and ally in Guinea, President Toure, has sent me a contingent of his best troops. They will keep the crowd under control," he said in a grave, steady voice.

Baccus Matthews leaned forward, placing his hands on the front of the President's desk.

"If you do that, sir. I guarantee you will bring on a deluge the likes of which no one in this country has seen before."

President Tolbert turned away, and leaning back in his seat, said, "Gentlemen, this meeting is over."

CHAPTER 31

PIERS

Darius looked out at the ocean through the window of his room in the small guest house he'd rented overlooking Mamba Point. It was close to the CIA office, and Piers could spend time there safely without fear of running into anyone she knew. He stretched out on the bed.

"I'd like to stay pretty close to home the next couple of days," he said to Piers. "I told the office to call here if they had any news. There was a big meeting with PAL the other day, and I need to know what went on."

"Oh, I know some of the people associated with PAL," Piers said. "I grew up with Amos Sawyer. He has just come back from America with a PhD in Political Science from Northwestern University. He was at the house the other day. He is full of lofty ideas about what he can do here in Liberia. Ultimately, he would like to have a life in academia, but due to the political unrest here he has become an activist. He actually ran for Mayor of Monrovia as an Independent rather than with the True Whig Party. He has plans to help me with my efforts to empower women and has been instrumental in being the voice of reason within the PAL."

"I have to say, it's hard to know who's who in this country, and which side they are on," said Darius. "Sawyer is Americo, yet he is connected with PAL. Shad Tubman too is rumored to be with PAL, but nobody knows for sure. And you'd think the adopted sons like Cheapo and Matthews would be grateful that they emerged from their hovels in the bush."

"Well, let's face it. You can be corrupt and duplicitous no matter what your family lineage is. By the same coin, you can be honest and endeavor to protect the common man if you're Americo."

"Your knowledge and logic never ceases to amaze me," Darius said with a slight smile.

"Just because I'm a Congo girl doesn't mean I don't know what the Government is doing. As you know, I've tried to help in any way I could, but believe me, there are a lot of angry people out there."

Darius propped himself up on his elbows. "Do we really have to talk about politics, baby? I'm telling you I don't want to go out, so you know what that means, right?" He held his hand out toward her to join him on the bed.

Piers was deep in thought for a moment. "No, really, life can be difficult here if you are the underclass. You just can't understand."

At once, Darius was alert. He stood up.

"Can't understand? You're talking to a Black man, a Black American, born and raised in the South, and you're telling me I don't understand? You think because you are 'sensitive to their cause' that you understand their plight? Not until you've walked in their shoes, baby, not until you have been spat upon and treated like dirt, will you understand!"

Piers sat up. "But you have succeeded. You are a Black man with a college education, a great job, and all that you could ask for!"

Darius took a deep breath to calm down. He really didn't want to argue with Piers, yet he was newly aware of a huge gap in their understanding of each other.

"Piers, baby, I know you mean well. But here you are the upper class. Your "reality" is wealth and privilege, just as the market woman's reality is hard work, fatigue, and poverty. Nothing can change that. Have you ever heard of 'benign discrimination'? In America it means that no matter how much education I have, no matter how much money I have, I am still viewed as a Black man. And that means even though people are polite, I will never, ever, fit in."

Piers seemed slightly puzzled, even disinterested, as though she believed it to be an exaggeration.

CHAPTER 32

THE DEBRIEFING

Honorable Williams waited a couple of days before contacting Craig and Darius. He did not want them coming to his office again and he did not want to be seen entering the US Embassy. He agreed to meet them in the operations office of West African Air Service. Sam and I were there, and Honorable Williams asked us to stay.

The two CIA men were on time. They seemed to have a built-in time mechanism that did not allow them to show up too early or late. They were dressed casually in short-sleeved shirts and light trousers, which did not blend in with the typical well-to-do Liberian. They glanced at me when they entered the office. Honorable Williams motioned for them to close the door. A desk fan was running but did little to stir the hot dry air in the room.

"That's the guy from the Ambassador Hotel. What's he doing here?" Craig asked. He then looked at me and asked, "Where's the monkey?"

"So, you have all met each other," said Honorable Williams. "Good. Ken is my operations manager and I asked him to be present at this meeting. And I asked him to keep the monkey home today."

Craig was skeptical and Darius bit his lower lip.

"So, why's he here?" Craig asked.

"Because he was one of my pilots back during the sixties, he has managed this operation for the past nine months, because I trust him, because we may need him, and because I consider him my friend."

Sam interrupted both of them, "The question is—why are *they* here? I thought you guys were mining engineers!"

Craig and Darius both glanced at me, and I met their eyes straight on.

"We are," said Darius, "in the broad sense of the term."

Sam was about to say something, but my eyes told her to stay quiet. I would find out what was happening from Honorable Williams soon enough. The two men agreed that we could remain. Honorable Williams proceeded to tell the two men about the details of the meeting.

"Essentially, gentlemen," Honorable Williams said. "It was a power struggle between the haves and the want-mores. PAL wants the price of rice lowered again, and the Government doesn't want to bear the financial burden. There were threats made that both sides meant. Talbot will use force if PAL takes to the streets. Plus, I have no doubt that he will jail the PAL leadership if they step out of line."

"What do you suppose this means?" Darius asked.

Honorable Williams buried his head in his hands, shaking his head as he did so.

"I don't know," Honorable Williams said. "I honestly don't know, but given the unrest and the tensions of this past year, nothing good will come out of this. And at the meeting, Tolbert was like a fish out of water; flittering and floundering about, gulping for air and not finding any."

"Was any mention made of the Russians or the Chinese?" Darius asked.

"No, nothing was said about them," Honorable Williams said, looking up from his desk. "This all seems to be internal."

"We've heard there will be a demonstration tomorrow," Craig said.

"Where?" Honorable Williams said. "I haven't heard anything about it. At the meeting, Matthews asked for a permit to assemble, but Tolbert refused it."

"Take our word for it, sir." Darius said. "I've heard rumblings on the street. It's not official or permitted, but it will happen. Matthews is keeping a low profile. He thinks if he just lets it happen, then he can't be blamed."

Honorable Williams looked at the two men with an expression of horror and bewilderment.

"This does not portend well."

CHAPTER 33

PAL DEMONSTRATION

"I knew something was going on," Sam said, "and those two guys have 'CIA' written all over them. Not only that, but I'd be willing to bet there's more to this than even Honorable Williams knows. What's the US doing in all of this? And what was that question about Russia and China about? I mean, who cares? The meeting was about rice, right?"

"You know, you're right," I said. "For the Liberians, the meeting was about rice, but our miner friends seemed to be more interested in who Tolbert is sidling up to for outside help. If it turns out it's the Communists, then the US would be very concerned."

We agreed to see if the "rumblings on the street" that Darius referred to would lead to an actual demonstration and wanted to attend. We decided we would observe from the periphery and would always have an avenue of escape in case things got too ugly. Winston let us out of his cab about a block from PAL Headquarters and Sam and I walked the rest of the way.

An expectant crowd began to assemble outside PAL Headquarters on Tubman Boulevard. I saw Craig and Darius quickly making their way through the growing crowd. Many were soldiers out of uniform, but most were from the poorest sections of Monrovia, smelling of decayed fish and the acrid stench of unwashed human bodies. Some carried crudely made signs that read "DOWN WITH THE TWP,", "I AM NOT YOUR SLAVE,", or "TOLBERT MUST GO!".

By noon, the horde had grown to where it filled the street. Someone started chanting: "Matthews, Matthews." The chant rippled through the crowd like a sine wave, and in what seemed like an instant, the mob amplified the chant—"Matthews! Matthews!"

The chanting became louder and more strident. Matthews, probably assuming the protesters would grow tired and disperse, did not appear for about thirty minutes. Then again, he may have been waiting for a substantial crowd. When he did appear, he looked out over the throng of supporters with satisfaction, then raised and lowered his hands to signal for quiet. The crowd grew slowly silent the way an ocean surf seems to calm down at sunset. Matthews then thanked everyone for their enthusiasm and promised that justice would be done, that there would be fair treatment for all, but they needed to disperse and return to their homes. He assured them that he and the PAL had met with President Tolbert and that all their grievances would be addressed.

The silenced crowd started to murmur, then they grumbled, and finally a unified roar erupted from the mob, and they started to move along the street toward the Executive Mansion, spreading out like a giant amoeba. Matthews's admonitions were drowned out by the collective tumult of shouts and chants.

We could see Craig and Darius following along on foot, outside the perimeter of the crowd, curious as to what would happen next.

The protesters reassembled on the grounds of the Executive Mansion face-to-face with a line of armed police and Guinean soldiers. The sight of Guinean soldiers had an electrifying effect on them. They yelled and hurled curses. Someone in the gathering threw an empty bottle at the police and soldiers. That was followed by a fusillade of bottles, stones, and anything solid at hand. The police fired into the air, which had no calming effect on the growing anger of the crowd. When it was evident the ambience was not subsiding, the soldiers then started firing into the crowd. Several protesters screamed and fell backward like flat targets in a shooting gallery. Sam and I had been through this before, so we ducked into a nearby building and watched from a window along with many others.

The Guinean soldiers moved forward without orders and continued to fire indiscriminately toward the rioters. Some police followed suit; others held back. One soldier moved ahead of the line and lunged into the crowd, firing as he went. He was quickly surrounded by the horde and seemed to be swallowed up as though he had been ingested. The Guinean soldiers regrouped and fired to kill. Abruptly, the mob seemed to burst and scatter, leaving a vacuum filled only with smoke, writhing victims, and lifeless bodies. The soldiers walked among the dead and wounded protesters, bayoneting some and shooting others until there was utter silence, except for the wind blowing off the ocean and the distant, faint rattle of palm fronds.

Craig and Darius came jogging toward our building, and I stepped out in front of them.

"What are you guys doing here? I thought this was supposed to be peaceful," I said. "Otherwise, we wouldn't have come."

"Uh, yeah," Craig said. "We thought so too."

"But I gotta tell ya," Darius said, "Guinean troops killing Liberians under Tolbert's orders. There's bound to be trouble in high places."

"What do you mean?" Sam asked. "I think you know more about this than you're letting on."

Darius looked at her with an expression of deep concern. "You're right. We do. And now we had better get back to HQ and start getting this thing set up."

Sam and I exchanged a quick glance, but did not say a word.

The crowd had fully dispersed by the time we found Winston and his cab. The troops had withdrawn and regrouped on the lawn of the Executive Mansion. The faint sting of tear gas still hung in the air.

"Whoa, boss! Is dat finish, oh? I beg you, ya. Les no do dat again!"

"I'm sorry, Winston," I said. "I had no idea it would be so dangerous. Let's get out of here."

CHAPTER 34

REPERCUSSIONS

President Tolbert had been watching the event through a window on the top floor of the Executive Mansion. He was visibly trembling. His lips quivered as he clenched and unclenched his hands. When the masses had fully dispersed and the Guinean troops reassembled, he turned to Honorables Wilson and Chesson and said that he wanted the traitors Sawyer, Matthews, and Cheapoo arrested and brought to him immediately.

"And tell them that if they try to escape, they will be executed immediately; and if they run, they will be hunted down like the animals they are!"

Honorable Chesson acknowledged these instructions with enthusiasm, and the two men left to find the Police Commissioner.

Commissioner Barnes was a short, obese man with large buttocks that pumped up and down as he walked. His neck and head seemed to be the same size and his arms hung at an angle outward from his body. He had been appointed Police Commissioner after his father died in office. That he had no experience and had never served on the police force was not of importance. However, he had served in the Army as a junior officer and had been assigned to the headquarters staff for a couple of years. Confrontation was repellent to him, and he would always seek diplomatic or concession solutions rather than conflict.

"Do we need to arrest them?" Commissioner Barnes asked.

"That is the President's order," Honorable Wilson said. "I've never seen him so agitated. If I were you, Barnes, I wouldn't dilly dally around. I would get some men out there now and bring Sawyer and the rest in."

Barnes pulled his hat down tighter on his round head, turned as though doing a military about face, and left the room, rolling from side to side as he did so, each step accomplished with increasing effort.

Honorable Wilson shook his head slowly.

"One of these days that man is going to have a great fall," he said.

"Yes," said Honorable Chesson, "and the earth will truly shake."

By late afternoon, Sawyer, Matthews, and Cheapoo were in handcuffs and waiting in the President's outer office with two armed policemen. Honorable Wilson opened the door of Tolbert's office and summoned the men inside, instructing the policeman to wait in the outer office.

President Tolbert lingered at the window looking out. He was not wearing his suit jacket. His tie was loose and shirt collar open. Beads of perspiration rolled down the sides and back of his head. He turned and glared at the three captives.

"Are you all happy now?" Tolbert shouted. "Is this what you wanted? My army is untrustworthy. My police force is disloyal. Is that what you truly want? Chaos and disorder in the streets and God only knows what is to follow! And you men are to blame for this. You have stirred them up. You have turned them against me! I should have you all executed for treason!"

"Where will that get you, Mr. President?" Matthews said. "We did not do this. You did this when you rejected the recommendations of the rice commission. We are not their leaders. This is a popular movement. Killing us will not change a thing."

"Maybe not!" Tolbert shouted, "but you all have families, you all have friends. I tell you this: if you don't go back out there and get control of that mob, you and your families and friends will suffer!"

He slammed his fist down on the desk. "Now get them out of here!"

"Sir," Commissioner Barnes said, almost in a whisper. "Do you want them released?"

"Yes, yes," Tolbert said with a wave of his hand. "Take them back to the hovels they crawled out of." He turned to the men. "You have two days. Two days to get the mob under control."

As the men were being led out, President Tolbert asked Commissioner Barnes to wait and instructed him to close the door. President Tolbert removed his shaded glasses, revealing tired, bloodshot eyes.

"Commissioner," he said, "I knew your father. He was a good friend of mine, and I know that he would be disappointed with the way you have handled this affair or, should I say, not handled it."

"Sir?" the Commissioner said.

"Do not interrupt me! Didn't they teach you that at that expensive school you attended in Switzerland?" President Tolbert pulled out his desk chair and sat down, exhaling deeply as he did so.

"You have one month, and if you haven't gotten your police force whipped into shape by then, you will find yourself seated at a not-so-comfortable desk somewhere in the basement. With the cellar rats crawling over your ankles. Do I make myself clear?"

"Yes, sir," the Commissioner said. "Very clear, sir."

"Then you are dismissed."

The Commissioner took one step backward, gave a military salute, and pivoted toward the door.

"And Amos, it would help if you looked more like a policeman."

The Commissioner paused for a moment as if he was about to speak, then opened the office door and left.

President Tolbert stared at the closed door for some time. He knew that the Commissioner was not up to the task. He reached for his phone and called his secretary.

"Albert, I want you to find Captain Roberts and tell him to report to me. Yes, I know he is no longer attached to the Army. Find him and get him here immediately."

CHAPTER 35

TWO DAYS BEFORE APRIL 12, 1980

Cian burst into the operations office. His brow was wrinkled, and it was obvious something was on his mind. I asked him if he had gotten things closed up at the airfield at Kolahun. He said yes, but suggested it be maintained as an auxiliary field. I said that it was a good idea and that I would pass it along.

"Then it's true?" he said.

"Is what true?"

"That you're leaving—returning to America."

"Yes, in about a month."

"I knew it! Just when the operation was starting to do well. Who's going to take over from you?"

"I don't know—do you want it? I can put in a good word."

"Oh Lord above, no! Not even if all the saints in heaven or hell got down on their knees and begged me. I hear that the great Captain Roberts has resigned his commission. Is that so?"

"Resigned, or was fired. I've heard nothing official."

"Well, if he's gone, then the Liberian people are a degree safer. I've seen his type. The British Army is full of them. But I suspect the good Captain isn't done yet—too much fire in the eyes."

"Do you remember that Catholic Priest we flew up to the mission a while back?" I asked.

Cian wrinkled his brow, then the moment of clarity came. "Oh, that I do. The one who looked scrubbed clean and as innocent as a babe—not a stain on his clothes. Just as though he had that bishop's hat always before him."

"What about what is in his heart?" I asked.

"Oh, I would not look there. It would be a waste of time, but if you could find it, and I seriously doubt you could, it's most likely covered with horrible stains."

"Maybe we shouldn't judge the man, Cian."

"So true, sir. Judge not, the Good Book says, but if I were to be his judge, I'd be willing to bet that beneath his shiny, clean exterior lies a dirty devil's soul."

"Let's look at it this way, Cian. He's a client, no better or no worse than any other client."

"Yes, sir. Those be wise words, sir. Wise words indeed." Cian said with thinly veiled mockery. "When do I pick him up?"

"Tomorrow. The weather looks good. I'd leave here this evening so you'll have time to take him to Robertsfield and get back here before dark." I picked up the flight schedule for the next day and started going through it. Cian took it correctly as a dismissive gesture.

"Yes sir. I promise on my sainted mother's grave that I will be as gentle as the blessed lamb with the good father," Cian said.

I watched Cian leave, and I could tell by the way he walked out to his car that this wasn't the sort of job he preferred. He would much rather have been transporting miners or Mandingos to wherever they were destined. He probably would have preferred taking Captain Roberts on one of his silly arms interdiction flights than transporting a scrubbed and clean-shaven priest back to Monrovia. Part of his thinly veiled resentment lay in the possibility that the Catholic Priesthood still held a mystical grip on his mind. He was still in awe of them even though he hated himself for it. It was something burned into him during childhood, and he would never transcend it completely.

CHAPTER 36

APRIL 12, 1980

Few things disturbed Darius more than ill-fitting clothes. He and Craig were dressed in Liberian Army fatigues supplied to them by Corporal Pennoh. Darius tugged and pulled at his crotch. It was nearly a size too small and pinched him there uncomfortably, as well as under the arms. Nevertheless, he took some comfort in knowing that this was only temporary, a necessary inconvenience until the job was done.

Craig's uniform, on the other hand, was too large, and he found it necessary to roll up his sleeves and pant legs. The shoulders drooped and the trousers sagged. Craig thought it a most unmilitary sight. He had darkened his face and hands with black theatrical grease paint. This was a weak disguise and wouldn't fool anyone up close, but he hoped that from a distance he would not be noticed.

The two agents were waiting at the rendezvous point just outside Monrovia. A car passed them and slowed down. The men simultaneously drew their weapons. Then the car picked up speed and disappeared into the night. A few minutes later, another vehicle approached. It, too, slowed and then stopped. Craig and Darius had their guns ready. A man stepped out of the back seat. He was dressed in army fatigues. Darius shone his flashlight at the man.

"It's Corporal Pennoh," Darius said.

"Follow us," the Corporal said, then turned and walked back to the car.

The two CIA men followed the olive-green Chevrolet into Monrovia, traveling past familiar shops and streets leading up to the Barclay Training Center. The Chevrolet stopped at the gate and the guard exchanged a few words with the driver, then stepped back, saluted, and waved everyone through. Craig and Darius followed, stopped outside a barracks-style building, and pulled up close to the Chevrolet. Sergeant Doe emerged.

Inside it was dimly lit, and once the men entered, surprisingly quiet. The small crowd of soldiers recognized Doe immediately and made way for him as he approached. He raised his hands and quietly asked for their attention. Then, in a loud voice:

"Listen hee! Our brothers, Matthews and Cheapoo are in jail. President Tolbert put them in jail! An fo' what? For heppin' the common man. Fo' heppin' people like *you*!"

The crowd groaned and mumbled. The few who had rifles banged them on the floor while the rest of the men stamped their boots loudly.

"An' now he going to execute them!"

The soldiers started yelling and jumping up and down with their guns and fists in the air.

Sergeant Doe raised his arms for quiet. After a long pause, he spoke softly at first, then raised his voice to a crescendo.

"Men," he said, "the time is hee. It is now we take our freedom and kill the past. It is now we find equality fo' all men an' fo' all men to be treated with honor. All our people will be honorable. Not just the big men who call themselves honorable."

There was a mumble of assent.

"We will wipe away the past. No more of this 'who is yoh fatta? Who is yoh family?' We will be our own men, an' no man or hee family will be poor. No mo' blood suckin' rich. We will rid ourselves of them fo' good an fo' all! We will all be 'honorables'."

The men raised their weapons in solidarity and shouted with ear-splitting fervor.

Doe raised his arms again, and again the men were silent.

"Now listen, my men. We will all go double quick time to the Mansion. We will meet on the beach behind the Mansion. You," he said as he pointed to eight soldiers. You come wit me into the Mansion. Da rest a' you, you gonna be backup. You gonna shoot any man who points a gun at you or tries to stop you, whether he be police or soldier. Don't hesitate, shoot him. We ha' men inside. All we do is"—he looked down and chuckled—"is knock on the front door. Our man will open the door. If he don't, then he not our man—then, Kuyo, you kill him wit yo knife, you know how to do it quiet. Once inside the grounds me, Corporal Quiwonkpa, Corporal Pennoh, and our friends from America will go up to the President's quarters and deal wit him. My man on the inside said that he would be there and not be spending the night at hees country house."

Sergeant Doe looked out and into the faces of the seventeen men gathered around him. "We have good men and women on the inside who are wit us. We can count on them. An' once the operation start, we can expect many of the guards, an' maybe even de police, to join us."

Sergeant Doe hesitated, then pulled out a large, folded paper from his shirt pocket. He unfolded it and spread it out on the center table. It was a building plan of the interior of the Executive Mansion showing floors, rooms, stairways, and elevators. Sergeant Doe focused his flashlight on the plan and pointed to connected chambers on the top floor of the building.

"These rooms are the President's living quarters. We will enta the building down hee." He pointed to the front door. "Our man will let us inside. There is an armory on the first floor, and we will go there and get plenty o' guns. Then we will make our way to the elevator on the opposite side, an' up to the President's room. We will," he smiled, "neutralize any enemy that get in our way.

"Once we inside, we will force President Tolbert to admit to hees crimes against the people. Our American fren will ha' a recording device that will capture the moment. In the meantime, you men," he pointed to nine of the men standing in the circle around him, "you will secure the grounds. I do not expect it, but if anyone tries to resist us, they will be eliminated."

Sergeant Doe hesitated and looked around intently.

"Now men, we mus' be very quiet. No one mus' know what we are about to do. No one mus' hear us."

"Sergeant," one of the men said, "what is de plan once de President is dealt with?"

"Ah yes. You men," he pointed to the men who would secure the mansion grounds. "Stay an' guard the mansion. You four men, including our American frens, will come back hee to de training center. Rouse the men an' tell them that Liberia is free, that there is a new day for them! I know they will join us. The rest of the men wit me will get to the radio station, an' I will announce to the nation that Liberia is free of oppression an' will be governed as a true democracy."

Craig thought that Doe spoke with conviction and confidence. Either he didn't know Matthews and Cheapo were set free, or he was using their arrest to provoke the men. But it made no difference. One could almost believe he believed what he was saying. He seemed almost exuberant. His eyes glistened with purpose. It was as though he were riding the crest of an historical wave that would sweep all before it.

"The President mus' be sacrificed. The way a chicken was sacrificed in the days of old for the good of the people."

The men around him cheered, and each held out their right hand for all to touch.

"Now check yo' guns. Use yo' knife when possible, an' let us go double-quick time to the Mansion. Be quiet as a mouse but strong as a lion, men. Now, follow me."

Sergeant Doe slowly opened the door of the barracks and stepped outside, looked around, then signaled for the men to follow. They ran, in a group, across the training center grounds on the beach side and on to Lynch Street toward the Executive Mansion. The roar of ocean surf muffled their tramping boots on the pavement and the clatter of metal weaponry. It was nearly 11:00 p.m. Street lighting was dim to non-existent and they saw no one. The Executive Mansion, however, was well lit, and guards were visible as they came within sight of the building. Sergeant Doe signaled for a stop, then waved his right arm for the group to divide and proceed to their prearranged objectives. Darius went with the group responsible for securing the grounds, and Craig followed Sergeant Doe's group to the front door.

Two guards in the exterior grounds noticed the loose group of men jogging toward them. The guards unshouldered their rifles and placed them against their guardhouse. One of the guards spoke into his hand-held radio and stepped aside as the men ran onto the grounds. Both guards saluted, and Sergeant Doe continued toward the Mansion followed by his men. Then Darius and the men assigned to securing the grounds broke off from the main group and dispersed in twos around the mansion grounds.

After a simple knock on the front door, a servant in formal attire opened the large doors and let in Sergeant Doe and his men. The servant stood aside with an expressionless face as Doe headed for the armory. There again, the vault was unlocked and ready for them. The men grabbed the rifles and pistols they needed and found them already loaded and ready.

The elevator was not operating so they started up the stairs at a run. No one seemed to care that it was a long climb to the President's residence.

When Doe and his men reached the seventh floor, the door to the Attorney General's office opened and a policeman stepped out. He was startled at seeing the heavily armed soldiers in full battle dress. He drew his pistol and started to speak but was shot in the chest by Corporal Pennoh. He fell backward with a look of surprise and bafflement.

Doe kicked the body aside and continued rushing up the stairs until he reached the top floor—the President's residence. Sergeant Doe opened the door slowly, then stepped into the darkness. Craig and Pennoh followed closely behind. A soldier stepped out of an adjacent room, holding his weapon, and lowered it to aim at Doe. Pennoh shot him before he could squeeze the trigger. The soldier twisted around and fell face-first onto the floor. Sergeant Doe ran up to the fallen soldier and held his head up by his hair.

"Where ees de President?"

The soldier moaned and pointed down the hall. Doe dropped the soldier's head, letting it bounce on the marble floor. His men gathered round him.

"Go in each of the rooms till you find him, then come get me."

He looked at Craig, Quiwonkpa and Pennoh.

"You men, come wid me."

Doe's men split up into units of two and started entering rooms. Doors that were locked, they kicked in. There were screams, then gun shots, then more screams. A soldier yelled for Sergeant Doe.

"He in hee, Sergeant! He in hee!"

Doe and his men ran the few steps to a room where soldiers stood crowded by a door. Pushing the men aside, Doe strode forward and shot the lockset off the armored door. He stepped through the doorway and shined his flashlight around the room until it finally landed on President Tolbert and his wife in bed. They were lying on their backs with the top sheet pulled up to their chins.

A soldier switched on a ceiling light. President Tolbert and his wife, startled, sat up in bed. Trying to exhibit an air of authority, he asked, "What is the meaning of this? What are you doing here?"

"We ha' come to free the Liberian people," one of the soldiers said.

At that moment, Mrs. Tolbert shrieked and called for help. The soldier yanked the bed sheet from her, and with one arm, pulled her, screaming, out of bed. She continued to yell until he hit her hard in the mouth, and she fell to the floor, a crumpled mass of flesh, still sobbing.

President Tolbert slid out of bed, wrapping the sheet around him like a Roman toga. He stepped past his sobbing wife and ran by a soldier to his private elevator in the hallway. He banged on the control buttons with the palm of his free hand, but the elevator was not operating. He turned and looked down the corridor, hoping to find someone who could come to his rescue but, except for the moaning soldier on the floor, the hall was empty.

Sergeant Doe walked slowly toward him, and Tolbert backed into his room.

The soldiers surrounded him. Craig searched his pockets for his mini recorder and pushed the record button.

"You cannot kill me!" Tolbert shouted. "That would be bad juju! I have magic! I am protected by all the gods! I am your President, your father. I am lawfully anointed by our Christian God for this office! It would be a sin against the fifth Commandment! You would be committing a sacrilege! The curse of Cain would descend upon you!"

Craig looked at Sergeant Doe, who stood in front of the President. Tolbert's threat of bad juju had hit its mark. Although Doe held his rifle bayonet in his hand, he was shaking. His lower lip quivered visibly, and his eyes stared at the President with terror.

"Do it!" Craig shouted. "Goddammit, do it!"

Sergeant Doe just stood there, transfixed and trembling. Beads of sweat now appeared on his forehead. Craig looked at the other men who, except for Quiwonkpa and Pennoh, were nearly as terrified as Doe. Craig, acting on impulse, grabbed Doe's bayonet, and in an instant, plunged it into President Tolbert's midsection. The President groaned and doubled over. Corporal Pennoh then straightened his arm, aimed his gun, and shot President Tolbert in the head. A melee of stabbing and shooting followed until finally, when the men stepped back, President Tolbert lay silent, curled up in a strange kind of fetal position with the bed sheet still covering him, now streaked with blood.

Victoria Tolbert looked at her husband's body with horror, her mouth moving to some sort of prayer, but she was unable to speak.

"Take dhat woman outta hee," Quiwonkpa commanded.

"You wan' we should kill her, Corporal?"

"No! Not now. Arrest her. Take her away and arrest her. And I am *Colonel* Quiwonkpa now! Do you unnerstan'!"

"Yes, Colonel, yes."

Two men dragged Mrs. Tolbert down the stairs, banging her feet on the stairs as they went.

One of the soldiers looked down on Tolbert's crumpled body. "What do we do wid him now?"

"Corporal Pennoh," Quiwonkpa said, "cut his manhood off and dhen feed it to the dogs. Dhen we must remove his right eye an' open his bowls. He has bad juju, an' dis is de only way to kill a witch doctor. He had the magic powers to take men's souls. When dis is done, we throw hee body on de dump along wid the odder trash."

Corporal Pennoh said nothing. He drew his army knife quickly, bent down, pulled the bloody sheet away from the President's naked body, and cut away the genitals. He then stood up holding the trophy above his head. The soldiers cheered and Quiwonkpa smiled broadly.

After this, Pennoh cut out the President's right eye like one plucking a large grape from its vine. He then cut open the President's abdomen and exposed his intestines. While this was taking place, the soldiers looked on in silence as if they were watching a sacred ritual. But when Corporal Pennoh held up the President's intestines in one hand and his right eye in the other, they cheered as though they were watching a soccer match and their team had won.

"Where is Sergeant Doe?" Craig asked, glancing quickly around, seemingly unaffected by what had just happened. The soldiers looked around, puzzled. Not finding him, they turned to Quiwonkpa.

Quiwonkpa motioned for some men to take the bloody corpse away. Four of the men slung their guns over their shoulders and each grabbed one of the President's limbs and half-carried, half-dragged what was left of the body down the stairs.

Craig and the rest of the men ran past them down to the lobby. There were two bloody bodies sprawled by the doorway, but other than that, the space was empty. Darius, some soldiers, a few policemen, as well as some of the mansion security force were waiting outside.

"The grounds are secure, Craig." Darius said. "Most of the men have joined us—that is, those who have not been 'dealt with.'"

Darius looked around. "Where is Sergeant Doe?"

"Here he is," Quiwonkpa said, pulling the Sergeant by the arm toward the assembled men. "He hidden in de rose bushes like a woman. What wrong wid you, man, dhat you tremble so, oh?"

"Bad juju, bad juju," Doe muttered.

"You're supposed to be an educated man, Sergeant," Darius said. "Educated men do not believe in juju."

Doe stared at him. Slowly, the fear drained from his eyes. He could withstand any assault except being called ignorant or uneducated. He pulled his arm from Quiwonkpa's grip and made a point of standing erect as though he were on military parade.

"I am Master Sergeant Doe and I am in charge here. I have eliminated the bad juju." The words spoken, almost as an outburst, seemed to give Sergeant Doe added strength. Quiwonkpa backed away and the other men were silent. All knew the power of juju over a man, and all believed that mortal men were powerless against it.

Sergeant Doe looked at the men now grouped around him. He seemed transfigured. He held his arms out as in a kind of benediction.

"Men," he said, "this is a new day for Liberia. All Liberia will now be free an' equal."

He turned to Quiwonkpa and said, "Go to the training center. Tell the men what ha' happened here. They will join us, I know. I will go to the radio station and announce the dawn of freedom."

Sergeant Doe pointed to several of the men, including Craig, and told them to join him.

"Sergeant!" Quiwonkpa shouted. Everyone went quiet. "What about de odders? De rest o' de Gov'ment. We can no let dhem live. Dhey will hunt us down. You know dhey will."

Awareness entered Sergeant Doe's eyes. They shifted from side to side like an automatic typing machine.

"He is right. You will have to remove them," said Craig. "Permanently."

Sergeant Doe bit his lower lip until it went pale. "Alright, dhen. We round them up and bring them to de training center. Dhere's a jail dhere."

"Ah, wat 'bout de Congo people?" shouted one of the soldiers from the group. "Dhose dat live in Sinkor and Congo Town. Dhey de same as de gov'ment. Dhey would hunt us down, kill us all soon as dhey could."

"The man knows his history," Craig muttered under his breath.

"We will deal wit dat tomorrow," Sergeant Doe said in a much more confident voice.

"Dhere might not be no tomorrow if'n we don't kill 'em today," another soldier shouted.

Sergeant Doe pretended to ignore the remark and pointed to Quiwonkpa, instructing him to take a few selected men and hurry to the training center and rally the men. Once the men were assembled, they were to be sent in separate squads to find all Cabinet Ministers and bring them to the jail. He, Craig, Darius, and five other men would proceed to the radio station.

Quickly and silently, the men broke into groups, one headed for the radio station, the other for the training center where the rest of the army lay sleeping in the barracks.

CHAPTER 37

BETRAYAL

The sunset was like any other in the tropics, rapid but gentle and beautiful. Our mission here in Liberia had been completed, and we were beginning to look forward to returning to the US and picking up where we had left off. I had enough diamonds to make the business solvent again, once cut and converted into capital. Honorable Williams was very agreeable and promised to visit us in the States. West African Air Service was now profitable and looked forward to a prosperous future.

We bantered pleasantly and discussed what we thought would be the final chapter in our latest Liberia adventure. Bao had been celebrating along with us that night. He was rambunctious and playful, like he knew good things were ahead. Toward the end of the evening, he cuddled up next to Sam, and I couldn't help but appreciate the small moment of domestic tranquility. Sam had obtained a health certificate to allow him to be transported on the plane, so we were hoping he would be able to go home with us.

Sam and I planned to go to bed early, but only after enjoying a nightcap. I was enjoying the last of the bourbon, whereas Sam had switched to beer a while ago.

"Sam, I swear, after over ten years of marriage, you are still the most enigmatic woman I know."

"Really? Why do you say that? I thought you knew me both inside and out," she said with a sly smile.

"I like to think I do, but take right now. I know that something's on your mind, and it has been for a while, but I can't figure out what it is."

"Well, Ken darling, you know women know things, right?"

I nodded, thinking, *Oh God, here it comes.*

"Well, I'm a woman and I know some things."

"Pray, continue."

"I'm pregnant."

"Pregnant! How's that possible? I don't mean that, I know how it's possible, but how now? We've been trying for years! And now, in one of the most dangerous places on earth right now, you think you're pregnant? And, and how do you know? You haven't been to a doctor!"

"Like I said, I know some things."

"Well to quote Cian: 'Holy Jesus and mother Mary!' I can't believe it!" I smiled, laughed, then went over to Sam and gave her a hug. Bao woke up and gave her a hug too.

"So, you're happy about this?"

"Ecstatic! Now let's go to bed."

Just before sunrise, we were awakened by a fierce banging on the door and someone shouting. I pushed the mosquito netting aside and staggered out of bed. I switched on the light. Nothing happened. The electrical power was off. This wasn't especially unusual in Liberia even in 1980. I grabbed the flashlight from the bedside table and headed for the door.

Outside, someone with a flashlight was frantically waving the beam at the front door. I decided to run back for my gun. Weapon in hand, I directed the light through the glass door panel. It was Winston. I quickly checked the gun at the front hall table and opened the door. Winston burst in. He was breathing heavily as though he had run all the way from Monrovia.

"Boss! Boss! Somtin' terrible happenin'!" He could barely get the words out. "Dhere be shootin' and killin' all over Monrovia. People be runnin' and screamin.'"

I told him to calm down and give me details. About this time, Sam came into the room with another flashlight—barefoot and wearing only her flimsy night gown. From the expression on her face, I guessed that she had overheard Winston.

"Are you okay?" she asked.

Embarrassed, Winston stared at the floor. Sam grabbed a nearby shirt and put it on.

"Is your family okay?" She asked. He nodded and added that most of the trouble was near the Training Center, and in Congo town, the Congo people were panicked and running scared. By now, the sun was peeking above the horizon and the first streaks of light were shooting through the windows and onto the floor where we stood. I could think of only one thing to do. As I ran into the bedroom to get dressed, Sam followed and grabbed my arm.

"Wait, you don't know what you're getting into. Let's see if we can get more information."

She switched on the transistor radio. The voice was broadcasting loud and clear over the only radio station in Monrovia.

"Long Live the People's Progressive Party! Long live the Republic of Liberia!"

I didn't recognize the voice, but it was shouting that the Liberian people were now free, that all men would be equal now, the end of 130 years of oppression, a new beginning for Liberia. What disturbed me most was a clear statement that all oppressors would pay for their crimes against the people.

"That doesn't sound good," I said. "A hundred and thirty years of oppression can only mean one thing. They've overthrown the Government. Overthrown the Americo-Liberians. We need to go check on Honorable Williams. We might be in a position where we can help him for a change."

"I'm going with you," Sam said.

I protested that she would be safer here. "We will be safer together," she said. "Two guns instead of one always makes a difference."

I knew I couldn't stop her, and I admitted to myself that she was probably right.

I called for James to get the keys to the beach house car. No answer. I shouted several more times, but it became obvious that he was gone.

"Winston, we'll need your car," I said.

"Yes, boss. You wan' I should go wit you?"

"No, Winston, stay here and make sure Bao doesn't get out. He goes a little crazy when Sam leaves."

By now, Sam was dressed and had slipped the .32 caliber in her waist belt. I grabbed my 9 mm off the table and stowed it, and we both ran for Winston's car. The stench of stale cigarette smoke nearly took our breath away as we jumped onto our seats.

"The first thing we should do is check on Honorable Williams," I said.

The engine turned over several times with a loud grind, then finally started. We took off and I pushed the pedal of the old Chevy to the floor, speeding as fast I could while still staying on the road. Smoke was billowing from the direction of Monrovia. There were a few distant flashes, but we could not hear any sounds of explosions over the engine noise and the innumerable metallic rattles of Winston's car.

The metal gate to Honorable Williams's driveway was open, and as we entered, several people ran by, all carrying large and apparently heavy bundles. I recognized two houseboys. They ignored the car as they ran past. When we got to the house a few moments later, some of the full-height windows were shattered and the front door was ajar. Maximum lay lifeless by the front steps.

We approached the door cautiously. Sam drew her .32 and pointed it down with her finger on the trigger guard. Inside, the place was in turmoil— broken vases and ornamental pieces scattered on the floors. It was eerily quiet except for the sound of our footsteps crunching broken glass. The household staff had vanished, and the looters had taken their booty and left.

Amid the chaos, at the far end of the living room, Honorable Williams lay in a pool of blood. Sam and I rushed toward him and knelt down by his side. I felt his carotid artery. He had a weak pulse.

"Sir," I said. "What happened here?"

Honorable Williams opened his eyes slowly and looked up at me, an expression of extreme sadness—tears filled his eyes and ran down his cheeks.

"I treated him like a son," he said.

"Who?"

"Toby. I brought him out of poverty, educated him, gave him a future, and this is what he did to me. Why? I don't understand. Why?"

"Did he take anything, sir?" Sam asked.

"No. He wanted nothing except my death. Why?"

"It's okay sir, we'll get you to a hospital."

"No. I want to sit. I want to sit in my reading chair," Honorable Williams said.

"Sir," I said. "We should put you in the car and get you to a hospital."

"Please," he begged, "please, no hospital." He gasped for air. "Don't let me die like a dog here on the floor. Put me in my reading chair."

"But sir!" I protested.

"Please," he said. "It would mean a great deal to me."

Sam and I looked at one another. I knew she was thinking what I was thinking. We picked up Honorable Williams as gently as we could, and with great difficulty, we carefully moved him into his wingback chair. He had been stabbed just below the right rib cage and was bleeding badly.

"Thank you," he said. "He must have had such hatred for me, all this time. I never once sensed it. He must have hated us all. Why?"

Honorable Williams shook his head slowly as though answering his own question.

"And the women," he said, "they took what they wanted and spat on me as they left. I know I have treated them fairly. I have paid them more than is expected. I have paid their medical bills. I have arranged schooling for their children, and they spat on me. One of them even stepped over me as she left—just like I was a pile of trash."

"Sir," Sam said, "something bad is happening in Monrovia. Ken and I think there may be a coup in progress."

She walked over to the large radio mounted on a bookshelf and switched it on. It was the same voice blaring out the same message that we had heard earlier about freedom and equality for all. Honorable Williams listened, and I knew from his eyes that he understood.

"You know," he said, "I've been expecting this. I tried to tell the President but he wouldn't listen. I tried to tell the cabinet ministers, but they only laughed, and now it's finally happened. Spike, I know you have to go, it's better that you go now, but there is something I want you to do for me—one last thing."

He didn't wait for me to acknowledge or agree.

"I want you to go to Sinkor, in Monrovia. Since you're white and American. You should be safe. I want you to rescue a friend of mine."

"Of course, sir," I said.

"Her name is Allison. Go to apartment twelve at Sixteenth Street in Sinkor. Find her and keep her safe. I tried calling earlier this morning, but my phone is out. She's British. Please get her out of the country as soon as you can."

Sam turned toward the dying man and stared at him quizzically.

"Yes," he said. "She is my—"

He hesitated then spat out a quantity of blood.

"Mistress?" Sam said.

Honorable Williams nodded.

"Yes, you could say that. We've been together for nearly twenty years. I know I shouldn't ask you to do this, but you're the only one I can trust. Just get her to Sierra Leone. She's a resourceful woman. She'll find a way to get back to the UK."

He hesitated for a moment and coughed up more blood. Then, after a few twists on his college class ring, slid it off his finger and put it into my hand—it had several specks of blood on it.

"Give this to her and tell her that I'm very sorry. And if you run into Toby, tell him that I forgive him."

"Sir," I said, "there is still time. Let us get you to a hospital. The US Embassy—"

He held up his bloody hand, indicating for me to stop.

"Do you know what the big cats do when they sense death coming?"

I shook my head.

"They go quietly off to a favorite place, a place they love, get themselves comfortable, and wait for it. That is what I want to do. It isn't far off now, and I'm in a place that I love." He grabbed my hand. I could feel the warm blood in my palm. "Now it's time to go," he said.

I looked at Sam and she motioned, quickly with her eyes, for us to go.

CHAPTER 38

MONROVIA BURNING

Cian landed at the mission an hour before dark. He tied the airplane down using metal twist stakes that he had brought along. He knew this mission had almost nothing in the way of facilities—not even a wind sock—so he congratulated himself in not forgetting to bring his last bottle of Irish whiskey, a full bottle which he handled with care.

The accommodation was primitive, as he expected—a circular wattle hut with a grass roof, single kerosene lantern, a frame cot, a small, crudely made table, and no mosquito netting. He had not forgotten to bring his new battery-powered cassette player and two hours of Irish folk music. The doorway was covered by folds of rough burlap emblazoned with 100 LBS. NET in red. There was a small wooden cup on the table, which Cian inspected in the yellow light of the lantern. He decided that drinking from the bottle would be safer.

He stretched out on the cot, took a long draught of whiskey from the bottle, and listened with pleasure to "Fields of Athenry" and "Molly Malone" until he was overcome by sleep.

He was awakened the next morning by a mission boy of about ten or eleven years of age.

"Mista pilot, de priest say you come to breakfast."

"Where is breakfast?" Cian asked.

"It at de mission house. You mus' come, oh."

"Tell the priest I will be there."

Cian had not relieved himself all night. His clothes were damp with sweat, the whiskey was half gone, the batteries were dead on his cassette player, and he desperately needed to drink a lot of water.

One of the nuns, Sister Martin, greeted him at the mission door. She seemed concerned.

"I don't suppose you've heard any news?" she asked.

"Oh no, my dear sister. Has the famine come back to Ireland?"

"This is no time for joking, Cian McNerney." Cian knew the nun's family from back in Cork County in Ireland.

"Well what, pray tell, has you so unhappy this beautiful morning?"

"Something terrible has happened in Monrovia. We heard it on the wireless not half an hour ago. Some man carrying on about freedom and equality and him saying for everyone to keep calm. Well, you know, when someone says to keep calm, that's a sure and certain sign you should not."

Sister Martin led Cian through the small, dark hallway to the dining room where the school children had their lunches: usually some variety of soup and a piece of bread or cassava. Father O'Brian was seated at one of the dining tables while one of the mission village women poured coffee into a heavy ceramic cup for him. He motioned for Cian to sit.

"What is this terrible news that Sister Martin was going on about?" Cian asked.

"It sounds like there has been a coup d'état in Monrovia, but no one here knows for certain. Would you like something to eat?"

"Lord, yes, but it's most important that I get some water to put out the fire, Father. Know what I mean?"

"It may taste a little funny," Father O'Brian said. "I've had a couple of gallons of sodium hypochlorite shipped in. If we mix one ounce per twenty gallons of water, that should take care of most of the waterborne disease without making it taste like chlorine. Here, try some."

Father O'Brian poured a cup full of clear water from a clay pitcher. Cian tasted the water, carefully at first, then swilled it down like a man dying of thirst. When he finished, he wiped his mouth with the back of his hand.

"I say, Father, 'tis the true nectar of the gods. Could I have another dram, please sir?"

The priest poured another cup full. Cian drank it more slowly this time, seeming to savor every swallow.

"Now, what is all this about a coup d'état?"

Father O'Brian reach down into the seat next to him and brought out a small, battery-operated radio. He switched it on and tuned it to the frequency operated by Monrovia's radio station. A loud male voice was announcing the end of the Tolbert Government followed by slogans of freedom and equality.

"It's been ranting on like this since I got up. That's one of the first things a revolutionary group does, isn't it—take over public communications and get the word out—'No point in resisting. We're in charge now.'"

"Damn!" Cian said. "Father, you had better get your things and let's get you to Robertsfield before international flights are canceled."

Cian couldn't interpret Father O'Brian's expression—was it fear, concern, or simply puzzlement? The priest excused himself and told Cian that he would meet him at the airplane. Cian finished his breakfast, grabbed his overnight bag, and hurried down the solitary dirt path to where the Cessna 180 was parked. Father O'Brian hadn't arrived. He untied the airplane and stowed the metal tie-down stakes in the baggage compartment. By the time he had finished securing this equipment, Father O'Brian was standing next to him holding his two cases. They were not heavy, and Cian placed them in the baggage compartment and secured them.

The priest's flight out of Robertsfield was not until 3:00 p.m., so there was ample time. Father O'Brian climbed into the passenger seat next to Cian and quickly fastened his seat belt.

"Don't worry, Father. There is plenty of time. You'll be back in New York sipping unconsecrated wine before you know it."

Father O'Brian smiled. Even though both men wore headsets with microphones, which considerably reduced the noise level in the cockpit, they remained generally silent during the flight. Father O'Brian occasionally gazed out of the side window at the cloud formations building off the coast.

"Can we make a short diversion over Monrovia?" he asked, as though he had awakened from an afternoon nap.

Cian nodded. "Sure thing, Father. Just one last look, aye?"

The priest was silent. They flew on until the thin, dark line of the coast started to appear below the horizon.

"That's it, the city, just over there."

The priest looked in the direction Cian was pointing. Several distant columns of black smoke surged and boiled upward until reaching cooler air aloft. The smoke then flattened out and drifted in the direction of the upper winds like blackened fingers, all pointing in the same direction. Both men looked at one another as if confirming the answer to their question.

As the suburbs of the city came in sight, Cian descended to six hundred feet above ground level. At this altitude they could see more detail and at the same time remain above most obstructions within the city. There seemed to be little activity in the suburbs. Some people were running in the direction of the city center, others were driving vehicles. Most people took no notice of the low-flying aircraft.

Cian flew on toward the rising smoke, which was growing larger and darker. They circled the Ducor Palace Hotel. There were crowds of people gathered on the grounds and standing on the balconies looking toward the city. Cian found the Executive Mansion a short distance away. It looked very different from the hotel. A few bodies could be seen scattered over the grounds and there were soldiers running about in all directions, some with weapons and some without. Other soldiers were marching in formation while still others seemed to be establishing a defense line around the Mansion. A few looked up at the sound of the airplane. Several pointed to the airplane and then raised their weapons. Cian banked sharply away and headed for the city center, still maintaining his low altitude. Though he had never been a combat pilot, he calculated that by flying low, hostile forces would have less time to see him and therefore less time to react. He dropped down to "tree top" level.

He located United Nations Drive, and keeping the street on his left, flew over the buildings. There were crowds running through the street, some pelting the buildings with stones and anything solid they could get their hands on. Others stopped long enough to break into buildings and loot all that they could carry. A few vehicles were burning. Cian banked again to fly over the American Embassy. US Marines were setting up sniper and defensive positions at various points on the roof. No vehicles were moving into or out of the Embassy compound. A crowd of people had gathered at the main entrance. They were pushing on the wood and metal gates, trying to open them. They were all well dressed. One person tried ramming the main gate with his Mercedes. Marines stood at the ready on the Embassy side of the gates, but they were not yet aiming their guns at the crowd.

Father O'Brian was pale and visibly shaking. Cian turned again and headed for Americo-Liberian neighborhood of Sinkor. Gangs of half-naked people were breaking into the lavish homes—most were unoccupied—and throwing items out of the doors and windows. A few houses were burning.

"Seen enough of your God-fearing fellow man, Father?"

The priest didn't answer but continued staring down at the chaos below. Cian decided to hold his low altitude until clear of the city, then climb to three thousand feet before contacting Robertsfield tower. On the way, occasionally banking to give the priest a look at what was happening below, Cian found Christ the Redeemer Catholic Church to give the priest one last look before climbing to safety. At three thousand feet they couldn't see individuals on the ground—only the amorphous shape of a crowd. Cian again circled directly over the church. The grounds were filled with people all struggling against one another to reach the interior.

"They believe they'll be safe in there, Father," Cian said. "The same thing happened in the Congo, only your boys locked the doors to keep the people out—didn't want 'em desecrating the Holy Tabernacle, I suspect."

Father O'Brian appeared bewildered, not angry as Cian expected him to be.

"Are we headed to Robertsfield now?" asked the priest.

"Aye, Father, as sure as Satan is rejoicing."

"No!" shouted the priest. "No! Take me to Spriggs-Payne! Take me to Spriggs-Payne!"

"But Father, you'll—"

"Don't waste time, dammit. Get me down."

Again, Cian altered course, and within a couple of minutes Spriggs-Payne came into view. Although it was not the safest way to approach an uncontrolled airfield, Cian decided to request a straight-in approach. This type of approach, even at a controlled airfield, requires acute vigilance on the part of all other air traffic. The control tower declared an all-clear. Cian acknowledged and continued to scan for other traffic. He did not see any other aircraft, so he continued his approach and landed smoothly.

Once on the ground and at the ramp, Father O'Brian jumped to the ground, and without waiting for Cian to exit the aircraft, grabbed his two bags and headed for the parking lot.

"Wait! Wait, for God's sake, Father!" Cian shouted after him.

Father O'Brian stopped and placed his bags on the ground.

"What are you doing? What do you think you're doing?" Cian demanded as he caught up with him.

The priest hesitated, then said, "I'm going into Monrovia. I'm going to do what I can to help. This is where I'm needed. This is why I became a priest." He stopped and looked Cian straight in the eye. "I realize that somewhere along the way I lost sight of that, and now I want to reclaim it."

"But Father, there is a riot there. And this is not your run-of-the-mill food riot. I suspect that the rioters are after blood, and you look like the perfect sacrificial lamb to me."

"That could be, and if it is, that is the way it will have to be, but I know beyond any doubt that this is what I must do."

The priest then picked up his bags and walked to the auto parking area and got into one of the many waiting cabs. Cian found it surreal that humdrum daily life activities, like waiting cabs, seemed to go on as normal even while the society around them was crumbling.

"May the saints protect you, you holy idiot!" Cian shouted after the cab as it drove away.

CHAPTER 39

THE OTHER WOMAN

When we got to Sinkor, it was strangely quiet. Gray-black smoke was rising from the city center, but there were no sirens or blaring horns. There were signs of looting—debris was scattered throughout the streets. But other than that, the place was devoid of human activity.

We found the address given to me by Honorable Williams. It was a modest but tasteful apartment in the upscale neighborhood. As I reached for the highly polished brass door knocker, I was surprised to see my disheveled appearance in its reflection. A small, middle-aged Liberian woman answered the door. At first she only cracked the door open wide enough so that I could just see one of her eyes, searching. Then she opened the door wider, still keeping the opening at the width of her body and managing a firm grip on the doorknob.

"We've come from Honorable Williams and need to speak to Ms. Allison Appleton right away," Sam said. The maid eyed us suspiciously.

"It's all right, Ella. Let them in," a woman's voice commanded from inside the house.

Ella showed us to an elegant living room overlooking the ocean in the distance. Allison—I resisted the urge to call her Lady Allison—was sitting in a Victorian parlor chair. She was a woman of about Honorable Williams's age and possessed the unmistakable aura of British dignity. She indicated, with a wave of her right hand, that we were to sit on the sofa.

"Ella, would you bring us some tea, please?"

Wiping her hands on her apron, and with a sideways glance at us, Ella turned and left.

Allison's dark hair was beginning to show streaks of light gray. She reminded me of an aging movie star, still desperately trying to hold on to her youth and beauty.

"You're the young man who's running the flight operation?" she asked.

I said that I was, and she continued by saying that Honorable Williams had spoken very highly of me. Ella brought the tea. I asked if she had listened to the radio. She had and wanted to know what it was all about.

"It's a revolution," I said, "and a pretty serious one."

"How do you know?"

"Look outside. That smoke you'll see is coming from the city center."

Allison walked the few steps to the windows and pulled the curtains aside. She gasped at the sight of the dark haze and jerked the curtains closed.

"Why have you come? Why didn't Robert call? Why didn't he come?"

It's never a good practice to defer bad news or to delay its revelation.

"I'm very sorry to have to tell you this, ma'am," I said, "but Honorable Williams is dead." I held out my hand, revealing to her the ring he had given me.

Allison looked as though she had taken a blow to the midsection. She put one hand over her stomach and the other over her mouth, then slowly made her way to the sofa and sat down at one end. After a few minutes she asked how I knew. I told her how Sam and I had found Honorable Williams and that his last wish was that she be flown out of the country.

She started weeping softly and wiping her eyes with a tissue. She wanted to know how he died, and after some hesitation, I told her.

"It's so hard to believe," she said. "I've met Toby many times in the past and he seemed very kind and thoughtful. Then he turns on his benefactor like that. It's hard to believe. Why would he do such a thing? Do you think it had something to do with what's happening on the radio?"

"I don't know, ma'am, but I do believe that what's happening out there is very serious and will probably escalate."

"Where is he now?" Allison asked.

"At his insistence, we left him where we found him."

"You mean you left him there on the floor like a dead dog? That will not do. He was a good Christian man and deserves a proper burial," she said indignantly through tears.

"He asked that we help him to his favorite chair, and that is where he died. There wasn't time to do anything else, ma'am. Honorable Williams's last thoughts were about you and your safety. He wanted us to find you and get you out of this country as soon as possible."

"Nonsense!" Allison said. "I will not leave him like that. I will refuse to go anywhere until his body is properly taken care of."

"Is your phone working?" Sam asked.

Allison walked over to where the telephone was resting on a separate marble stand. She picked up the handset.

"Yes, it seems to be."

"Call Nathan the undertaker and tell him we will be coming by in a few minutes," I said.

Nathan was a small, thin man whose body seemed constructed of flesh strings. His sinewy neck looked like dark wire rope supporting his head, which was covered with a dark film of tightly drawn skin. His white shirt collar, bound by a neatly tied Windsor knot, was too large for his neck. He kept his hands folded, immobile, in front of him as though he was making an effort not to disturb the pressed creases in his dark blue suit. Yes, he was aware of the current disturbance and was expecting, as he called it, "an increase in demand."

He didn't seem the least bit surprised or moved in any way by the news of Honorable Williams's murder. It would be tomorrow before he could retrieve the "remains."

We explained that there were no family members to be consulted, and the disposition was to be cremation. Then he cleared his throat and, after a slight pause, quietly asked about payment. Allison said that she would pay.

Nathan bent slightly with an obsequious bow of his head and said through tightened lips that there would be a small deposit of 500 US dollars. He then lowered his head slightly and waited.

Allison wrote out a check and handed it to him. Nathan, with his head still lowered, softly thanked her, slowly backed away behind the black curtain that concealed the inner chamber, and disappeared from view.

"I guess that's it," Sam said. "Let's get out of this creepy place."

"I want to see him," Allison said.

I didn't think that was a good idea, but she insisted. It had only been a few hours since his death, so I thought the condition of his body may not have deteriorated substantially.

Honorable Williams was as we had left him. Allison walked over to where he remained in the chair with his head bent forward, and knelt beside him. She stroked his head gently. I half expected him to revive and raise his head, but it was clear, from his color and the fact that he was completely motionless, that he was dead.

"Why would that boy do this? Robert loved him and treated him like a son. Why? How could he have hated him so much?" Allison's eyes were filling with tears.

I thought it best to distract her so I said, "I wish I could answer that for you, Allison. Maybe, through no fault of our own, we all get caught up in the tsunami of history and simply get swept along, unable to understand or affect the outcome."

Allison looked at me dubiously, then raised a determined eyebrow.

"I want to stay here until the undertaker comes tomorrow," she said.

"I really don't think that's a good idea," Sam said. "His last wish was that we get you out of here as soon as possible, and besides," Sam continued hesitantly, "he may not look the same or smell the same tomorrow."

Allison looked offended, even a little angry, but something in her eyes registered that Sam was right.

"What about looters?" she asked.

"As you can see, this place has been pretty well gutted already. But with the body here—this is bad juju. They won't come in here until the body is removed," I said.

"Then can we at least wait somewhere until tomorrow?" Allison asked.

"If you insist on waiting, you'll have to spend the night at our place," said Sam. "Sinkor is still a target for rioters and looters. They will be hunting out Americos soon, and even though you are white and British, I doubt they would make much of a distinction." She paused and said kindly, "We've been staying at Honorable Williams' beach house. And I'm afraid you'll have to travel with what you have. We'll be leaving in our plane. It's a small plane— not a lot of extra room." Then she added, "Maybe when this is all over you can come back and reclaim what is valuable to you."

Allison stared at her for a long moment, her eyes slowly welling up with tears. She wiped them away with the back of her hand and quickly regained her composure.

"Yes. Let's make sure he is cared for tomorrow, then we can leave."

"That depends on what tomorrow brings," I said.

CHAPTER 40

MISSION ACCOMPLISHED

The odor of burning wood, tar, and trash hung in the streets like an omnipresent foul spirit. A thin, gray cloud of smoke drifted slowly over the US Embassy and floated over the grounds like a miasmic fog. Craig and Darius waited in their car for the marine guard to complete his examination of their IDs. The guard had seen them many times before, knew who they were, but once things went on emergency alert, everyone went by the book no matter how familiar you were.

The guard handed them back their ID badges, smiled and saluted smartly. Craig touched his right eyebrow in a mock salute and drove onto the Embassy grounds and around to the employee parking spaces.

Larry was leaning back in his chair with his feet crossed atop the desk. As Craig and Darius entered the office, Larry dropped his feet to the floor, stood up, and extended his hand to the men.

"Great job, men. Great job. Mr. Ellis wants to see us right away, no delays. Have you heard the news?" he asked, not waiting for the men to answer. "The rebels have arrested the government ministers and locked 'em up. They're gonna put 'em on trial, maybe tomorrow!"

"How about Tubman? Where's he?"

"The Honorable Shad Tubman, Jr.," Larry said, as if making an announcement, "attended an international governmental conference in Norway and is now taking a short break in New York. Not sure when he will be back."

"How about Wokie, his wife?"

"We've made sure she is safe. They will both probably end up in the US at some point. It's not going to be safe for Americos around here for a while. Though his help has been invaluable and PAL recognizes what he's done for them, he really won't be safe from the ordinary man on the street for quite a while."

"Great. Okay, let's go see Mr. Ellis."

Mr. Ellis was seated on his sofa, with a cigarette dangling from his mouth, casually throwing darts at a board across the room.

"Something I picked up from our British friends. It's amazing how relaxing it is. A few minutes of this and your concerns just seem to take on a milder perspective."

He stood up and lobbed one more dart, which missed the board and stuck in the wall. "Oops," he said with a giggle.

He walked over to his desk and stood gazing out the window.

"Did things go as expected?" he asked.

"Pretty much as expected sir," Darius said. "My assets that were tracking the Russians and the Chinese report that they have already left town."

"Yes, well, they would know about revolutions, wouldn't they?" Mr. Ellis said. "What about your recording, Miller? Did you get anything worthwhile?"

"Not really, sir. It's all audio, so all there actually is, is a garbled mess of screaming, moaning, and pleading. Tolbert and his wife were the only easily identifiable voices. I did yell at Doe to get on with it right before I grabbed his knife, so to be on the safe side we destroyed the tape. Keep the word 'clandestine' in our moniker, if you know what I mean."

"Good point, Miller. Give it here."

"We've also gotten reports," Larry added, "that President Tolbert's body was hacked up and thrown into a drainage ditch along with some loyal soldiers and civilians. Residents, mostly from the poor sections, spent the day pelting the bodies with stones and garbage."

"Revolutions are ugly things, truly ugly things," Mr. Ellis said. "Any action against whites or foreigners?"

"No, sir," Craig said. "Not that we know of. There was no history of white colonialism here sir, so there's no significant white resentment."

"I know that, Miller! I didn't get this job because I'm ignorant."

"Sorry, sir," Craig said.

"Once the killing starts, the lines between good and bad get blurred and sometimes disappear. There are groups who will destroy anything or anyone in their path. I want to know who's controlling them now. Where is Sergeant Doe in all of this?"

"Doe is still considered the leader," said Larry, "although he couldn't go through with the killing of Tolbert. Nevertheless, he is the highest-ranking enlisted man, which is to say, of all the conspirators, and he is a Krahn. He likes fine things, cars, and woman. He's already strutting around in a clean, pressed uniform with as many medals and ribbons as he can find to pin on it. We call him Herman."

"Why Herman?" Mr. Ellis asked.

"He reminds us of Hermann Göring, sir."

Mr. Ellis laughed, "Yes, that would be appropriate, wouldn't it? Very good, Larry."

"The really dangerous ones are Quiwonkpa and Pennoh. Quiwonkpa is a mindless brute and Pennoh is a killer, a true psychopath, but they're probably smart enough to know that they can always blame Doe for their crimes. That's why they let him strut around like a barnyard rooster."

"Good," Ellis said. "If we ever need to sanction Doe, we can nail him for war crimes. People are always prone to believe the worst when it comes to that. I want you two men to get back out on the streets. Get your assets working. Find out where this is headed. We don't want to lose control of this situation. It's been the ongoing policy of every Administration since Harry Truman to limit Communist influence around the world, especially in these backward, undeveloped countries."

Mr. Ellis waved his hand in dismissal and started scanning reports stacked up on his desk.

"Thank you, sir," Larry said, following Craig and Darius out of the office. They stopped at the door outside Larry's office.

"Now that we've unleashed the dogs of war, how do you plan to control them?" Craig asked.

"We've got two transports of marines coming. They should be here in four days. We'll set them up on the Embassy grounds. When we're ready for this thing to end or if events start to get out of hand, we'll deploy them. PR will spin it to the press that we are reestablishing order and preventing further bloodshed. Craig, I want you to follow the trials, keep a low profile. Don't let anyone take your picture. I want to know every detail. Go in disguise and try to blend in. Don't be recognized. Darius, find out what's going on at street level—who the leaders are, what the plans are. How good is your 'Merico' speech?"

Darius mentally thanked his involvement with Piers. "Sir. I can pass, but I will take great pains not to be identified as an Americo by the opposition."

Larry smiled confidently. "Right. Great. Let me know what you need in the way of resources. And gentlemen, if push comes to shove, shove."

Darius immediately thought of Piers's safety. She could be a little naïve when it came to the common man in the street. She had worked with so many, she really felt that she would be safe among them.

Darius placed a US diplomat tag on the dash of his car so that it could be seen and drove slowly through the milling crowd. Most of the throng ignored him, some saluting in a military fashion and a few cheering. He made his way slowly into Sinkor waving and smiling to groups of people.

Looters had started hurling bricks, bottles, and anything else they could find, at nearby houses. Occasionally, Darius could hear glass shattering. Someone would scream, but he heard no gunfire, no explosions. He checked his gun. It was loaded with a round in the chamber, and he had an extra clip in his pocket. He hoped, he even felt like praying, that he would not have to use it.

As he approached Piers's house, the crowd thinned out and he was able to pull in front of her courtyard gates, and got out to push the intercom. He was approached by several people dressed in ragged shorts and shirts.

Some were carrying pangas, the Liberian equivalent to machetes. He smiled at them."Brothers and sisters," he said, "I am an American. I am with the American Government. I am one of you. I have come to arrest these Congo people and take them to justice."

Some of them raised their fists and pangas and cheered.

"We will have justice and equality," Darius shouted.

The crowd cheered again and danced around in circles.

Piers opened her front door and saw Darius. She quickly unlocked the wrought-iron gates. He put his arms around her and gently moved her out of sight. Her eyes were wide with terror.

"What is happening?" she cried. "What is going on?"

"There's a revolution in progress out there, Piers, and you're not safe here."

"What do you mean 'not safe'?"

"President Tolbert has been murdered and the people are celebrating, looting, and looking for revenge."

"Revenge? Revenge for what?"

"Piers, do you remember reading about the French revolution in school?"

"Yes, I do, but I don't remember much about it."

"That's what's occurring out there. Tolbert is Louis XVI and you Congo people are the French aristocracy. Surely you remember what happened to them—the reign of terror."

An expression of horror swept over her face.

"But you don't expect that will happen here, do you?"

"It's already happening. Doe's revolutionary Government is quickly rounding up high-level officials in the Tolbert Government, throwing them in jail, and preparing to try them. There can only be one end to this. I've come to take you to the US Embassy and from there we can get you to the States. Where is the rest of your family?"

She seemed hesitant, bewildered, as though struggling with the reality of a catastrophic collapse of everything she had known.

"They're spending the next few months in Switzerland. I don't expect them back until maybe September."

"Good! Let's go now!" Darius took her by the arm and started leading her to the car door.

"Wait! Wait! I can't just leave. Not like this! I've always been for the country people. I know they've been treated unjustly, and I've said so publicly. Why would they harm me?"

"They don't believe you. They probably think that you're a spoiled rich kid who's rebelling against her family, but when the chips are down, like they are now, you'll side with your people."

"We both know that's not true."

"Yes, you and I do, but we're dealing with a mob mentality, and the mob is like a beast from hell with the scent of blood in its head. They are likely to kill or destroy anything that gets in their way. Now, we have to go!"

"No! I should try to talk to them. I can't leave like this, running away like some coward."

"Yes, you can! Our lives depend on it—now. This instant!"

She was still staring at him as he dragged her out of the courtyard and into his car. He tried to make it appear that she was in custody, so onlookers would not interfere.

"Lock your door," Darius shouted, "and keep your head down."

Darius reached the Embassy in about twenty minutes after dodging around milling crowds of people and various roadblocks. His car, despite being marked as a US government vehicle, was splattered with eggs, rotting vegetables, and animal feces.

The Marine guards were in battle dress and carried their weapons at the ready. There were two guards at the main gate; one checked Darius's credentials while the other vigilantly looked around constantly for possible threats. The guard looked over at Piers. He seemed very young, barely out of high school.

"I'm taking her for interrogation. It's important."

The young guard seemed doubtful for a moment then waved them through.

"Why are we here?" Piers asked.

"This is the only place I knew you would be safe for a couple of days. I have arranged for you to stay in the secure area of the Embassy."

"Then what?"

"Let's just take this one step at a time. I don't know what. But you can't stay in Monrovia. Why don't you consider it for a while? I have work to do, so I have to go. But I'll be back soon."

"What? Work to do? What does a 'technical engineer' have to do in the middle of a revolution?"

"I'll explain everything later. What I can say is that the secure area you will be staying in is CIA Headquarters for Liberia."

Just then, Larry appeared in the Embassy lobby. The two men nodded to each other. Darius gestured to Piers to go with Larry, then turned and left.

CHAPTER 41

KANGAROO COURT

Craig decided not to take the government car. By now the crowds in the streets made movement in a motorized vehicle nearly impossible. He would, instead, walk from the Embassy to the Barclay Training Center. Per Mr. Ellis's instructions, he would go undercover. He went as a journalist. He knew from experience that victorious revolutionaries liked to get the word out. It was the first step in establishing legitimacy.

He thought horn-rimmed glasses, a false mustache, and a wide-brimmed military hat would be a good start. Then he added a khaki hunting vest with numerous pockets—the type that he had seen many foreign correspondents and photographers wear. As a correspondent covering a successful revolution, he didn't expect to be scrutinized too much but he did have the office make up some fake credentials.

After donning his limited disguise, he strapped his professional Nikon F3 with telephoto lens over his shoulder and slipped his press pass around his neck so it was clearly visible. He took his gun out of his safe, looked at it for a few moments, felt its familiar form, its angularity, its curves, its hard, uncompromising steel, then slowly put it back in the safe. If he were stopped by the police or military and they found a gun, it might be difficult to explain. In a revolution, suspicion, paranoia, and distrust run high.

As he expected, motorized traffic had come to a standstill. Soldiers and police were running in all directions. The crowd was cheering in places and singing tribal songs or Christian hymns. Occasionally someone would run up to him, beer in hand, and say "the day of deliverance has come" or "dignity, equality, and fair treatment" or other slogans they had probably heard on the radio. Two soldiers, reeking of stale beer, walked up to him and demanded his camera. Craig said that he was a reporter for the *New York Times*, whipped out his pad and started to interview them. He explained with authority that the camera was not their property and that the *New York Times* knew many big men in Liberia.

"Dar are no mo' big men in Liberia. We are de big men now and ha' wan' yo cam'ra."

"If I give you my camera," Craig said, "then I will not be able to show the injustices of the Congo people to the world. I will not be able to show what good you have done."

The two men looked at each other and then at Craig. They smiled. Craig slowly exhaled, hoping that they bought this.

They stepped back, watching Craig closely. Craig dug in his pants pocket and brought out two $5 bills. It would go a long way to assuage their sense of loss and pride. They took the money and smiled broadly.

"You tell de world what has happened hee. You tell dhem dhat God ha' spoken—dis hee is justice."

Craig assured them that he would. He stepped away from the two soldiers and resumed his journey down United Nations Drive toward the Barclay Training Center, stopping long enough to see the two soldiers break a shop window with their rifle butts, kick open the door, and enter. He slowly threaded his way through the agitated crowd of soldiers and citizens to the building where the trials were to take place.

He had reached the first landing of the entrance stairs when he heard the shouting. He looked over the heads of the mob and saw a group of men, all stripped to the waist, being led through the throng.

People were hurling insults and cursing the men. Some threw rotten fruit. Craig recognized the prisoners as President Tolbert's cabinet officers. He counted them. There were only thirteen—some were missing.

As they were led up the stairs, Craig was close enough to touch them. They smelled heavily of bodily odors and rotten fruit. Strangely, they didn't seem frightened, only resigned to what they knew their fate would be.

Craig assumed it would be a kangaroo court, although it had not been discussed at station Headquarters. His job, along with others working on the project, had been to destabilize the Tolbert Government. What the citizenry did after that was outside the interest of the company, and none of his concern. As company employees were fond of saying, this was above his paygrade. Nevertheless, judging from the way the tribunal was going, Mr. Ellis had nothing to worry about.

This, ostensibly, was a trial whose purpose was to publicly charge the Tolbert Government with corruption, malfeasance, and suppression of civil and human rights and treason. The crowd chanted out the charges in unison "Treason! Murders!" etc. The accused officials standing before the court of five military officers were permitted no defense. Their crimes were considered indefensible and their guilt unquestionable.

The trial was the strongest public declaration of legitimacy for the revolution and the final purgation of nearly a hundred and fifty years of dominance.

All was over for the Americo-Liberians, thought Craig. *And they had better run.*

After leaving Piers, Darius went to his locker and slipped into Liberian army fatigues with the rank of corporal on his sleeves. He put on the well-worn fatigue hat and pulled the brim down to just above his eyes. He knew Craig would be at the trial, and he needed to find him to touch base.

Sergeant Doe had announced that any soldier caught looting would be shot, but Darius doubted very much that this order would be carried out. Nonetheless, he knew he had to watch his back at all times.

He made his way down United Nations Boulevard through swarms of people who were still cheering and dancing as though it were a street festival. His rank of corporal identified him as "Country," so many insisted on shaking his hand, others on patting him on the back. Most were smiling and laughing.

These people believe the Messiah has come and will lead them to the Promised Land, Darius thought.

There was another cheering crowd when Darius arrived at the Barclay Training Center. The verdicts had been announced, and it was no surprise to Darius that it was death by firing squad.

Craig, along with the other spectators, was coming out of the improvised courthouse. He recognized the news reporter and photographer cover— Craig had used it before. Behind them walked the condemned.

The prisoners had been cleaned up for the trial and were fully dressed, but now they were being led away to be stripped again and subjected to the wrath of the crowd. The men were handcuffed and chained to one another. They were loaded onto a bus and driven a short distance to a nearby beach. There they waited on the bus and watched as the workmen completed their grisly chore of preparing for their execution.

Craig arrived with the rest of the mob and started taking his disguise as a reporter seriously. He prepared the settings on his camera and started taking photographs.

After some time, the prisoners were led by soldiers to where large wooden poles had been erected in the sand. The poles resembled telephone poles—far too oversized for the purpose but very effective is sending a strong message. One by one, each man was tied to a pole—a single rope around his waist or chest. The soldiers, all considerably inebriated at this point, were laughing and joking and shouting vulgarities at the condemned. There were only nine posts erected, so the four remaining men had to watch and wait in the bus for their turn.

The soldiers, staggering, lined up in front of the men in an attempt to form a firing squad. They clumsily tried to load their weapons; all old, all in various states of disrepair. Most of the rifles were old World War II M-1s, used by the US armed forces. Some had Uzis and a few had automatic weapons.

One of the elderly government ministers had soiled himself and had apparently fainted. His legs had given way and he had slumped down to the ground, his head dangling like a large ball.

A soldier with a megaphone shouted, "Now we weel ha' justice!"

There was a brief moment of heavy silence; then the order was given to fire. This was followed by a fusillade of deafening gun shots. The impact of the bullets on the bodies was strangely inconsequential. Most of the condemned men were merely wounded in their extremities, if hit at all. The drunken squad started shooting randomly at all of the ministers. As bullets popped and sprayed around them, the random prisoner fell forward, slumping against his restraints.

All, that is, except for Honorable Cecil Dennis. Honorable Dennis stood erect with his head held back against the pole. He looked forward, alert. When the firing started, bullets hit the ground all around him— but rather than fall, he locked his knees so that he did not slump. Many of the other ministers looked down in fear or to the heavens in prayer, but Dennis did not. He stared directly at his executioners, and it seemed that this one act unnerved the soldiers to the point that they continually missed him.

More shots were fired. This time most of them hit, but still Dennis didn't fall. Many of the soldiers focused their rifles and pistols on him. Bullets tore into him. They hit the ground around his feet, sending up small geysers of sand, but still he didn't slump or fall. Finally, one of the soldiers walked up to him and shot Honorable Dennis in the head, which knocked him to one side. But still he didn't fall. There was a general mumbling among Dennis's executioners as they backed away from the semi-erect body. This was bad juju, so it seemed very important to the soldiers that he fall.

When he finally did, the remaining prisoners were led from the bus where they had been watching the carnage. The inebriated executioners grabbed the four men and made quick work of their death sentence.

Darius joined Craig standing with a silent group of foreign correspondents. No one spoke and most avoided eye contact. Even the most callous of them could not help feeling a little shame and some stirrings of outrage.

"Did you get Piers out?" Craig asked, pale and shaken.

"Yes, she is safe in the Embassy."

"Good, very good," Craig said. "I think our work here is done. Ellis should be proud."

"Have you seen Sergeant Doe?"

"I've heard the Sergeant has promoted himself to General, and most of his merry men are now high-ranking officers. Have you been able to learn anything?"

"No, not much." Darius said. "Our General Doe seems to have had a string of good luck. This seems to have gone off without a hitch. He's been parading through the neighborhoods where the people are cheering him on and even trying to touch him. They believe he has good juju." He paused. "How long do you think the bloodbath will go on?"

"I suspect Ellis will wait until the Marines get here, then he'll inform the new General. That should bring it to a close. I doubt that there will be any Congo people left alive here by then."

"What about the ones who made it out?" Darius asked.

"This new Government doesn't have the resources or the wherewithal to go after them. As long as they stay out of Liberia, they'll be safe. Remember, most of 'em own houses and estates in the US or Europe and they probably have their money in foreign banks. They'll definitely be better off outside of Liberia."

"Could you write this up?" Darius asked. "We need to get this to Ellis ASAP, and I'd like to check on Piers before I see him."

Piers was sitting on the bed clasping her handbag on her lap when Darius walked in her room.

"Hey babe, you okay?"

She looked at him with serious eyes but with no evidence of tears. She waited for him to explain.

Darius was under oath not to divulge his actual job and rank, so he focused on her destination and her safety. He knew that there was a US Navy helicopter carrier and two other ships headed for Liberia, and it would be about three more days before they arrived off shore. He suggested that he make arrangements for her to go back to the States and stay with her relatives in DC.

She smiled but could not keep tears from reemerging in her eyes.

"It will be okay," he assured her.

She smiled broadly and managed a short laugh, but her hands were trembling as she took his.

"I've decided to join my family in Switzerland," she said. "Your coworkers have been very friendly and helpful. They say they can get me out of the country today. Once out, I know how to get to our villa in Switzerland."

Darius gently wiped the tears away from her cheeks.

"You've been very kind, Darius," she continued. "I even thought there was a possibility of having a real relationship. Now I know that with your line of work, whatever that is, that a relationship has always been out of the question."

"Hmm. Well, yeah." He paused. "Switzerland sounds good. I'm glad you understand. But I want you to know that I've always admired you and want what is best for you. Please take care and stay safe."

Darius hesitated for a moment then kissed her softly. "Hey, when this is over, I'll get to Switzerland and look you up."

She smiled without a word.

"And here, take this." Darius reached in his shirt pocket and took out a blank white card, jotted his initials and DC phone number on it. "If you ever decide to come to DC, call me. It's not such a bad place."

She took the card and clinched it in her right hand. Darius kissed her again, then turned and left for his meeting with Mr. Ellis.

CHAPTER 42

ESCAPE

"Are we coming back?" Sam asked as we left the beach house.

"I think so. We have to take care of Honorable Williams's body. Once that's done it may be too late to depart for Sierra Leone today, so maybe just one more night here."

"No, I meant are we coming back to Liberia, ever?"

"Right now, I see no reason to. All of our connections here are lost—no, I don't think so."

Sam led Bao into the kitchen and closed the door. "Just to make sure he doesn't destroy the whole house," she said.

Winston, who in my estimation was the most reliable taxi driver on the planet, was waiting for us in the driveway. Allison, looking very stately in a silk Chanel dress, was waiting by the car. She appeared dressed as though she was ready to board the Queen Elizabeth II complete with heels and a wide-brimmed hat decorated with various species of birds and flowers. I have always been amazed at this obsession, or whatever it is, that English women have for hats and the seemingly inappropriate places they don them.

She looked at me curiously.

"We are going to a funeral, aren't we?" she said with wide-eyed assurance.

A large sign had been tacked onto the door of Nathan's funeral home.

WE CLOSED UNTIL FURTHER NOTICE. WE REGRET INCONVENIENCE.

"The little son of a bitch!" Sam said. "Do you suppose Honorable Williams is in there?"

"I seriously doubt it," I said.

"Can we go take a look?" Sam asked. We got out of the car, leaving Allison to deal with the heat. The entrance was locked and all shades had been drawn at the windows.

"Nathan's no idiot," I said. "He's staying out of sight until this madness is over. Let's go back to the house. I'll bet he's still there."

Honorable Williams was where we had left him, sitting slumped in the chair. In some grotesque way, he looked at peace. Allison was not. She was clearly shocked at the swift deterioration of her lover's dead body. With a trembling hand, she slowly and tenderly reached to touch his face. His cold skin caused her to recoil quickly.

"How horrible death is!" she said, covering her mouth with her hand. "It takes away everything—who we are, what we were, and what we could become. Why did this happen to a good man?" She wiped the tears away from her cheeks.

I suggested that we bury him on the ocean side of his house and that maybe, when times were better, he could be moved to his family cemetery. Allison agreed but had no intention of getting dirty.

"Where's Winston? Can he help?"

The plan was to wrap Honorable Williams in a clean sheet, then in something waterproof like a tarpaulin.

Fortunately after some searching, Sam found a roll of dark plastic sheeting in a corner of the garage. I was dragging it out on my way to find Winston when a small convoy of army jeeps and trucks drove up and stopped at the entrance to the house. Several soldiers jumped out of the truck and I instantly recognized the officer who stepped out of the passenger side of the jeep. Captain Roberts walked up to me. I knew that he had recognized me too.

"What are you doing with that?" he asked.

I didn't answer.

"What do you think you are doing? You are just a common looter, just like all the rest. Do you want to be held complicit in a felony charge?"

"I'm not stealing anything," I said. "My question is, what are you doing here?"

"I've come to arrest Honorable Williams for conspiracy and high treason."

I couldn't resist making a facial gesture of disgust hoping the Captain would notice it. If he did notice it, he ignored it the way a performer might ignore a heckler.

"Oh, so you've changed sides now, have you? You sucked up to Honorable Williams when you thought he had Tolbert's ear. But even Tolbert fired you for being inept. And now Tolbert is dead. The mobs are killing the Big Men left and right! Now you have to prove your alliance to the PAL. To the Cause!"

"Fired? Me? Not at all. Those cowards didn't have the guts to take that risk! I was too brave for them, so I quit and joined the PAL. Those men know how to keep law and order! So now, lead me to Honorable Williams!"

"You're too late. He's beyond your justice."

"What do you mean by that?"

"He's in the house. Why don't you go and arrest him?" I said.

Captain Roberts signaled to his men to follow him. He and his men burst into the house and I followed behind.

"Who did this?" Captain Roberts asked in a loud voice. "Was it you? Did you do this?" he insisted, looking straight at me.

"Captain—are you a captain again?—you know damn good and well that I didn't do this."

"Then who did? Tell me now."

"It was Toby, his adopted son. And the household staff are gone—stole as much as they could carry."

"Where is the boy, Toby, now?" the Captain demanded.

"I have no idea," I said. "But I suspect he's returned to his tribal origins, wherever that was. We've come to give Honorable Williams a decent burial. Nathan couldn't manage it."

"You will do no such thing. We will take charge of the body," the Captain said, motioning to his soldiers. Rigor mortis had already begun to set in. Allison turned away and started sobbing.

"What will you do with him?" I asked.

"He has been charged with treason and conspiracy and will be put on trial."

"That is ridiculous! It's absurd!" I shouted. "The man is dead! Murdered!"

The Captain moved close to me and leaned into my face. "You are an American and therefore have some protection, but you had better watch what you say or you, too, my friend, you could be brought up on charges by the Progressive Alliance of Liberia."

His eyes glistened with rage and hatred, and as he spoke, he unconsciously fondled his sidearm. The soldiers wrapped Honorable Williams' body in the plastic and threw it into the back of the truck. It made a sickening thud as it hit the floor of the truck bed. Captain Roberts glared at me as he stepped into the front passenger seat.

"Do not leave Liberia without permission of the PAL," he said.

I thought for a moment that he was going to shoot me right there. He gave a signal with his hand and the driver put the jeep in gear and drove off, spraying orange dirt from the rear wheels.

"I don't like this one bit," Sam said. "That guy's a snake. And somehow he's got it in for you. We ought to get to the airport as soon as possible and get outta here, regardless of what the little dictator said. What's he gonna do once we're gone?"

I turned to Allison. She was dabbing the tears from her eyes with an embroidered handkerchief. I explained what we were about to do. She nodded, the wide brim of her hat flopping gently as she did so.

Winston had wisely parked out of sight during the Captain's visit. He now made his reappearance. On our way back to the beach house, I told him our plan to depart Liberia.

"Boss," he said, "I know ya wan' go to Spriggs-Payne. But de soldiers ha' block all de main roads. Dhey shootin' anybody dhat don't stop and robbin' dhem that do. I know anodder way not many people know of."

He must have noticed my skepticism.

"You know how it be when drivin' a cab—you know all de ways."

I had to admit that he was right. If Captain Roberts wanted to vent his fury on me, he could well have given my description to all the roadblocks leading to the airport.

"Okay, Winston," I said as he pulled up to the beach house. "We have to get a few things. Wait here."

Winston put his finger to his hat brim in a kind of salute.

Bao was more restless than usual when we returned to the beach house. He didn't like being enclosed in the kitchen and he seemed to know something was up. Sam spoke to him soothingly then took him in her arms to calm him down. A couple of bananas helped, but he became very clingy to Sam and wouldn't let her go.

"Bao-Bao, this is not helpful, baby. Mommy has to go and get ready."

Bao looked at her skeptically, then held her a little tighter.

"Oh, you're coming too, Bao! We're going to go fly in a plane!"

As Bao started to relax, Sam's face became determined. Yet there was a glint of excitement in her eyes. She looked at me and I thought I noticed a slight smile. As she extricated herself from the chimp, she strapped her .32 caliber on her waist and checked her spare clips. She told me she had about thirty rounds, then took Bao by his wrist. He jumped up and down and hooted loudly.

"Do you want to stay here and become bush meat?" she said to him in a rather strong voice. He seemed to understand, or at least he understood that she was upset, and when he sensed this, he always became reluctantly compliant.

I grabbed my 9 mm and a box of extra clips. "Sam, where are the diamonds?"

"I have them sewn into my shorts."

"Not those. They were in that damned Furbank book, but I can't find the book. Do you think James found them and took 'em?"

"No. But I thought you mailed it."

I stopped and looked at her. "I never had a chance to speak to Honorable Williams about it and I just couldn't trust the mail."

"In that case, they could be anywhere. James probably moved the book when he was neatening up."

It turned out to be quite simple. James did, indeed, move the book— he put it in the bookshelf in our room. I would have been proud to have thought of that myself.

With a sigh of relief, I tucked the book into my flight satchel, then we both threw a change of clothes in a small duffel and ran out to Winston's cab, dragging a bewildered Bao with us.

I paused and said to Sam, "You okay?"

"Yeah, why? Oh God, I should never have told you!"

"Okay, okay. Just checking."

Sam opened the rear door and threw the chimp in next to Allison, then jumped in after. I got in the front passenger seat, and the instant I got the door closed, Winston floored the accelerator, spun the rear wheels, and we were off.

"He smells!" Allison exclaimed. "Do you really have to? I mean, couldn't you leave him with a friend or at a zoo or something?"

Sam turned to her. "Allison, I'm sorry things are turning out this way, but if you don't want to go with us, Winston can stop the car and you can get out. It's your choice."

Allison turned her head up and toward the open window. She was breathing heavily, and her nostrils were pulsating like fish gills.

Winston drove down streets and neighborhoods in Monrovia that I didn't know existed. They were strangely quiet and empty. Sam theorized that everyone was in the city center. She asked Winston where all the people were.

"Dhey in town at the trial and execution," Winston said.

"How do you know there is going to be an execution?" I asked.

"Oh, dhey is gonna be. Dhey woud'na ha' a trial less dhere is gonna be executions."

At last, Winston turned onto a road that I recognized. Then, shortly before we entered the airport property, we were stopped by a roadblock consisting of two poles resting end to end, on top of emptied, rusted fuel drums. There were two soldiers with rifles standing by the barrier. We came to a full stop.

"Wha yo bidness hee?" one of them asked. Winston didn't hesitate.

"Mr. Ken hee," Winston pointed to me, "he de boss and he come to check on his bidness."

Both soldiers looked through the driver side window at me.

"You de boss?" one of them asked.

"Whutch you got in da bag?" the other asked.

"Yes, I am the boss." I pointed to my flight bag. "This here is my business, and this is a very important British lady."

"Do she know de queen?" the other soldiers asked.

"Yes," I said loud enough to stop Allison's protest.

They weren't buying it and one eyed my bag suspiciously. Just then, Sam pulled Bao closely and repositioned herself to try and hide him.

The soldiers saw the cringing chimp.

"Oh ya! Dat be too funny, oh! Da queen an' da monkey! He look like good bush meat! Gimme dat chimp."

This was clearly getting out of hand.

"Here," I said, reaching across Winston, and handed the soldiers $50 apiece. They glanced at the dash, pleased but a little astonished, hopefully thinking that Allison must be very important. Winston's jaw dropped a little. The guards smiled and waved us through.

"Boss!" Winston said. "Why so much dash? No one pay that much dash to soldiers."

"It got us through the roadblock without much palaver, didn't it, Winston? Sometimes you have to pay large when it's important."

Winston nodded in agreement.

When we drove up to the operations shack, most of the pilots and ground personnel were gathered in the waiting room. The cacophony ceased when we walked into the room. Even Bao was quiet and stood holding Sam's hand. Everyone turned to me with unveiled concern on their faces.

"Boss," Cian said, "what's going to happen? What should we do?"

Paterson was there next to Cian. He knew his world was crumbling and he looked it.

"Paterson, while I'm talking, could you take Miss Allison, here, and help her into my plane?"

"Yes, boss, yes."

I turned to the assembled group. "As you all know, there has been a coup d'état. The old Government has been replaced, and I'm told that all of the government ministers have been put on trial. I suspect, although I don't know yet, that they will all be executed."

An audible groan rose from the group.

"I can tell you this, and it gives me great sadness to do so, that Honorable Williams is dead."

Shock registered on their faces, then changed to expressions of pain. They wanted to know how it happened. I told them as succinctly as I could and recounted how Honorable Williams's body had been taken by Captain Roberts. I said I doubted that he would be given a decent burial. I gave them a few moments to digest this bad news, then explained what I knew they all wanted to know.

"The company, West African Air Service, essentially doesn't exist anymore. The money and assets have been confiscated by the revolutionary Government. It's been a pleasure, men, and I regret to say that from this time on, you are on your own. My advice to you is to get the hell out of

Liberia as soon as you can. We are flying out in my airplane. As far as I'm concerned, those of you who want to go can take one of the operational company planes and fly with us to Freetown in Sierra Leone or anywhere you want."

This was followed by a general outcry of agreement.

"Then let's get the hell outta here!" I shouted.

Most of the pilots followed me and Sam out of the building. I ran up to Winston's cab, stuck my head through the open window, and handed him $400.

"Your last installment, Winston. Don't spend it all in one place!"

"Oh, boss! Dis hee way too much! You jus' pay me somtin' lass week oh!"

"Winston, you need to get out of here, now! Take the money and make sure your family is safe. This coup is for the rise of the working man, I know. That's you. But there is a lot of drinking and shooting, and if some guy with a gun decides he wants your car, he'll just take it! So get your family out of Monrovia until all the rioting calms down. Go now! And stay safe!"

Several pilots were running toward the airplanes to board them and get underway. Just then, an army jeep and truck appeared and came to a screeching halt in the parking area. They were the same vehicles that had stopped at Honorable Williams's house.

I put my hand on my gun.

Captain Roberts leapt down from the passenger seat of the jeep and drew his .45 caliber, a vintage 1911 pistol. A group of four soldiers jumped from the truck, all carrying M-1 rifles. Captain Roberts started toward Sam and me. He stopped just outside of an arm's-length distance.

"You were not planning on escaping against my expressed orders, were you? I could shoot you where you stand and it would be lawful. But never mind that now. I have come to confiscate all aircraft and material assets of West African Air Service." He squinted his eyes against the glare of the sun. He was smiling as though tasting the sweetness of revenge.

"By whose authority?" I said, hoping to find a way to stall for time.

The Captain snarled, "By the authority of the PAL. That's who."

"The PAL? You said that before. PAL's not the Government. It's just an opposition party."

"You know nothing!" The Captain seethed, "Doe is in charge now! He has established a new Government and he is its chairman! He is promising a complete overhaul of Liberia's society, economy, and political system." The Captain's voice was getting louder. "President Doe has promised the replacement of the corrupt system of the past and restoring respect for the rights of the Liberian people."

I seemed to sense that some of the pilots were quietly reaching for their guns and this was not what I wanted.

"So, if I turn everything over to you, what will happen to us, to all of us?"

"You will be taken into custody and given a fair trial."

"No doubt like the one they gave Tolbert's ministers?"

Bao had been restless and tugged at Sam's hand. Now he started hooting and jumping and even seemed to lunge at the Captain.

Captain Roberts stopped smiling and a look of rage came over his face. In an instant he raised his pistol and fired at Bao. The bullet hit Bao with enough impact to knock him out of Sam's hand and send him rolling several yards onto the dirt parking area.

"Goddammit!" someone yelled, and Captain Roberts instinctively turned toward the voice. At that moment another shot rang out and the Captain crumpled over at his midsection and fell face forward, dropping his pistol as he fell. During the momentary distraction, Sam pulled out her .32 and shot the Captain, and then shot him again before he hit the ground.

I knew what would happen next. I pulled my gun out and shouted for everybody to run for their aircraft. The soldiers took cover behind several parked cars. It took a surprisingly long time for them to start shooting. I, and most of the other pilots, fired back, all the while running for our aircraft.

I shouted for Cian to get into the left seat and start the engine. Fortunately, Paterson had seated Allison in the rear passenger seat and had told her to wait. She looked bewildered, unable to take in what was happening. I told Sam to get in next to her and that I would cover her.

"No!" she shouted. "I'll take care of this."

She got down on her right knee and started shooting at soldiers behind the parked cars. She emptied one clip and quickly injected another and continued shooting. I jumped into the front passenger seat just as Cian got the engine started.

"Get in! Get in!" I shouted at Sam. She stood up and leapt into the seat next to Allison, who by this time was hyperventilating and muttering "Oh God, Oh God," between breaths. I could hear bullets thudding into the fuselage as Cian pushed the power up with the intention of getting the airplane airborne as quickly as possible.

The bullets stopped hitting the airplane soon after we started the takeoff run. We were heavy. From the sound of the engine, one bullet, at least, had done some damage. Cian held it down, gaining speed on the runway so that we could do a rapid climb out. He held the airplane at treetop level, hovering just over the tops of houses and buildings, making it extremely difficult for the rifle fire to hit us.

Cian put his flying expertise to work. He said that the controls were responding relatively well, and that we should be able to get to Freetown. I could see that most engine and flight gauges were operating as they should, but I was concerned about the fuel. There were a couple of holes in the fuselage, and a small stream of leaking fuel glistened over the wing. Cian kept the airplane at rooftop level until he was out over the coast, then climbed to eight thousand feet, which kept us out of the effective range of small arms.

Cian had just leveled off and lined us up on a heading to Freetown when I heard Allison exclaiming, "Oh God! Oh God!"

I looked back and saw that her dress was stained with blood on her right hip.

"Are you hit?" I asked.

"Am I hit? What do you mean by that?"

"Have you been shot?"

"No, no, I don't think so."

No," Sam said, "but I have."

It was one of those moments you didn't want to believe. She was wincing in pain.

"I can't feel my legs. I think I've been hit twice. It's a little difficult to breathe."

I told Cian to descend as quickly as he could. We would be crossing the border soon.

The engine seemed to cough. I looked at Cian in alarm. His face stared straight ahead in deep concentration.

"Hang on, Sam," I said softly. "I'll get you some help."

CHAPTER 43

FREETOWN

Once we crossed the border, I called the tower at Freetown. There was no contact. I tried again, then again and again. Finally, a voice hailed me back. I told him that we were inbound from Monrovia with a wounded passenger who needed medical assistance right away.

The tower operator said that there were no emergency vehicles available, then he informed me in a formal voice that the tower would be closed in thirty minutes. It was getting dark. Lights were beginning to spring up from below. I told the operator that we were only about forty-five minutes out and that it was an emergency. He again repeated in the same monotone voice that the tower would close in thirty minutes. I asked him if he could leave the runway lights on. Again, he repeated that the airport would be closed in thirty minutes. I asked him if there was any transportation available, and after a long pause he said that I might be able to get a cab, that sometimes cabs hang around the airport after closing in case of late arrivals.

I looked back at Sam. She appeared unconscious. I reached over the front seat, and with a great deal of effort, managed to reach Sam's hand. Her pulse was steady but weak. Allison had her face turned toward the back seat window and was holding a thick handkerchief over her mouth to muffle her cries.

After about twenty minutes, I spotted the airport beacon and Cian quickly lined up on a compass heading that put the beacon on the nose of the airplane. I checked my watch. Then, just as the tower operator said it would, the beacon went black.

The engine coughed again. Then sputtered a little.

Cian descended some more and held the heading for thirteen minutes.

He then turned to line up on the magnetic compass heading off the runway. Cian switched on the landing light and started a slow let down. We both scanned the dark ahead for any sign of the airfield. I expected at any moment to see a building appear in the landing light, followed by the terrible sounds of impact.

I remembered listening to a cockpit voice recording of the crash of a corporate, twin engine aircraft. The pilots had entered instrument flight conditions from visual flight conditions. They were unsure of the mountainous terrain around them. The next sound reminded me of a flyswatter coming down hard on a bug. It was all over in a second—none of the extended drama of a Hollywood movie. They hit the side of a mountain and were crushed in an instant.

I was just about to tell Cian to try and add power and climb when we noticed runway lights come on about ten degrees to our right.

"God bless him for a saint!" Cian shouted. He turned for the runway and landed the plane as it gasped for fuel.

The tower operator kept the light on until we were clear of the runway and had taxied to the main ramp. While Cian was shutting the airplane down, I rushed out of the passenger side and ran to the terminal hoping the doors were not locked. They opened, and breathing heavily, I ran out into the front parking area where there was a single taxicab. The driver was asleep and was startled awake when I opened his door. I pulled him out of the cab. I was in no mood for argument or pleasantries.

"We've just landed. We've come from Liberia. My wife's been shot and I need to get her to a hospital."

The driver, still stunned and stuttering, seemed bewildered.

"Let me put it to you this way. Do you understand English?"

The driver nodded.

"Then if you don't help us, I will blow your fucking head off and take your cab. Do you understand me now?"

The driver nodded again, this time vigorously.

I took him by the arm and pulled him through the break in the fence.

Allison was out of the airplane, confused and still wearing her wide-brim hat. Her dress was covered in blood. Sam's blood.

Cian and I eased Sam out of the rear seat as gently as possible. She choked the pain down and tried to muzzle her cries with her hand. Allison extended her arms to receive Sam. We got her into the cab and somehow managed to squeeze ourselves in too. Sam's body was stretched over Allison's and my laps. Allison held Sam's head gently and caressed her forehead as I held her body to protect her from the bumpy ride. I was directly behind the driver and Cian rode up front.

"Take us to the nearest hospital!" I shouted.

"Dat be the gov'ment hospital, boss, but don't know if dhey be open now."

"I don't give a damn! Just get us there as fast as you can push this thing."

The driver did his best. Unfortunately, the suspension in his cab had long since worn out, and we bounded and banged over every imperfection in the road. I held Sam as tightly as I could. Then, just as we drove onto the entrance ramp of the hospital, the exhaust muffler and tail pipe caught on the edge of the pavement and was ripped off, making a noise similar to empty metal trash cans rolling around in the street.

The cab driver started to slow down; I placed the mussel of my gun against his head. His eyes opened wide with fear, but he understood and pressed this foot on the accelerator.

The hospital was a single-story building that had been built in the '50s with pale green paint peeling from the plywood siding and with the remnants of a faded gray trim. There was no emergency service. Once the cab came to a stop, I dashed out and ran into the building.

A very gaunt woman with extremely large eyes was sitting at a battered wooden desk, the victim of innumerable collisions. I explained to her as quickly as I could what I needed. She looked at me indifferently and sighed, then picked up a phone handset and called someone—she never said who.

A few long minutes passed until a woman, wearing a dirty white apron, came from down the hall toward me. I assumed she was an orderly, but she introduced herself as Nurse Johnson and asked me what the problem was. I said that my wife had been shot and needed immediate emergency assistance.

Nurse Johnson understood and instantly yelled for help. A stooped man who appeared to be in his late sixties emerged from one of the rooms. He was pushing a gurney with one wobbly wheel. It was covered with a thin mattress and over that was a cotton sheet that was stained with faded red and yellow spots.

The two of them followed me out to the cab, with the gurney making a loud rattling noise. Allison was still holding Sam's head, and helped Nurse Johnson ease her out of the back seat. Sam was now unconscious and still bleeding. It took three of us to then lift her on to the gurney.

Nurse Johnson said, "We take her now. You wait in de lobby."

The cab driver followed me, and just as we were entering the hospital, he grabbed me by the arm and wanted to know, in a loud voice, when I was going to pay the fare and that I was to pay him for the damages to his cab.

"Ya can neva get de blood out," he said. "Bad juju. An de spirits weel know o' de blood an' come into de cab. It won' be fit to drive no mo'."

I gave him $50. He seemed disappointed, even angry.

"What! You want more?" I shouted in his face. "Get the hell out of my sight. I'm in no mood to be shaken down."

He must have sensed that I had my hand on my gun again because his expression changed to fear, and he backed away slowly without taking his eyes off mine until he was back in the cab. Allison was still in the back seat and had started whimpering.

I went back into the hospital. Cian was inside, waiting in what passed for the lobby. He asked about Sam, and I just stared at him unable to speak. I didn't know.

"Cian," I said. "It's best if you get out of here as soon as you can. There's a very pissed off cab driver who, I'm sure, could be convinced to help you out, given the right amount of 'coaxing'. Then take Allison to the nearest decent hotel and disappear. We don't know where this will end. The problems in Liberia could easily spill over into the border countries."

Cian nodded in agreement.

"Aye, they all seem ripe for revolution, don't they? And what should we do with the aircraft, sir?"

"Leave it back there," I said. "It's no longer a concern of mine. I think it got shot up pretty badly. No one owns it now. I suppose you could say it's part of the spoils of war, at least Captain Roberts thought so."

As Cian was turning to leave, I stopped him. "By the way, Cian, what happened to that Catholic priest, Father . . ."

"O'Brian."

"Yes, that one."

"Ooh, the poor soul up and got religion all of a sudden like. It was like he had this glorious beatific vision appear before him. He wanted to land at Spriggs-Payne, and once there, he announced he was going into town. He said something like duty called him there. Just as though his good angel was talking to him. I told him that was no way to gain that bishop's miter, but he just smiled and left. Just like a barefooted saint on a pilgrimage. It was a rare sight to see. A miracle, sir. A real miracle."

"It is amazing what adversity will do to some people," I said.

At that, I took Cian's hand and wished him a safe journey.

"If there is a God, sir, maybe he'll look after good people," he said.

I watched as he walked out of the hospital into the black night.

I found where they had taken Sam. She was in a long ward with what looked like hundreds of other people, although it was probably no more than fifty others, all suffering from various ailments. Bad smells drifted throughout the room. Some were moaning, others were weeping, but most, like Sam, were silent.

There was another nurse, a European, wearing a blood-stained apron, standing at the foot of Sam's bed.

"What can you do for her?" I asked.

"The most we can do for her now is to make her comfortable. We have very little medicines—no antibiotics, little morphine, and the surgeon does not come until tomorrow. He will bring medicines with him tomorrow."

She paused and looked at me, and in that instant, I knew what she was trying to tell me.

I found a rickety chair nearby and put it next to Sam's bed. I took her hand in both of mine. Her hand was limp and did not respond to my touch, but it was warm, and I could feel her pulse. Her pulse was weak and slow, but she was alive. I had no idea what to do or how to help her. I had reached my limit.

I stayed with her, holding her hand, for several hours. Most of the lights had been turned off and only a doorway light, a single light at the other end of the ward, remained on.

Then I remembered the diamonds. Lovingly, I caressed her hips and removed her shorts, then stuffed them into my flight bag. They were safe for now.

The hours passed. I listened to every labored breath she took, counting the seconds between breaths. Then the count slowed down. I watched her face. Her expression was surprisingly peaceful. I could see in the dim light that her mouth was slightly opened, and then, I could feel that she had no pulse. I don't know how long I sat there looking at her. I didn't know what to do.

Finally, I went to find someone on duty. It was an old woman who would have been well past retirement age in the US. She was asleep at the desk in the entrance lobby. I woke her up, much to her irritation, and told her that I thought my wife had just died and that I wanted her to call a doctor.

"Wha' fo'? If she dead, she dead. No docta can bring her back to life. Wait till morning, doctor come around dhen."

She glared at me, then put her head back down on the desk. I returned to the ward and resumed my place in the chair next to Sam. I couldn't help thinking of King Lear looking down at the body of his beloved daughter,

Cordelia, and lamenting, "Why should a dog, a horse, a rat have life, and thou no breath at all?" What is that terrible mystery where someone like Sam can be Sam one moment then "dead as earth" the next moment?

It was well past dawn when a young doctor came into the ward. He walked down the rows of patients, looking at each like a drill sergeant inspecting his troops. He stopped when he got to Sam's bed. He hesitated as though waiting for me to stand to attention. He walked up to Sam's bedside and looked at her for a few moments.

"Can you bring her back to life?" I asked.

He looked as though I had slapped him across the face.

"Will you sign the death certificate?"

He motioned for me to follow him to his office.

"When did death occur?" he asked.

"Last night," I said.

"Do not play the smart aleck with me!" he shouted. "At what time did she die?"

"It was around 01:00."

He asked me a few more questions, then signed the paper and handed it to me across his desk.

"Show this to the nurse at reception." He had obviously been trained at a fully staffed, fully funded hospital, probably in Europe. "She will contact the necessary people. Please wait in the lobby."

"No," I said "I'm going to be with my wife."

It was clear that the young doctor was not used to having people say no to him. His face hardened. There wasn't the slightest indication of empathy in his eyes.

"As you wish," he said. "But it's highly irregular."

CHAPTER 44

HOME

Someone at the undertaker's had stolen the rough diamond ring that I had given to Sam when we first met. The owner denied it, of course, and threatened to call the police and have me arrested. I didn't want that kind of palaver, so I dropped the matter and arranged to have her body shipped to Seattle. I stayed with her all the way back to Seattle and took the unpleasant but necessary steps of arranging her funeral and having her placed in the family's cemetery plot. Next to her grandparents.

There were more people at the gathering than I had expected. Many of her college friends came, a number of people she knew in high school and some from the Peace Corps. Most of her aunts and uncles were there, all with fond stories of her childhood. She had cousins too, more than I knew. Weddings and funerals are both dreadful events to me. They are where old wounds are reopened, old feuds revived, and old scores beg to be settled.

Sam's aging parents glared at me during most of the graveside service, and when it was over I waited for the inevitable as Sam's parents made their way toward me. Her mother's cheeks were wet from tears and her blue eyes red from weeping. She walked with a cane that she also used as a pointer or prod, whatever was needed. Her father, somewhat older than her mother, pushed a metal walker in front of him and stood behind his wife, staring at me unblinkingly.

"This would not have happened had she not met you," said her mother. "She went to Africa to do good and now look what she has come to—my beautiful, brilliant daughter." Her father shook his head in agreement. "You are responsible for this, and I hope you live the rest of your life in shame."

He shook his head again. Then they both turned to leave, but not without one more look at Sam's coffin.

They were right and I knew it. I was responsible for Sam's death, and I would have to bear that guilt for the rest of my life. I did not tell them about the baby. It would only have added to their pain. It didn't matter now anyway. Once again, death had rendered life meaningless.

When I left Seattle, it was raining and cold. A Northwest wind was blowing off the Pacific Ocean, lashing the city and shrouding the top of the Space Needle with mist. For a moment I wanted to stay—make my new home here, be here to visit Sam occasionally, but no, I had another life and other obligations.

I flew back to New York and took a cab to the diamond district. I sensed that New York had changed. The cab drivers, mostly immigrants, were polite; even the general population seemed quieter, more reserved, even considerate—not the rude, noisy, blusterous, shove-you-out-of-the-way New York that I knew in 1968 when I first returned from Liberia.

Sam's friend in the diamond business had given us the name of a Mr. Abe, a highly qualified lapidary in New York. I had contacted him about the rough diamonds while still in Liberia and now, fortunately, he was able to see me right away. I went to his three-story walk-up office on Forty-Seventh Street and handed him the Ronald Furbank book. Without missing a beat, he opened the book, leafed through to the cut-out, and dislodged the cloth bag of uncut diamonds. It was obvious he had seen this ruse before. I then handed over the remaining diamonds I had removed from the hem of Sam's shorts.

The next day, Mr. Abe called to say that once cut, the diamonds could be worth over $1M dollars—would I like him to proceed? That was a lot of money in 1980. I was approaching forty and wondered, briefly, if retirement would be possible. I didn't consider the idea of ever remarrying—there would never be another Sam out there.

But no, my original intent was to acquire enough money to get my air carrier business up and running, and now I had more than enough capital for that. So, yes, please, Mr. Abe, please cut and sell the diamonds for me.

I will stay in New York until the diamonds are cut and sold. Then I will think more about the future.

ABOUT THE AUTHOR

A retired Aviation Safety Inspector for the FAA, Daniel V. Meier, Jr. has always had a passion for writing. During his college years, he studied history at the University of North Carolina, Wilmington (UNCW) and American Literature at the University of Maryland Graduate School. In 1980 he published an action/thriller with Leisure Books under the pen name of Vince Daniels.

Dan also worked for the *Washington Business Journal* as a journalist and has been a contributing writer/editor for several aviation magazines. In addition to *Blood Before Dawn*, he is the author of its prequel, the award-winning novel, *The Dung Beetles of Liberia*, as well as two other highly acclaimed novels published by BQB Publishing.

OTHER BOOKS BY DANIEL V. MEIER, JR.

First Book in The Dung Beetles series

2019 Grand Prize Winner—Red City Review

Based on the remarkable true account of a young American who landed in Liberia in 1961.

"The blend of fictional action and nonfiction social inspection is simply exquisite, and are strengths that set this story apart from many other fictional pieces sporting African settings."

—D. Donovan, Midwest Book Review

Nothing could have prepared him for the events he was about to experience.

Ken Verrier quickly realizes the moment he arrives in Liberia that he is in a place where he understands very little of what is considered normal, where the dignity of life has little meaning, and where he can trust no one. It's 1961 and young Ken Verrier is experiencing the turbulence of Ishmael and the guilt of his brother's death. His sudden decision to drop out of college and deal with his demons shocks his family, his friends, and especially his girlfriend, soon to have been his fiancée. His destination: Liberia—the richest country in Africa both in monetary wealth and natural resources.

Author Daniel V. Meier, Jr. describes Ken Verrier's many escapades, span-ning from horrifying to whimsical, with engaging and fast-moving narrative that ultimately describe a society upon which the wealthy are feeding and in which the poor are being buried.

It's a novel that will stay with you long after the last word has been read.

Satire at its best!

In this indelible and deeply moving portrait of our time, two young people, Beckman and Malany, set out on an odyssey to find meaning and reality in the artistic life, and in doing so unleash a barrage of humorous, unintended consequences.

Beckman and Malany's journey reflects the allegorical evolution of humanity from its primal state, represented by Beckman's dismal life as a dishwasher to the crude, medieval development of mankind in a pool hall, and then to the false but erudite veneer of sophistication of the academic world.

The world these protagonists live in is a world without love. It has every other variety of drive and emotion, but not love. Do they know it? Not yet. And they won't until they figure out why no birds sing here.

Meier's writing is precise and detailed, whether the situation he describes is clear or ambiguous. Fans of Franzen and Salinger will find Meier to be another sharp, provocative writer of our time.

A gripping account of survival in America's earliest settlement, Jamestown, Virginia.

Virginia, 1622. Powhatan warriors prepare war paint from the sacred juice of the bloodroot plant, but Nehiegh, the English son-in-law of Chief Ochawintan has sworn never to kill again. He must leave before the massacre.

England 1609. Matthew did not trust his friend Richard's stories of Paradise in the Jamestown settlement, but nothing could have equipped him for the violence and privation that awaited him in this savage land.

Once ashore in the fledgling settlement, Matthew experiences the unimaginable beauty of this pristine land and learns the meaning of hope, but it all turns into a nightmare as gold mania infests the community and Indians become an increasing threat. The nightmare only gets worse as the harsh winter brings on "the starving time" and all the grizzly horrors of a desperate and dying community that come with it.

Driven to the depths of despair by the guilt of his sins against Richard and his lust for that man's wife, Matthew seeks death. In that moment of crisis, when he chooses death over a life of depravity, he unexpectedly finds new life among his sworn enemy, the Powhatan Indians. What will this new life mean for Matthew, and will he survive?